What reviewers are saying about the stories in Paranormal Mates Society Vol. I

Matchmaker's Match — Willa Okati

"Not only is this book hilarious from front to back, every page pushed the story forward. With quick wit and three dimensional characters that pull you in the fun, this book is a hit."

—Stacey Brutger, Road to Romance

Finders Keepers —Lacey Savage

"The sexual interaction of the two was just delicious. Ms. Savage handles her characters with a light but deft touch."

—Kirra Pierce, Just Erotic Romance Reviews

Long Tall Furry — Rachel Bo

"Rachel Bo has done a tremendous job creating an imaginative, tantalizing, and rewarding story full circle."

—Shayley, Fallen Angel Reviews

Chunkybuttfunky — Dakota Cassidy

"There is comedy throughout the entire plot and the characters never fail to bring out the laughs."

—Angel, Romance Junkies

www.ChangelingPress.com

Paranormal Mates Society Vol. I

Willa Okati
Lacey Savage
Rachel Bo
Dakota Cassidy

ISBN: 978-1-59596-811-1

Publisher:
Changeling Press LLC
PO Box 1046
Martinsburg WV 25402-1046
www.ChangelingPress.com

Printed in the U.S.A.
Lightning Source, Inc.
1246 Heil Quaker Blvd
La Vergne TN 37086
www.lightningsource.com

Anthology Editors: Katriena Knights, Maryam Salim, Crystal
Esau, and Sheri Ross Fogarty
Cover Layout and Design: Bryan Keller

Paranormal Mates Society:
Matchmaker's Match

Willa Okati

Chapter One

"No! No, no, no! Look, how many times do I have to tell you? The question is not 'will they' talk about sex. The question is, 'when will they' talk about sex? Do I have to spell it out for this crowd? S-E-X. You know, the thing none of you are ever going to enjoy again unless you make — this — work?"

A crowd of demons, sulfurous, scaly, and one hundred percent scared shitless, cowered beneath a view screen covering the outside wall of their boss's office. Not middle management either. The Big Boss. Larger than life and more than miffed. Positively pissed off.

They could tell because he was smiling. Satan's smile never boded well. The Boss knew as much, and put the facial tics to best effect by saving them for special occasions, when someone's soles were about to fry.

And since they, the dread creatures of the Pit charged with — what was it, again? *Customer Surface?* — in Lucifer's newest scheme, had been called together for a meeting that started with their chief of operations being blown into chewy chunks, they didn't think it would go uphill from there.

* * *

Scratch drummed three fingers on his view screen. "I am not about to have my entire plan blown out of the lake of fire because of some spineless, brainless, hornless, one-eyed purple people eater morons! Do you know how much time I've put into PMS?"

"The — the monthly affliction of women?" Frajni the Horrendous quavered.

A piece of cold pizza decorated with pepperoni and mold flew through the air and bounced just above Frajni's three horns. The missile thunked home between the demon's eyes, which crossed as he stumbled, staggered, and fell down, out cold, which was saying something in Hell.

"Anyone else have any questions? No? Good. Okay, demons, I'm going over it one last time. This is what you do when a new sucker signs up, so you better have the protocol down.

"One: get their credit info. Full checks. I want everything from how much they're worth to how much they're gonna be worth. Ever. Understand?

"Two: run a cross-check on what kind of powers they have. I didn't log fifty-seven point five hours worth of admin time just to have someone fry my computers with a thunderbolt when they get mad.

"Yes, they're going to be angry. In case you forgot, angry is the point. What, you thought this was about making people *happy*?

"Third, and most important: no one finds out who I am, or why I'm doing this. You breathe one sulfur-scented word to anyone outside this Hellhole and I'll toast you on your own pitchforks. Are we clear?"

A select group of demons — massive warty creatures decorated with dripping horns and multiple eyes — crowded together in a tight huddle, making a serious effort to look small as possible and properly humble.

The effect was unbelievably silly. Kind of like King Kong trying to play chimpanzee. Scratch leaned forward in his computer chair, ignoring its squeaks and wobbles from one broken leg. "I asked you if we were clear. A question needs an answer, boys. I'm waiting, and I do not have all millennium. Talk!"

"Yes, Lord," quavered a demon with more muscles than a wrestling pro. "We obey your commands."

"Oh, I'm sure of that. You're real go-getters, every one of you. Too bad you have this problem with actually doing anything right." Scratch glowered at the cowering creatures of nightmare and legend.

"Master, please, have mercy!"

"Mercy? Right." Scratch laughed. The demons trembled. Somewhere on earth, a three-headed calf was born.

His face fell back into dark, threatening lines. "Mercy," he repeated, drawing the word out like Hell's finest burned salt-water taffy. "How quickly they forget. Refresher course: I don't do mercy. I do business. I also do pain. Also, just to remind you, I'm not much on stupid questions."

"Master, no!"

"Bye-bye, brain-dead bogey head." Scratch moved his mouse pointer over a desktop icon labeled *incinerate*. One click hoisted Mr. Big-and-Bad smack on his own petard.

Or, in this case, melted him into a puddle of yellow goo that looked like recycled toad pâté.

The demons squeaked and did a quick two-step away from their fallen comrade. Unfortunately, this meant they couldn't cling together like little girls.

Scratch glowered. Lightning zigzagged over the demons' heads. A deafening crack of thunder shook the walls of Hell. "One more thing. I'll be a really nice guy and tell you this one last time. It's not 'master.' It's not 'the prince of darkness.' Not 'the father of lies,' 'the morning star,' or even 'sir.' It's Scratch. Not 'the old Scratch.' Just Scratch. As far as anyone out there knows, I'm an ordinary Joe, a computer geek in charge of some seriously stupid lackeys. Peons. Employees. Whatever. I'm the good guy around here. Mr. Go-To."

"Yes! Yes, Mas—Scratch. Just-Scratch."

Criminy. Well, getting that far with this crowd was a decent morning's work. "Fine. Get out there. Everyone has a cube. Find it, park your butts in front of the computers, and don't leave unless I say you can go. You're customer service for PMS, Incorporated, and it's up to you to make our no-life, loser clients think they're happy until the hammer falls."

"Master, I mean, Scratch, please, a question?" A goaty variety of Hell-spawn groveled without looking up to meet Scratch's eyes on the teleconferencing monitor.

"Let me guess. You don't understand something."

"The cubes, your Dark Lordship. What did we do to deserve placement in five-by-five boxes with gray felt walls, designed to be adjusted yet welded in place?"

Scratch shrugged. "This is Hell. You expected a corner office with a view? Idiot. Get to work."

Their exit speed would have impressed Scratch if he hadn't been more or less beyond blasé about, well, everything. Hell wasn't big on entertainment, and watching condemned souls do the hokey-pokey on hot coals got old after the first couple centuries.

Boredom was why he'd come up with PMS. Both kinds, in point of fact, but more recently the computer dating service for the few creatures of fantasy and legend still walking the Earth. They'd do anything to fall in love or even have one good moment with someone who understood where they were coming from. Lonely and desperate for sympathetic company.

Easy, easy pickings. Dangle the "perfect match" bait as candy on his hook. Reel them in. Partner them with profiles so unbelievably wrong they'd swear off love forever.

At least, that was the plan. Might work out, might not. His test run between a fire imp and a mermaid had actually been amusing. Poor bastard imp was so desperate for a lay he jumped into the ocean and, well… he'd made a nice sizzle, going out.

Scratch grinned his most pleasant grin, took a screen shot of himself, and uploaded it to every demon's computer as a background and screen saver. For fun, he burned in the scrolling text: *I'm watching you.* He cocked his head to catch the sound of terrified screams coming from the cube farm he'd built over a tar pit and nodded in satisfaction.

He clicked on the minimized tab that brought up a display of the PMS gateway web page. The counter of users logging on looked like a bomb countdown in reverse, numbers ticking up and up and up.

Not a bad morning's work. Reasonably satisfied for the moment, Scratch rolled back from his main computer station and across the cluttered room to snag a lightweight laptop and resume his current run-through game of "Death By Humvee 4." He'd almost made it to SUV level. With any luck, he'd get to start mowing down mopeds soon.

What was he, besides the fallen angel of legend? A guy who moved with the times. He'd taken his lumps and figured, since it looked like he wasn't going to find a "get out of jail free" card in his e-mail anytime soon, he might as well have some fun.

Not much else to do when you were alone. Always alone.

"Just another day in paradise," he muttered, picking up a joystick. "Me, myself, I, and a Hell full of demons too dumb to figure out what WWW stands for. Let's rock."

"Meow."

Scratch blinked. "Okay, that's new."

He glanced down to see not a demon, but what looked exactly like an innocent tomcat. Seriously big for its breed, not quite bobcat size but not too far off. White with a spattering of black spots. The beastie trilled at him again, way too innocent-sounding for anything interested in a visit to Hell. Or its Master, all things considered.

Tail lifted high to show off its goodies, the cat picked a finicky path through the mess of papers, junk food wrappers, tangles of wire and bits of demon strewn across the floor of Scratch's sanctum sanctorum. Finding no clean, empty spaces, it plopped down on both hind legs and began to wash one forepaw while shooting Scratch a dirty look.

You didn't have to speak Feline to get the message loud and clear: *Yecch.*

"Yeah, well, me? Not much on the kind of company who really cares about how long it's been since Housekeeping made a stop." Scratch thought. "Or since I flash-fried the last demon who knew what a vacuum cleaner was."

The cat began to purr. "Fried does not equal food," Scratch informed it, returning to his game. He felt the green eyes roaming over his present form, examining him from horns to toes.

Way too curious.

If he's a cat for real, I'll start eating pussy again. Scratch smirked. *Whoever's playing games, they're a class-A dumbbell.* Did they actually expect Scratch to believe a grade-normal Earth cat could find its way down where he lived? Sure. Contrary to the old-school belief, felines weren't exactly his friends. They didn't like the competition.

Scratch focused on his game—or pretended to. "So," he said, one corner of his mouth turning up. "How'd you get down here? Not that I know for sure who you are, but I'm gonna bet Loki."

He glanced at the cat, who was staring at him as if he'd just taken away the best dead mouse ever. "Been a long time, Jokester."

"Well, you're no fun," the cat said sourly. The air rippled as it changed shape, shivering from feline to human-approximate. A man in his early thirties sporting long spiky hair and something tunic-shaped. Might have been in Nordic fashion a couple millennia ago.

"Here's some advice for free," Scratch said, returning to his game. "Go shopping. Quickly. It's safe to say Asgard hasn't been the look for a while. At least discover the softer side of—"

"How did you know?" Loki snapped, getting to his feet. "Thor's balls, this place is disgusting."

"You expected what in Hell? Five-star awards for sanitation?"

"Stop dodging the point."

"Spoilsport." Scratch lifted his shoulders without looking away from the laptop's monitor. "I had a hunch. Besides, the way today's been going, it pretty much makes sense for an old enemy to show up, looking to pick a fight. So. You want to go, Trick?"

"Don't call me 'Trick.' Never call me 'Trick.'" Loki shuddered. "Your penchant for nicknames is appalling."

"Yeah. I'm a real pain in the ass sometimes."

Loki folded his arms, scowling. "You'd be wise, little fallen angel, to show respect to those who are still gods among men."

"Right, uh-huh. So, how many people still think you might be real?" Scratch flickered with black light, his eyes emptying into deep, dark wells of absolute nothingness. He glanced at Loki, smiling at how the little old god tried to hide his flinch.

"Thought so. Now," Scratch said softly, "how many people know for damn sure I exist?"

Loki drew back. Doubt crossed the face of the Trickster.

"Want to play games with me now?" Scratch asked, his grin lingering like the ghost of a nightmare. "You think you can take me on?"

Loki cleared his throat. He tried to meet Scratch's level stare, but had to look away. "No."

"Wise choice. Now scram, huh? I'm busy."

"Yes. I'd heard about your latest scheme. It's quite the talk of—"

Scratch let a little more of the faux humanity drain from his eyes. Just like water down a drain. A darker shade of damnation. He didn't say a word. Didn't have to.

Loki paled. "I suspect you'd rather be left alone though," he said. "Very well. I have no need to stay. I've seen enough to satisfy me."

Scratch nodded once, up and down, very slowly. Smiling. "Careful with the first step. It's a doozy."

"First step? I—"

One keystroke and a hole opened up beneath Loki's feet. With a seriously undignified yelp, like a man who's just slipped on a banana peel and can't believe karma has the balls, the Trickster plummeted down, down, down. Scratch stared at the pit as it slowly closed.

"I figured I'd see you again some day," he said. "You should have remembered, though... curiosity kills the cat. Or in this case, dumps it headfirst into the demon latrines. Kind of a shame we're enemies, you know? Guys like us should network. But, eh, what do I know?"

Scratch leaned back and took another look at the steadily rising counter of logged-in PMS clients. Tick, tick, tick; up, up, up.

Suckers.

* * *

Several million miles below Scratch's Hellish hackery, as the metaphysical crow flew, and as far from where he'd landed as he could make it in one single, horrified leap, Loki quivered with the threat of an impending nervous breakdown. Gagging, he ripped and tore at his clothes in an effort to get them off, away, and possibly destroyed as fast as possible.

Finally naked, if still smeared with demonic effluvia and things best not thought about, Loki wrapped both arms around his chest and shuddered with disgust.

Shit! The little fallen angel had dared drop him—*him!*—down a U-bend!

In days gone by, no one would have had the nerve. They'd respected and feared him more than any nasty-tempered outcast from Heaven, as well they should have.

And yet, no matter how it galled Loki to admit it, Scratch had been right. He'd gotten lazy. Spent too much time away from the playing fields. Men had forgotten the games Loki could play with their lives.

He began to grin, white teeth sparkling in the near-pitch darkness.

"You think yourself better than me?" Loki asked, peering up the porthole he'd fallen through. "We'll see about that, scorpion. I think it's time for a small lesson in manners."

Loki clapped his hands together and vanished in a cloud of smoke, headed for the first vacant five-star shower he could find.

He'd just clean up a bit, and then he'd see what was what. They all would.

He knew exactly how to make Scratch pay for his insult.

Loki's laughter shook the earth he soared through, causing a tectonic shift that would, sooner rather than later, result in a tsunami off Greenland.

Oops.

* * *

Far and away, a creature, man-like in form, tall and solid as the grove of trees he knelt among, leaned on the hilt of his fiery sword and gazed up at the sky. Beautiful and fierce, a lion running free in Central Park.

Someone had, very politely, requested a word with him... after his own fashion. This did not involve any audible communication.

As he listened to his summoner's request, the being made no sound. Not even the whisper of drawing or expelling breath.

He needed neither.

Long moments passed as the not-quite-human communed with something higher than the clouds. His expression never wavered, nor did he flinch away from the flickering flames of his blade as they climbed high enough to lick at his hands.

Finally, he nodded. Stood, and slid the sword into a scabbard on his back.

Then, snapping open a set of six bronze wings, he took flight. Not upwards, to dance in the clouds, as one might expect.

Down.

A long, long way down.

He had a job to do.

Chapter Two

Scratch sorted through his morning mail brought to him by the three-inch-high ghost of a bulldog. It whimpered, tail between its legs, as it offered him a mouthful of soggy envelopes.

"Good boy," he said absently, reaching down to pet the dog's vaporous head. It whined and scampered away through the mess on Scratch's floor.

Scratch watched it go with idle curiosity. "Always something new," he muttered. The dog had shown up maybe twenty, thirty Earth years ago, scared out of its pea-sized canine mind, and hadn't gotten any less skittish with time. He had yet to figure out the whole story, but somewhere out there a mailman with deeply scarred calves was laughing his ass off.

Sometimes the depths to which humans could sink impressed him.

All the same, if anyone ever asked Scratch about the plastic bag of Doggy Delite Bakon Bitez hidden just out of sight but still in reach, he'd deny its existence to his last days and flash fry anyone who'd dared bring them up.

He'd already had enough PMS for one day. He'd matched a spider princess with a bug-phobic Yeti, an exotic dancer who used music as her magic to a preacher deaf as a stone, and a were-bird to a were-sloth. After those, the "regular" Joes and Janes were pretty dull.

"Screw it," he said, switching off the PMS observation monitor but keeping the server running. Just in case, right?

Besides which, he had better things to do, or wish he could do. He'd loaded up his favorite porn site, full of ripped, naked men with huge cocks poised to jack themselves off for his pleasure. And a quick call to a fast-food joint Above brought him a bag full of greasy faux Mexican fast food.

Porn and cholesterol. It got no better.

I call an official ten-minute break, or I would if I'd actually been working. He figured after the push, deadlines, and countless hours of programming he'd put into PMS, he deserved some slacker time.

* * *

A crumpled piece of paper lying next to one of Scratch's overflowing trash bins shifted, rocking back and forth as if it were laughing.

As a matter of fact, it was.

Or rather, Loki had been caught with such a fit of giggles he couldn't hold still a moment longer. Disguising himself as a discarded, badly spelled memo written in purple crayon from a lesser demon—a stroke of genius, if he did say so himself.

As for how he'd gotten in, not even Satan would notice a flea, once attached to a mail-dog's hide, hop off and scuttle away. When Scratch had been distracted by the porn streaming onto his computer, Loki had shifted shape.

I am, and do remain, he exulted, *number one with a prank. You'll soon regret your insults, Scratch. No one shames Loki and lives to tell the tale.*

Fine, he's immortal. He'll live. Nonetheless, he'll be toasting on his own pitchfork before I'm finished here.

Loki manifested a pair of eyes in the shape of a double set of parentheses and peeked up at one of Scratch's security feeds. More precisely, the one that treated them to a view of the Dark Road, with its thronging crowd of damned souls pushing and shoving their way into Hell.

There appeared to be, approaching from the rear, someone clearing a path. Most of the condemned tended toward crankiness, and cutting in line wasn't taken lightly.

For this fellow, they moved at speed. After all, someone a good few feet taller than your average human, waving a fiery sword about like a blind man's cane, was probably someone best not tangled with, even after death.

If he'd had hands in this form, Loki would have rubbed them together and cackled in glee.

It appears to me the Devil is being called to pay his due. In other words: show time. Loki wiggled in delight.

* * *

Few things annoyed Scratch more than being interrupted in the middle of a good session of love with his sinister hand. So it was that when a klaxon began to blare and pop-eyed demons dialed up emergency HellIM windows chiming at him like a clock-maker's workshop gone mad, it pissed Scratch off more than it usually would.

He bypassed crankiness and went straight to rage. X-ing out each HellIM window as it popped up, he put the whole gaggle on block, then picked up a system-wide microphone, bellowing, "What the *Heaven* are you idiots doing now?"

A chorus of terrified squeals and insane clattering clamor started instantly. Scratch rolled his eyes and flicked on the view screen.

He smiled down at his demons.

They shut up, most in mid-wail. Wide eyes stared at him from shaking Hell-spawn the size of small mountains.

"Let's try it again," Scratch said, every inch the kind and patient employer, just to see how many of the monsters would faint. He counted. Three. Not bad, although, of course, he'd done better. "One of you. Just one. How about the golden calf in the middle? Start talking."

"M-m-master?" the ex-idol peeped. "M-m-me?"

Scratch inclined his head gently, adding an extra note of boyishness to his grin. "It's all right, Bessie," he said, as if his intent were to soothe.

Two more demons toppled.

Much better.

"Bessie? I'm waiting."

The golden calf swallowed its cud but, possibly motivated by the death glares from its fellows, spoke up in a small voice. "An angel, Master. There's an angel come to Hell, on the broad road of damnation."

Scratch blinked. "You mean a fallen angel? Someone else up there copped 'tude?"

"No, Master." Bessie's brown eyes grew wide enough to show a ring of white around its irises. "A true angel of Heaven. He has wings, all six, and a sword of fire."

Scratch let that sink in. "Uh-huh." He tapped his fingers in a staccato rhythm on one knee. "And this Clarence type is on his way. Coming here. Now."

Bessie nodded.

"Do you know who sent him?"

The demons glanced at one another. "No?" Bessie ventured.

"Wrong answer."

Click!

Scratch wouldn't put an end to the old milk cow, but for the moment, it made a great statue, its mouth frozen in a moo of terror. He admired the sculpture briefly, then leaned forward, every last trace of gentle good humor gone. A negative cloud of dark halo swarmed over his skin, smoldering across his face with searing heat.

"Find. Out," he said, low and dangerous, and switched the outer view screen off.

He knew better than to trust his crew of pea-brains to get anything accomplished. That would mean they, oh, had an ounce of common sense between them. Sure. And the angel with a fiery sword was there to hand-deliver an invitation back inside the pearly gates.

"When you want something done right, or possibly done to death," Scratch muttered, re-routing his vid-cam to an infrequently used feed, "you do it yourself."

He grinned again, for his own pleasure, shimmered once with black fire, and punched a final keystroke.

* * *

Loki-the-paper-wad wriggled. *Yes, yes, yes! I knew he wouldn't fail to rise to such a tasty bait!*

Now, for a better view...

He rolled to the right, peeped out through purple crayon eyes, and gazed up gleefully at Scratch's dust-covered monitor.

Ahh. Much better.

* * *

The angel didn't bother speaking as he calmly but firmly made his way through the ranks of dead souls on their way to Limbo, Purgatory, or a lake of flame, depending on individual belief systems. After a few well-considered, gently insistent nudges to semi-corporeal backsides with the tip of his sword, the majority decided it would be wise to step aside.

A horde of demons rushing out of Satan's rusty iron gates, however, did not display the same native intelligence, nor any sense of self-preservation.

Never once changing expression from placid blankness, the angel simply lifted his sword and cut the scaly nightmare beasts down easily as swatting flies. His blade slid through their hides with the ease of a hot knife cutting slices of soft cheese.

They snarled at him, slavering yellow-green froth from opened jaws with an overabundance of teeth.

He gazed back, thoroughly unimpressed and not bothering to hide it. If need be, he'd remain in place until every one of the former host lay bleeding at his feet. Whatever he deemed necessary to provoke their master out of hiding.

The man he'd come to see.

"You mind telling me what in the Masons you think you're doing?" a young male voice with a trace of New York snapped above the angel's head. "Hey! I'm talking to you, stupid. Nooo, not down there. Up here. Look up. I'm betting you know how. Come on, come on, come on!" Fingers snapped impatiently.

With a complete lack of hurry, the angel glanced up to a flat-screen monitor mounted above the gates to Hell. He tilted his head slightly, which was, for him, the equivalent of pop-eyes and a dropped jaw. Scratch did not look... quite... as he had often been described.

No crimson skin, no cloven hooves for hands; neither fangs nor scarlet eyes; not a fallen angel of immense but miserably grieved beauty or a snarling, disfigured beast.

He looked, actually, more or less like a disheveled mortal who shaved when he felt like it, had a penchant for James Dean's mode of dress, and wore rectangular-shaped black plastic glasses. With the exception of two small, gilded horns, Lucifer looked... ordinary.

Attractive, to be certain, but not the force of nature he had been led to expect.

It threw his plans a little askew. Fortunately, thinking on his feet while never revealing a glimmer of his thoughts happened to be one of the angel's specialties. He planted his fiery sword point down in the dirt, leaned on the hilt. Patiently waiting, utterly silent.

The Devil blinked at him. Not surprisingly, he would have been prepared for the voice of God delivering an unpleasant message in no uncertain terms. "You—hey, you are an angel, right?"

The angel nodded.

Satan glanced to his left and to his right. "Don't tell me they figured out a way to get a Candid Camera crew down here," he mumbled. "You're not so much what I'd... so, the androgynous look is out of style Upstairs?"

The angel shrugged.

"Not much with the small talk, are you?"

Shrug.

Satan, the angel was pleased to note, seemed still further thrown off track by his continuing silence. Almost, one might say, unnerved.

"You have a reason for being here?" he asked, eyeballing the angel up and down.

Shrug.

"Can't you talk?"

Shrug.

The Devil made a huffing sound of impatience. His glasses slid down his nose to be sharply pushed back into place with one finger. He stared at the angel for a long moment, thoughts beyond the ken of any other being obviously churning away at light-speed behind his eyes.

Finally, he spoke again. "So, you want to come up here for a meet? Man to—er—demon to angel?" He made a come-hither gesture with his finger. "*Mi casa es su casa.*"

The angel smiled and disappeared from his place before the gates to Hell, reappearing seconds later in the middle of the Devil's private domain. The place was positively reminiscent of Dali and Escher with its peculiar geography and mutable nature, and had a dash of Warhol as well, the angel decided, flapping his wings to clear them of dust.

He didn't notice a crumpled ball of crayon-scribbled paper go tumbling over and over in the breeze to land near his feet. He folded his hands together on the pommel of his sword, grip loose and ready for swinging if necessary.

The Devil, wiry and tough in the flesh, flicked a few strands of dark hair out of his eyes. "Don't tell me," he said dryly, "Let me guess. Someone wants a word with me, and you're here to deliver the message."

The angel nodded.

"Problem being, the way I see it—you don't talk. Jabber. Flap your lips. So, to make this an even better day, I have to figure out what the message is. Am I on the right track here?"

Nod.

"Isn't that just jim-dandy." The Devil sighed. "Okay, fine. You mind if I check the stats on a little web project first?"

Shake.

"Great. Won't take a second. Clear off a chair, if you can find one, and sit down." Satan turned, the movement casual, but the stiffness of his shoulders betraying him.

The angel considered his Enemy's actions and decided he had no idea what to do next. Therefore, sitting seemed as good an option as any. He scanned the piled-high chairs and discarded clearing one off as a bad idea. He'd never fit in one anyway. He checked the floor next, deciding it wouldn't be too bad to sit on top of scattered printouts. Near his foot, he spotted a reasonably clean ball of thick construction paper. He frowned at the thing, instinctively not liking it. The double parentheses reminded him uncomfortably of eyes, staring greedily out at the room.

It was a small and petty action, but at least being able to destroy one of the Devil's memos provided a little satisfaction for his hungry blade. With one easy glide, he jabbed the point of his sword through the wad, pinning it to Satan's floor, and sat cross-legged behind it.

He frowned. Satan hadn't made a sound and neither had he. From whence, then, hailed that peculiar squealing? It reminded him of a cat in heat.

* * *

Loki's purple-crayon eyes had all but popped off the paper. Squirming to get free, he voiced the only thought on his mind at the moment:

AIIIIIIEEEEEEEEEEEEEEEEEEEEEEE!!!

Chapter Three

The angel sat quietly on Satan's floor. Silence hadn't been his native tongue, but he not-spoke it with efficient fluency. He found the skill came in handy during any number of situations. Quiet unnerved the talkative, and caused their lips to part and spill out secrets like falling rain. A somber hush chilled the souls of the guilty, making them feel without fail they'd been weighed in the balance and found wanting. Failing to rise to an enemy's bait drove them absolutely insane.

In this case, the angel merely hoped it lent him an air of purpose that suitably masked his puzzlement. When he had accepted his assignment, the prospective employer had not bothered to fill him in on some finer details. Details he felt, with a sting of annoyance, he would have been far better off being aware of.

For example, the fact that Satan called himself "Scratch." That he'd remade himself over in the image of a modern mortal man with a taste for computers, junk food, and pornography.

Rather... the angel tilted his head again... *intriguing* pornography, indeed. As yet, his own augmented anatomy seemed to be behaving itself. Augmentation it simply would not do to let the Enemy know about.

Or the Man Upstairs, for that matter.

Androgyny remained quite in style within reach of St. Peter's gimlet glare. However, as a roving "free agent," the angel had taken advantage of certain loopholes, technicalities, and ended up a bit... different, one might say. If one were able to speak between gasps of outrage, or peculiarly inflamed perversity of hormones.

Hormones, yes. Testosterone for one. If he'd known they were part and parcel of a "package," he might have taken a different fork in the road. Pheromones tended to make one's body act in the strangest of ways, with or without the mind's consent.

By the glassy seas, why hadn't anyone told him Scratch's current appearance just happened to be... attractive?

Perhaps they hadn't thought he would find the intellectual look appealing. They had been wrong. Native cunning and the knowledge of how to use it made a devastating aphrodisiac, and when combined with an apparent vanity that had led Scratch to shape himself with defined abdominal muscles and long runner's legs...

The angel suspected he might well be in trouble.

Ah, yes, there went his anatomy, misbehaving itself.

He would have prayed Scratch should take no notice, but deemed bringing his plight to the attention of higher powers somewhat unwise.

Sighing, the angel shifted uneasily and spun the point of his flaming sword where he'd wedged it through the ball of crayoned paper on Scratch's floor. He frowned.

What *was* that peculiar squealing, and from whence did it hail?

* * *

He was up to something. Had to be up to something. No angel set so much as a single pearly-pink piggie on the Brimstone Path without a—well—"damned" good reason.

Scratch didn't trust the silently hulking presence behind him. As far as he was concerned, turning his back on the angel showed who had the biggest balls on Hell and Earth, yes sirree. Of course, size didn't matter when said organs were trying to crawl back up into the safety of a guy's innards.

Scratch shivered. New, different, and not a pleasant sensation. He couldn't help it though. A guy—angel—like this set the hairs on his neck bristling like a wet hedgehog's spikes.

Carefully, carefully, Scratch manifested a tiny single eye beneath the fall of tousled hair on the back of his skull. He got a single peep at the angel, sitting ever so patient and calm behind his flaming sword, before the creature in question met his "gaze" and held it steady.

Zap! Scratch popped the eye out of existence. Too late though. He could *feel* the angel smirking, even if it would never show up on his solemn face. His rugged... roughly chiseled... all but leonine... completely gorgeous... face...

Oh, crap. Scratch manipulated his mouse, navigating carefully but with the greatest of ease through a minefield of spam e-mail, HellIM requests for technical assistance, and clumsy attempts at flirting with him from genuinely fugly PMS customers. Deleted the whole shebang while trying not to think about the angel's face, much less the creature's powerful chest, corded arms, rock-hard stomach, or legs like strangely attractive redwoods. The fifth time he caught himself trying to think of a synonym for "bulge," he gave up.

Fine. He turns me on. Someone up there better be satisfied. Mission accomplished. But get this clear: I do not give up the golden ticket without a fight.

He clicked and deleted, clicked and saved, cursed his disobedient loins currently sitting up to beg for attention, and kept a careful watch on the angel.

Ashes, I just wish I knew who sent him here. Then I might know who to kill later, but for now, I'd love to get a clue about this guy's weaknesses. He's got to have at least one.

Scratch saw his eyes, reflected in the monitor, turn dark with the black halo of the damned. *Trust me. I know. There's always a reason when someone draws battle lines in the sand between Me and Them.*

He'd figure it out.

In the meantime, though... "Hey, you hear that weird squealing? Sounds like a stuck pig."

* * *

Loki knew the meaning of pain. Quite well, in point of fact. Had he not spent ages upon ages being tortured at the whim of Odin himself? Tied to a rock with half-human entrails, sticky-wet and never quite cooling down from blood heat. A snake dangling above his head, venom dripping from fangs roughly the size of harpoons.

He'd had Sigyn, of course, on and off, styling herself as his "wife." They weren't on what one might call speaking terms, yet some odd quirk of loyalty, or delight in his punishment that went so far as wanting a front-row seat, had moved her to join him in his cavern. She'd even held a bowl beneath the drooling poison, catching the viscous strands of toxin before they dribbled into his eyes.

A small bowl. One she'd had to walk away and empty rather frequently. An errand she seemed to perform with tremendous slowness of motion.

He never *saw* her smile or *heard* her laugh, but there are certain things a man simply knew. A heart, once he'd had a look inside, would forever after be an open book to him.

Sigyn's pages were full of revenge poetry.

Loki shuddered for three reasons: first, remembering the searing pain of the snake's venom. Second, recalling Sigyn's atrocious grasp of meter and rhyme.

Third, possibly the most important and certainly the most relevant, the bloody, massive, fiery sword planted through the general area of his guts, insofar as he had guts while in the shape of a crumpled wad of paper.

For some reason, he had yet to burst into flame. He supposed Scratch would have ignition-resistant writing materials though. However, his crayon wax was melting and dripping to cool in violet puddles from a Jackson Pollock best-selling nightmare on the floor. If not engulfed by flame, Loki found himself most certainly feeling the heat. Unpleasantly.

He whined again as he tried to slither away from the sword's point. No luck. Too much obvious movement would give the game away, or he'd be tempted to tear himself in half just to gain freedom. Dissolving into a cloud of mist and floating free, his preferred method of dealing with pointy objects thrust through his innards, was not a viable option.

Who would have suspected a holy weapon could foul up his powers of changing shape? Crossovers between pantheons were not in any rules of play he'd ever read. Not that he tended to obey the rules, but that was beside the point.

Point. Ah-ha-ha-ha. Loki winced.

Right, enough was quite enough. When he managed to wiggle loose, Loki decided he'd be having a word with this angel. Preferably several. Loud ones. Followed by the breaking of a sword across his knee to be used as a spanking switch.

And then, with regard to Scratch, he'd —

Loki paused to sniff the air. What was that peculiar smell?

Oh, blast.

* * *

Okay, that was it. Final straw, the one that cracked the camel's back. Scratch didn't do sitting around, waiting for the Enemy to strike first. He bit before they could sink fangs, punched before their hands had time to fist up, and yanked the rugs out from beneath any leagues of extraordinary sycophants before they got a good running start.

So. No more sitting around, no matter how many sets of creeps this angel gave him. Time for the Old Scratch to make his move.

He grinned an *extra*-special grin. Far above, in Denmark, a major dairy farm's herd began producing curdled yogurt mid-milking.

Let's get this party started.

Lesson the first: always keep 'em guessing. That he could handle. Scratch was good at taking people by surprise.

He kick-swung around in his computer chair. It creaked in protest, but he ignored the sound. "You hungry?"

The angel blinked. Scratch compared the reaction to past behavior, and decided it'd be roughly equivalent to "Who? What? Huh?"

Good enough for a start.

Scratch scooted himself, chair and all, over to a small work table piled high with junk mail, fast-food leftovers, and some plans for a 3-D double-sided tetragonal jigsaw puzzle which claimed, when put together, would be in the shape of Marilyn Monroe. Totally unsolvable, yeah, but that was more or less the point. Scratch cleared off a space and started rummaging.

"Hungry, I asked. You know, as in food? Snack time? Or are angels still not into between meal munchies?" He chuckled, rifling through a Burger Boom bag for leftover French fries. They were only a few weeks old. "I got all kinds of stuff around here. Anything you could ask for. What profit the whole world if you can't enjoy a good pizza, huh?"

The angel tilted its head.

"Knock it off, already. You're making my ears ring with all the nonstop yakkety-yak."

The angel blinked. Again.

Scratch hid his grin this time. He also scooted his chair just a bit forward to hide his male body's definite reaction to a guy that ripped looking confused as a lost puppy. *Down!* he ordered his cock. *Down, I said! Bad boy!*

He would have sworn the organ in question blew him a metaphorical raspberry before boinging up like it was enjoying quality trampoline time. *Traitor. And, hello? Since when do I get a boner off the harps and halos crowd?*

Ecch. Hardly bore thinking about.

Scratch distracted himself by digging around again, finally coming up with an unopened packet of plastic utensils. "Sorry about the mess," he said offhandedly, knowing with painful precision just how hard nonstop chatter about Absolutely Nothing Important would jerk the chains of a strong silent type. "The Big Guy Upstairs didn't really budget in domestic staff as such, you know?"

He paused, fingering his chin. "Actually, I take it back. I did have this one demon a few years back. Far as I could tell, female, or at least she liked to pretend the gender. Smartest beastie ever damned to the Pit, let me tell you." Scratch whistled. "That dame cracked like a whip. Sometimes I almost started thinking she might launch her own counter-attack on Hell."

Scratch leaned back, drawing out his story far longer than strictly necessary, mostly because he *thought* he saw one corner of the angel's left eye developing a tiny tic. "Still, I figured keeping her around was worth a little worry. Never knew an idea doll like her. The things she could do with dried macaroni, glitter, and an empty egg carton... amazing.

"Sent her up to Earth maybe a decade ago. Two? I can't remember. Anyway, last I heard she got a syndicated TV show and she's having a royal ball. Torture's her specialty. She shows hopeless housewives how to make an ellllllllllegant window treatment out of ragbag scraps and offers DIY shortcuts to recipes a frikkin' graduate of French cooking school couldn't handle without growing three extra arms."

Scratch sighed fondly. "She's got six hundred and forty-seven complete and total nervous breakdowns to her cred." He pretended to wipe away a tear. "I do miss her."

The tic at the corner of the angel's eye was no longer by any means a figment of Scratch's imagination. *Score!*

He turned his attention back to the plastic ware. "Would you look at this," he said, turning a cellophane packet of the things over and over in his hands. "Never say I don't know the value of creativity. Let me introduce you to true evil."

Tearing the wrapper open, Scratch brandished his brain-child high. "My good sir, I present to you... the spork."

The angel's eye spasmed mid-tic.

"Fabulous, huh?" Scratch asked, just barely keeping down an attack of the giggles. "Is it a spoon or is it a fork? Men have gone insane trying to figure that one. Also from trying to use them for eating." He petted the brittle white plastic. "Good times, man, good times. But eh, well. Back to the hunt."

Even though he figured he was enjoying himself way too much for this not to come to a messy end, no way Scratch could stop now. Always had been a design flaw in his nature.

So, Scratch kept up a running commentary as he rifled through bags and boxes. "Got half a burrito here, only sort of fuzzy... no? Hey, how about some fried chicken—no, wait, sorry, nothing left but bones. Kinda greenish. I could do you a slice of cold anchovy pizza."

He paused for effect. "Or, hey, the ultimate snack food: instant ramen. Hey? Hmm?"

In the utter stillness, Scratch could have sworn he heard that dromedary's vertebrae snapping like cheap rice cereal.

The angel whipped his fiery sword out of the ground, flicking aside a smoldering wad of paper it had skewered, and held the sharp blade aimed straight at Scratch's head, ready to throw.

"Whoa, big guy, take it easy, huh? No ramen." Scratch dropped the neon packet, then put his hands together and twiddled the thumbs. "Let's try this instead of food then," he said, voice low. Glancing up through spiky eyelashes, he said, "Tell me who sent you and why, or I'll nuke a cup of soup and pour it down your throat. And they say I don't move with the times. Morons. We clear about this?"

The angel glared.

Scratch glared back. "I asked you, are we clear here?" Black fire flickered around his head. "I should warn you, I'm not a fan of waiting."

And the angel said… nothing.

* * *

Loki bounced across the floor, smothering his own flames with frantic squeaks of pain and dismay, no longer caring if Scratch or the angel saw him on the move.

He'd rolled several feet before he remembered he could change shape now. Deliberately, he chose a form with arms, a diminutive toy T-Rex, so he could smack himself in the forehead.

Then again, if confronted over playing the fool, Loki suspected he would be exonerated after pointing to the extenuating circumstances. Actually, it might make a fine joke if he gave it the right spin…

But first, to the situation at hand. Loki cocked his tiny reptilian head and peered at the two male-type beings, devil and angel, facing down over a table of the worst petty torture devices ever visited on mankind. Especially the ramen.

Loki shuddered. By Odin's one eye and both of Thor's basketball-sized nuts, he'd always suspected some truly twisted mind lay behind the invention of the horrifying snack in question. Why else would it be so inexpensive and so foul, yet addictive as crack cocaine all at once?

Pay attention! Are you growing senile? Look at them, old god. Look!

Loki looked... and laughed. Oh, but this was just priceless! Hidden beneath a tabletop and a sturdy, oversized tunic, respectively, both angel and devil sported paranormally impressive erections. Cocks all but pointing at one another, straining at their tethers.

Better than he'd dared hope for. Love had been his intent, turning Scratch's weapon back again him, but lust? Lust would do quite nicely. Perhaps better.

Let's see what happens when we increase the frequency just a bit. Say, up to eleven.

Loki scratched a set of tiny runes in the floor with one molded claw. A little trick Freyja had taught him ages past, in return for a favor. It worked well enough on mortals; he didn't see why it wouldn't have the same effect on those that lived forever. After all, its purpose was merely to remove all of one's inhibitions. Get people to let their hair down, so to speak. Or their horns, in this case.

Loki completed the rune set and watched it begin to glow. Above him, the angel and Scratch froze in place, save for their heads slowly rising, gazes locking in a stare intense enough to be almost frightening.

Almost, Loki insisted to himself, swallowing hard all the same. He scuttled back a few dino-steps, just in case.

A good thing, as it turned out.

* * *

Scratch stared at the angel.

The angel stared back.

A light sweat broke out on Scratch's forehead.

The angel's skin flushed dark.

Scratch's zipper broke.

The angel stood. Throwing down his fiery sword, he took three steps to cross the room and yanked Scratch out of his seat with one seriously large fist.

"What are you—" Scratch began to stammer, then stopped.

Words were kind of difficult to shape when there was a tongue, not your own, mind you, jammed down your throat.

I should probably not be enjoying this quite so much, Scratch thought vaguely. *Hey, while he's distracted, bet I can grab that sword out of his other hand and... oh, oops, not a sword.*

The angel snarled in Scratch's ear before biting the lobe.

"Well, as they say down here," Scratch muttered, "the Hell with it. And by the way, just what took you so long anyhow?"

Chapter Four

Surprisingly enough, there were no Words from On High, thundering down indignant, disgusted wrath.

Shockingly, Hell fell silent, as if all the demons had decided the better part of curiosity was opting for nap-time.

The cause was probably a natural reaction to reality bending on itself and the Devil falling for an angel. Scratch didn't care. He'd just re-discovered what a shameless slut he could be with proper motivation. For example, the offer of actual, sticky, real sex involving his personal person. Pretty much a turn-on no matter who was offering.

So, he'd never figured to get a lay out of a player for the Manger Squad. Didn't mean he was about to turn down a free orgasm when it came served up on a silver plate. Answers could wait. Scratch couldn't.

How many *centuries*—?

He'd do the math later. Right now? He was busy.

The angel had torn away Scratch's worn T-shirt easily as wet tissues, tossing the rags aside and leaving him bare from the waist up. *You had to stop there? The jeans, guy, jeans! Take a hint*!

Scratch complained in silence, however, his mouth being otherwise occupied. Very well occupied, namely by a pair of angelic lips and a tongue which, given how they never exercised themselves in talking, had surprising but definite talent when it came to deep, wet, raunchy kissing.

The angel reached up and jabbed his fiery sword—the metal one—into Scratch's overhead lights. *Poof*! Instant darkness surrounded both Heavenly Host and devil, minus a blue glow from dozens of computer screens.

Kinda romantic, in a bizarre way, Scratch thought dizzily, before the angel sucked a lower lip into his mouth and reduced his thought processes to, *Bibble*!

Huge, strong hands plowed down Scratch's back. He arched, shameless, as the angel grabbed his ass and began to squeeze. Scratch heard a rough rumble of satisfaction, and mentally thanked whatever passed for goodness he'd taken the "vain" road when shaping his present form. Great abs and a tight butt? Absolute necessities.

Judging from the angel's reaction, mostly the other variety of sword jabbing Scratch in the cleft of his thigh, Mr. Wings would be inclined to agree.

Also, not inclined to make this slow or romantic, which suited Scratch just fine. Who needed hearts and flowers when you could have a good nine inches up your hole or in your mouth?

So I'm not a poet. Sue me.

Scratch rolled his head around on his neck as the angel parted his thighs with ruthless hands. The jeans tore more like wet cardboard than sopping tissues, but hey, they were off in a jiffy. He wasn't gonna complain, especially seeing as how the angel was then letting Scratch's own hands help him scrabble open his hard-wearing canvas trousers and push them down.

Scratch caught the angel's cock in his hands, muffling a gulp. The guy was size-proportionate. Tall as a mountain, built like a boulder, and endowed like a stalactite. Or possibly a rhino. Scratch never minded mixing metaphors when they applied.

"Whoa," he said, measuring the cock with all ten fingers. "What are you, kidding? And who the Heaven did your upgrade because, I have to tell you, don't believe everything you see in *Playgirl* is real or anatomically correct, 'cause I—*ack!*"

Ignoring Scratch's commentary on the size of his equipment, the angel had opted to simply pick him up easily as a kitten and dump him across the cluttered table. Didn't even bother to sweep the junk off first. Scratch found himself nose-to-nose with a strangely smug-looking spork.

He didn't pay it much attention. Apparently, the angel could see just fine in the mostly-dark, and he wasn't one to waste good fucking time. Zeroing in, a dart to the bulls-eye, he parted the cheeks of Scratch's ass and dived in. A cool, wet tongue rasped at his pucker, sadly virginal for far too long, and proceeded, with seriously perverted and fervent energy, to rim like a thousand-dollar hooker.

Scratch yowled in surprise and almost turned inside out. Hard but not cruel, the angel smacked his ass with the flat of one hand.

Guess he wants me to be quiet. Okay, I can do quiet. I can. Sure. No problem.

I—

"Gyarrrrrrrrgh!" Scratch howled as the angel began to fuck him with his tongue.

* * *

Loki-Rex had ducked behind one leg of the table, out of the reach of huge and holy feet in solid boots, but hadn't been able to resist a cockroach scuttle across the way for a better view.

And, oh my, what a view it was.

He had often heard the descriptor "bugged-out eyes." However, he'd never seen anything that made his own sockets bulge with equal parts shock, glee, and… well, all right, more than a little voyeuristic arousal.

Loki was only male, after all. His gender was known for appreciating a good show. This looked to be one fit for recording in the grand annals of history.

He stared, amazed and delighted, and knew he could be no happier.

Popcorn would have been nice though.

* * *

The angel flipped Scratch over, sprawling the Devil's naked male form ass-first over a cascade of memoranda. He spared a brief thought to wonder if even he, with his "unusual" rank and privileges, would be doomed to damnation for what he planned on doing—yet somehow, he couldn't seem to care enough to stop.

He paused long enough to scrabble for a tiny, dust-covered bottle of mouthwash he thought he'd seen earlier, beneath the chicken bones—yes! Swish, swish, wipe the lips, spit—and there, sanitized and ready for further action. He wasted no time.

With his cleansed mouth soon fused to Scratch's, the angel reached down to grab a handful of demonic horn—so to speak. Ah, yes, there it was, easy to find. Nicely sized, though naturally smaller than his own. He measured it by finger spans, enjoying Scratch's yelps and yowls. He took his time at the task. A job worth doing was, after all, worth doing well.

He found himself surprised to discover Scratch had a pulse, blood throbbing through the length and breadth of his horn. A glance proved it to be deeply rosy, swollen fit to burst, and smeared with sticky strings seeping from the uncut tip.

He approved.

The angel dragged his fingers hard and heavy around a few strands of pre-come, then shoved them into his mouth for a taste. The flavor exploded with wasabi burn, tandoori spice, and the bitter scorch of raw cloves. He couldn't hold back a small groan of enjoyment.

Beneath him, Scratch managed a breathless laugh. "What, you like your meat charred?"

Frowning, the angel took one last lick at his forefinger. Charred? Not the word he would have chosen. But now, he found himself curious. What would he taste like to the Enemy?

A question deserved an answer.

The angel vaulted onto the table gracefully as a dancer, landing with one huge bare knee on either side of Scratch's well-built shoulders.

Scratch stared up at him, mind clearly attempting to work at its usual processing speed but hindered by the natural male regression into a troglodyte when hormones started running high enough. "Rruh?" he questioned, lips parting to form the sound.

It could have been considered an invitation. The angel didn't feel inclined to debate technicalities. Especially not with such a well-shaped mouth already opening up. He nudged his cock against the plumpness of Scratch's lower lip, painting it with his own over-anxious drops of seed.

Scratch stared at him, boggling. As much as he would have liked to slide his sword deep in, over the teeth and past the gums, the angel drew back and waited.

After a moment, he nudged Scratch and gave him a meaningful glare.

"Oh," Scratch said, peculiarly breathless. "Got it." The tip of a red tongue flickered out to swipe the drops of angelic semen from his mouth. The smears of holy seed left behind small burned spots, but as Scratch didn't seem worried by them, the angel decided not to dwell.

He had better things to contemplate, such as the way Scratch's eyes rolled back into his head, his mouth fell wide open, a rattling groan of impending orgasm burst from his throat, and his hips jerked up in sync with the arch of his spine.

The angel suspected Scratch rather enjoyed his taste.

Scratch was kind enough to confirm his theory. "What are you," he panted, "made of chocolate-covered opium? More!"

The angel shook his head. Perhaps later, or another time. At the moment, he had other plans.

Scratch raised his eyes hopefully. "How about you fuck me then?"

The angel grinned. He nodded.

"Hallelujah," Scratch whimpered. "And by the way, hurry it up!"

The angel gave him a look that indicated he'd been planning on that very thing.

Then, he got on with the show. Chances were he would indeed be punished for his violations; therefore, he would violate with a right good will and make it a roll in the spreadsheets neither would ever forget, come what might…

* * *

Loki boggled. *Oh. Oh, my.*

I didn't know that particular position was possible, given the limitations of human form.

If I had known Freyja's runes held so much power, I might well have put them to good use in my favor long before this!

Speaking of which, Loki glanced across the room to be certain his carven spell still glowed with sufficient power.

He blinked at what he saw.

Uh-oh.

* * *

Dignity? So long as no demons were playing Peeping Damien, Scratch decided pride could go get bent. He didn't want *anything* putting a stop to this.

The angel was kissing him again, strong, sharp teeth worrying at the skin just above Scratch's impatient cock. Not to worry, though. His hand slid down the pulsating length of Scratch's seriously horny horn, callused and rough as sandpaper. He knew exactly how to play the game man-style. It hurt like yowzah, and he knew from hurt, but also, it felt so good he let out a caterwaul of approval.

Thing was, much as Scratch hated the notion, if the angel didn't stop now, he was headed on a one-way power-jet track to shooting his brains out via his cock. Then it'd be over. Too soon. He wasn't gonna stand for that, or lie down as the case might be.

"Hey, cowboy!" Scratch managed to growl. "You in a hurry to cross the finish line? Ease up!" He bucked his hips, gyrating hard against the angel's hand. His own clever fingers, too nimble to play fair, stole down and got a nice solid grip on the angel's, er, sword.

The Heavenly being's eyes crossed. Scratch grinned. Apparently hours "wasted" playing video games did help with hand-eye coordination, after all. Who'd have thought?

He fondled the angel's cock, still shell shocked by the size but getting used to things. Already synced up with anticipation, truth be told. The thought of a cock like that one, a massive snake of an erection hard as chiseled granite, shoving up inside him— deep, rough, merciless…

Scratch wondered if he might not actually see stars for the first time in millennia.

"Get on," he panted, "with the good stuff. Okay? Foreplay, check. Now how about you—"

A small growl rumbled in the angel's chest. Scratch shut up. Fast. Mostly because as the angel made one of his rare noises, his baseball mitt of a fist squeezed Scratch's cock like it was a banana he wanted to pop out of its skin. Scratch didn't need the angel to speak his piece out loud. He figured it went something like, "Push me one more time and I'll tear off both cock and balls and feed them to you. Understand?"

Sweet mamma, yes.

So he got off on pain. He was *Satan*. Pain was his game.

The delicious threat of abuse sent a cascade of shudders ripping through his stomach. Deliberately, Scratch grunted and pushed harder into the angel's hand. His eyes glittered and teeth gleamed as he rasped, "Threat? Or promise?"

The angel snapped.

About time too.

Huge, rough hands reached down to grab Scratch's ass and spread him wide. Fingers shoved inside his all-but-virginal hole, the trimmed nails sharp as little knives. No lube, no condom, no need, eh?

Scratch rolled with the pain like a sailor re-learning how to walk on sea legs, releasing high-pitched yelps of horny impatience. "Harder," he ordered. "Go on! What're you afraid of?"

The angel caught Scratch's chin between two fingers of his free hand. The power in his gaze captured the Devil and held him still for a long moment. Wanting know if Scratch was sure he wanted to do this with him.

"Idiot." Scratch burst into flame. Literal flame. Handy party trick, and it got his point across. No pain, no charring, and it definitely impressed the current audience of one. He twisted, writhed, flipped, and slithered his legs up and over the angel's shoulders. Heels to Jesus, hallelujah, amen! "What do *you* think?"

The angel closed his eyes. Probably praying in thanks or for absolution. Most likely both.

Not that Scratch cared. The tip of a holy fuck tool was pressing against him, ready to slide into home base.

Prayers could wait.

Scratch arched *just* right and impaled himself on the angel's cock. Six sets of wings flew straight upwards in shock, and the angel's eyes popped open.

He stared at Scratch in utter disbelief.

Then he shrugged, and finally, finally, got on with the thrusting action.

After that, Scratch more or less forgot his own name, never mind where he was or who he was with.

The quest was on. Two immortal warriors on pilgrimage in search of the almighty orgasm, an orgasm straight from the Almighty. Their mingled howls all but raised the roof on Hell's antechamber, echoing off the walls. A casual observer might think they were slaughtering each other, and maybe they were. Who cared?

Grasping both of Scratch's hands in one of his, the angel pinned them above Scratch's head on the table while he gave a live-action lesson on just how to ride inhuman cock. Scratch felt things rip and tear deep inside himself, sharp enough to make his eyes water, and it was just — so — good. Just what he'd needed — wanted — burned after, for way too long.

Still, Scratch knew no matter what the plan, neither one of them was gonna last much longer. Felt too good, it'd been too long — so when the angel groaned mid-thrust, balls drawing up tight beneath his cock, Scratch let his own need for speed out to play. Nothing better than coming in tandem with a great top, like they had some hidden charge between their bodies that kicked in exactly — as — needed —

* * *

The sounds angel and devil made as they orgasmed would have woken the dead and sent them running for cover deeper than six feet under. Closer to home, it shocked Loki, his own hand rather busy at the moment with a most excellent wank, into losing control.

Completely losing control.

As in, materializing, full-size, naked, spent cock dangling in his hand and belly coated with spunk, on the floor of Scratch's computer haven.

He felt two sets of eyes on him. Amazed, disbelieving eyes.

Also, a rising sense of powerful wrath pointed in his general direction.

He dared to peek up. At any other time, he would have applauded at the sight of flushed, tangled limbs, thoroughly tousled hair damp with sweat, and chests heaving from the power of climax.

Still a tempting notion, or would have been if the angel hadn't been reaching for his fiery sword, and Scratch aiming a spork at Loki's head.

Loki struggled for a convincing lie, but even he knew when he'd been bested at his own game.

"Well, damn," he sighed, sitting back. "Was it good for you too?"

Chapter Five

On further consideration, it might have been wise to say nothing at all—if the way the spork almost snapped in Scratch's grip was anything to judge by.

Loki swallowed nervously, scooting backwards on his half-naked ass. One hand for leverage, one hand up in the classic gesture of, "See? I'm unarmed, helpless and quite willing to cooperate. Provided, of course, you don't bury, plunge, or insert those unpleasantly sharp-looking weapons anywhere that either has nerve endings or a sad tendency to bleed, please and thank you."

Scratch didn't seem inclined to mercy. His dark halo appeared, swirling with a rainbow miasma of dull mud and dried-blood crimson, a bit like the rainbow in a gasoline spill from a car engine.

The angel regarded Loki with a face blank as a store mannequin's. At the moment, a type to be featured in a porn emporium's back window, but otherwise still and emotionless as the surface of a stagnant lake.

Loki attempted a smile. "Do be reasonable, gentlemen. I've an excellent reason for being here." He thought quickly and grabbed up an old standard. "You see, you're in terrible danger. I've been sent to warn you."

"Loki?"

"Yes, Scratch?"

"You really, really deserve this. I only wish it'd hurt more."

"I beg your par—*ow!*" The spork, hurled with precision and force, buried itself surprisingly deep just below navel level in Loki's stomach. "That hurt, you prick!" he snapped, looking up just in time to see—

The angel, still calm as a force of nature, looking down at Scratch. Absolutely nothing resembling emotion appeared on his face as he moved his arm slightly up and across with perfect precision. The sword in his fist burned a sudden, cerulean blue.

"Scratch," Loki had time to say, earning himself a puzzled look. Not the direction Scratch should have glanced.

If he'd looked upwards instead, he might have seen and been able to stop the angel's arm as it arced down, slicing his fiery blade clean as butter through Scratch's neck and deep into the table beneath.

The Devil's eyes opened wide as flesh parted from flesh. Smooth as silk, and almost as elegant as a surgeon's first incision save for the particularly unappealing meaty crunch of metal through bone. Loki almost fancied he caught a twist of disgust on Scratch's lips even as they gaped wide with shock.

Still pressing down with his blade, the angel shook his head. He looked somewhat close to grieved by his actions. As would a mother to her newborn child, he lowered his face and pressed a gentle kiss to Scratch's forehead.

Then, with an even gentler flick of forefinger and thumb beneath Scratch's chin, the angel knocked his severed head off the table. Thumping to the floor, it bounced and rolled like an oddly angular rubber ball, coming at last to a nauseating, wet *splat* atop an empty, flattened bag of microwave popcorn.

"Not quite the sort of afterglow a man expects," Loki murmured, staring at the severed head, which was a little too close to his foot for comfort. "Heated skin, running sweat, sticky sexual fluids, yes. Blood, generally not. Decapitation is somewhat rare, to say the… least." Unable to stop himself, he prodded Scratch's slack cheek with one toe.

Scratch's dull eyes stared back at him with the stupidity of the well and truly deceased.

Loki shivered. "I must admit I'm curious," he said. "Do you generally finish your assignations with a bit of hearty slaughtering? Or is this was what you came to do in the first place, and found sexual congress the only way to work around Scratch's sense of self-preservation? Males do tend toward stupidity if an orgasm is in the offing." He scratched the back of his neck, which was prickling in a way he was certain he did not like. "You have no answer for me?"

The angel gave Loki a long, expressionless look with no hint of sorrow or regret. He slipped backwards off Scratch's limp body, landing on his feet gracefully as a cat. A large cat. What out-ranked a lion?

Much to Loki's discontent, the angel kept his gaze fixed on him as he retrieved his bloodied sword with one massive fist on the hilt. It'd sunk deep into the old wood of Scratch's table, which gave it up with some reluctance, a screech and a groan, but near-zero effort on the angel's part.

Folding his wings, the Heavenly being picked up a scrap of Scratch's shredded T-shirt and began to clean the length of the blade. Loki scooted back a few more feet. Mind you, he had seen many a dreadful thing in his time—had, in point of fact, caused most of them and stayed to enjoy the show. A naked angel, splattered with blood and semen, wiping down his flaming sword with the remnants of a Stones concert shirt proved a bit more disconcerting than even one of the Asgard could handle.

He'd be blasted if the sight didn't bring a pain to his stomach.

Pain? Stomach? Oh, wait, yes. Loki reached down and tugged Scratch's plastic projectile utensil out of his belly. Retrieval proved rather painful and surprisingly... red. "Quite an arm on that old fellow," he said, tucking the spork into a pocket.

The weapon used to strike Scratch's last blow would fetch quite a price as a conversation piece in any number of circles. Loki might be feeling a touch of nausea, but he had not grown stupid with his shock.

Come to think on it, a few more souvenirs might not go amiss. Loki nudged Scratch's severed head a second time, thoughtful. "Would you mind if I helped myself to a few locks of hair?" he asked. "Possibly a horn—or two? All in the name of free enterprise, you know. As in, now you're dead it would be free to me, and I could make a successful enterprise out of selling you off piecemeal."

The angel paused in his diligent sword-cleansing to quirk an eyebrow at Loki.

"Here, don't look at a fellow like that," Loki protested. "He's dead, isn't he? Shuffled cleanly off the immortal coils?"

The angel narrowed his eyes.

Loki squirmed. "I don't suppose you'd be kind enough to turn around while I make myself decent?"

The angel wasn't. At all. Rather, he scanned Loki up and down, as if he were a butcher and Loki a prime beef carcass... a not-unexpectedly displeasing mental image, all things considered.

His sword burned a tad brighter and hotter. Perking up, as it were.

"Your blade has a taste for blood, I presume?" Loki asked, summoning up his best "harmless" smile. "Tell me, is it sentient? I've always had a sort of curiosity about the weapons of the Host."

The angel continued to show no reaction whatsoever.

Loki squirmed. He'd never thought anyone could best Odin when it came to staring a fellow down, one eye notwithstanding, but this angel could give the old Norse a run for his gold.

However, aside from continuing to absently polish his sword, the angel made no move. Right — that was it. Loki had always known cowardice to be the cunning flipside of valor. He who turned and ran away lived to fight another day, yes?

"I'll just be on my way," he said cheerfully. "But I do think I'll take a few odds and bobs with me. You've no need of them, I'm sure, and I don't believe Scratch is in a position to protest."

Scratch's eyes popped open and blazed at Loki. Literally. "You wanna bet?"

Loki screamed like a little girl.

The angel blinked.

"Give me a break," Scratch grumbled. "Did you actually think that would kill me? Please." His disembodied head rocked disturbingly from side to side. He laughed, a thoroughly unsettling peal of mirth considering the source and situation. "You two? You got a lot to learn about me. Flaming swords, decapitation, give me a *break*..."

Loki and the angel watched in fascinated horror as Scratch's corpse rolled off his work table, landing lightly on the balls of its feet. It shook itself dog-fashion, droplets of blood and semen flying off. Then, as if this were perfectly natural, the body began to stumble towards Scratch's head.

Loki realized, vaguely, that the entity in question was continuing to bitch *sotto voce* all the while. "You know, a guy like me really needs to spend time working on glamours. Glamours, that's what I need. Make one of my Hell-spawn look halfway attractive, right? Get my rocks off with someone who's got a decent pair of balls, but not the kind that lead to playing guillotine master. Speaking of which, way to kill the afterglow, jerk."

Scratch glared up at the angel, who looked very close to dumbfounded. He snorted in disgust. "Gorgeous and stupid, huh? Figures. I always fall for the dumb ones — well, granted they have a decent cock or a nice set of boobs. Possibly both. I'm not picky. If a guy has to have every hair curled just right, he'll never get laid, and I'm here to tell you the opportunities are few and far between in Hell, in case you hadn't guessed."

Scratch's head hopped forward a few squelchy, bouncing feet to meet his body halfway. Loki made a small noise, which, to his dismay, sounded much like a mouse caught in a trap.

"Like you've never seen this trick before," Scratch scoffed.

"As a matter of fact, I haven't."

"No kidding? Huh. Remind me never to teach you how it's done." Scratch's smile turned nasty as his hands reached down to gather up his head. "Don't leave yet, kids. It's just the intermission."

"Pardon?"

Scratch balanced his head on the stump of his neck, paused, and said, "In case you're wondering — this does hurt like a sumbitch."

He inhaled a wet, gargling breath that rattled deep down in his lungs. Strands of skin extended, spaghetti-fashion, from stump to stump and lashed themselves together. A flicker of flame, the smell of cheap hot dogs scorching over a campfire, and Scratch was whole once more.

Wincing, he cracked his neck joints. "I really hate it when someone tries to kill me," he mused, poking at the join site.

Too quickly for angel or old god to follow his movements, Scratch flung a letter opener at one and a broken shard of CD-R at the other. He grinned as both made choking noises when the missiles hit home and sank in deep. "Score."

Loki stared at Scratch with disbelief, while the angel slowly, silently folded to his knees in a definite state of anguish.

Scratch leaned back against his table, folded his arms, and smirked. "Bet you didn't see those coming."

"And I very well never may see myself coming again," Loki croaked. Despite knowing a peek at the damage would only increase the pain, he couldn't resist glancing down. Yes, Scratch's projectile had landed exactly where he had feared.

Fortunately, nothing had been severed. Yet.

The angel whimpered.

Scratch raised an eyebrow. "You cut off my head..." he said, his voice trailing off. "Seemed like fair payback to me."

He rummaged through the clutter on his table until, with a small, satisfied grunt, he emerged with two broken No. 2 pencil stubs and brandished them high. "I wonder how hard I'd have to throw something blunt to make a decent puncture?" he mused aloud, tossing the pencils up in the air and catching them, juggling aimlessly.

"May I request you not attempt to find out?"

"Nope." Scratch's attention riveted itself to the pencils, tracking their lazy arcs through the air. He sent one hurtling toward the angel and knocked his flaming sword skittering out of an already loosened grasp.

He smiled. Loki was beginning to appreciate why man and beast alike feared Scratch's smiles. "So," he said. "How about we start with the basics? Great sex, killer technique, no pun intended, but I'd really, really love to know how an angel got working parts, learned how to use them, and didn't mind applying those skills to someone currently of the same gender."

Loki began to crab-crawl backwards. *Odin, Freyja, Thor, let him not notice me…*

No such luck. Another pencil stub zoomed across the way to score the top of Loki's scalp. "You're not going anywhere." Scratch cut him a narrow glance, dark as bitumen and pitch. "Got a few questions for you too, as it happens. Why did you pick now to come around for a visit? I'm doubting you just missed me. Why did you come back and play Peeping god while I was having my fun, as long as it lasted? And, most important, would those scratches on the floor be one of Freyja's little love spells?"

Loki gulped. "Er… yes?"

Scratch sighed. "Figured as much." He bit his lip, as lost if in thought. "Okay. How do you want to die?"

"I beg your pardon?"

"Die. End it all. Take that final leap into the great wide open. I'm talking to both of you, by the way, just so we're clear. You came into my home, took advantage of my good nature, cut off my head, and played around with spell casting. Me, I'm not the forgiving sort." The broken pencils zoomed back into Scratch's hand. He made a fist around them and squeezed. Wood crumbled into ashes and fell through his fingers in a powdered flurry.

He looked up. "I learned a long, long time ago that when you ask for forgiveness, you usually get the shaft. Not the fun kind, either."

Again, neither being saw Scratch move, but only registered a flash of motion before Scratch had both pinned against a wall. The fact that both were taller in their current forms, as well as bulkier, mattered not a whit. He held them high and fast by the neck, easily as rag dolls.

He sighed. "You know, it's kind of a shame. We could have made some beautiful music together, and hey, I remember you weren't so bad yourself one upon a time, Loki-boy. But you had to go and screw with me."

Scratch looked from face to face. So far as Loki could tell, the angel remained expressionless — unless — was it his imagination, or did his eyes give a small twitch? The briefest of glances in Loki's direction.

An idea popped into his mind. Divine inspiration? It would be a laughable concept under normal circumstances, but Loki did not deem this a good day to die.

He licked his lips, slow and languid. "It isn't too late," he suggested in a voice low and sibilant as curls of smoke.

Scratch frowned. "Say what, now?"

"One always has several choices close to hand," Loki crooned. He let his eyelids droop over a flare of feigned desire. "And a last request is traditional."

"What are you talking about?"

Loki was in the middle of forming his next sentence when that which he'd least expected came to pass: the angel opened his mouth.

"Sex," the angel said. "All three of us. One good fuck for the road. Deal?"

Chapter Six

"Huh."

Scratch didn't feel too inclined to release either Loki or the angel from where he'd pinned them to his wall. Granted, there had been an urge to yelp and jump back when Flyboy opened his lips and used them to make actual words, so hey, Scratch figured he could give himself a pat on the back for hanging tough.

It sounded like such a good idea he went ahead, extruded a third arm, and thumped himself between the shoulder blades. Loki made a strange peeping sound, and while the angel had returned to his usual Joe Stoic deal, he did raise one eyebrow a couple centimeters.

Probably because Scratch hadn't bothered to waste energy making the arm look overly human.

But meh, what did he care? He raised his stalky, hard-shelled new appendage and gave his prisoners a cheerful wave. "How's it hanging?" he asked, smiling at each in turn.

Loki swallowed, but to give him credit, Trickster did look to be getting over his attack of the inner X chromosome. He even managed a decent glare. "You do realize you look as if you've sprouted a lobster claw."

"Yeah?" Curious, Scratch angled the arm to peer at it. "You think?"

"Plucked from a tank, boiled alive, and served up on a tawdry Melmac plate with pretensions of fine china." Loki added a dash of "sneer" to his expression. "Is it your intent to frighten us with such a ridiculous thing?"

"Scare you? Nah." Scratch sucked his third arm back inside the human shell he wore. "If I wanted to scare you, I'd do this."

He dropped his mask and let them see, just for a moment, his true face. The one he'd been forbidden to wear when he fell from Heaven. He could only abide its burn for seconds, but now seemed like a great time to show the visage off.

Loki gaped, lips first frozen open, then struggling for words. The angel's gaze never wavered. His only sign of acknowledgement was a single crystal tear slipping from one eye to evaporate on his cheek.

Scratch was… beautiful.

"They didn't call me the Morningstar for nothing, boys," Scratch said, almost under his breath. "Cleopatra? Helen of Troy? Alexander? David? They had nothing on me. *Nothing*. In those days, we could walk whatever worlds we wanted—you do know there's more than one—and do anything we liked with whoever tickled our livers."

Curls of sunlight gold tumbled against Scratch's cheeks as he stared at his captives through eyes he knew, he remembered, were an unimaginably beautiful blue. The deepest shade of blue ever painted by a master's hand.

"I was crafted special. The best and most beautiful of all. To look at me was to want me, and to want me was to burn for me. One glance and anyone I wanted craved me like no drug on earth, then or now, from opium to Ecstasy. I had it all. Everything I wanted. Anyone I wanted."

The memory of his long-lost halo began to fade. Scratch's hair straightened and darkened into coal black. Irises shaded from heartbreaking blue to the dead dullness of a raven's corpse, spreading to cover the surface of his eyes. Diamond pupils of blood red popped open in their centers.

He couldn't see it happening, but he knew what it looked like. He'd watched it before in mirrors, in the surface of still waters, and had it etched fire-deep in his memory. From mortality to Glory, falling down to damnation. Wasn't pretty. Not even the rough-and-tumble good looks he liked to dress up in.

"So now you know who I am," he said in a voice like a heart going flat-line. "The package deal. And here's the kicker: I'm stuck here, like this, forever remembering who I was and what I looked like, and not able to do a thing about making amends.

"You, Loki, you can be whatever you want, go wherever, do anything, and what's the worst you get? A few centuries playing with snakes. Is that fair? Don't think so. But hey, I didn't make the rules for your Ass Guard."

"Asgard," Loki croaked. He was staring at Scratch with a mixture of horror and hey, cool, some respect.

"Whatever. And you, Wing-Fling, looks to me like you figured out a way to bend the rules I tried to break. Got yourself a great package in more ways than one, and you know how to use the goods inside. But you still have the wings, and you still work the mission. Got to admit, it confuses me."

Scratch tightened his grip until he heard vertebrae creak. "I don't like being confused."

Loki made a garbled noise. Scratch shook himself wet-dog style, melting back into his generally preferred physical shape. "Oh, hey, sorry. You wanted to say something?" He pressed harder. "I can't really imagine it's anything I'm interested in hearing."

"Will you listen to me then?"

"Crap! Stop *doing* that!" Scratch glared at the angel. Implacable, naturally. "Either start talking as a habit, or keep your trap shut, okay? Otherwise we might find out if a heart attack kills me when a sword won't."

The angel half-smiled. "I'm not a man of many words."

Scratch rolled his eyes. "Where's my trophy for Understatement of the Year?"

"A preference for silence doesn't mean I'm stupid, or unable to speak when I want." The angel gave his solid shoulders a roll and popped out of Scratch's grasp.

"Hey!"

"Sorry. You'd rather I stayed put and played the victim?"

"Well, not now," Scratch grumbled. "Was all that just you humoring me?"

"More or less." The angel's lips quirked. "I do think Loki's in some discomfort, though."

"One out of two." Scratch glanced back at Loki. And cracked up. The old god's form shifted and melted like cheap gelatin. Watch it wiggle, watch it jiggle, then pop right back into shape. He made it halfway to a baker's dozen of forms that could slip loose or break the Devil's grip on his throat, but no dice. His form always reverted to default.

"Having trouble?" Scratch asked innocently.

If looks could kill... but then again, none of the three in that room could really die, as such. Granted, the knowledge made holding Loki up like a moose head pointless except for the entertainment value, but what the heck.

"You want down?" Scratch smiled. Loki paled, but managed to nod.

"You want down?" he repeated. Loki glared, nodding again.

"What's the magic word?"

Loki hissed.

"Uh-uh-uh. Strike one. Try again."

"I would," the angel said diffidently. He'd turned aside to polish his sword.

"What is it with the Host and elbow grease?"

The angel shrugged.

"Great, it's quiet time again. Fine." Scratch turned back to Loki. "Tick tock, old god. I can't kill you, granted, but I know for a fact and according to Odin, the one-eyed bastard, I can make you wish for death."

Loki gargled out something like a sigh. His eyes telegraphed: *I can't speak, you moron. Exactly what do you want me to do?*

"Use your imagination."

Scratch could hear Loki's teeth grinding. Murder in his eyes, the Trickster raised both hands and clasped them together as if praying Christian fashion.

"Good enough." Scratch dropped Loki, without warning or ceremony, to tumble into a tangled heap of arms and legs on the floor. He turned his back to walk away.

"That, gentlemen, concludes today's entertainment," he said, sitting down at his computer and pulling up the PMS control console. "Which, just in case you were wondering, means 'scram.' I have business."

The angel peered over his shoulder. Scratch backhanded him in the chiseled jaw without looking. "Snooping? Not appreciated."

He heard Loki scrambling awkwardly to his feet. Then, a few squelching noises. Silence. Some grinding sounds.

"Damn."

"Problems?" Scratch asked, bored. "It's like listening to someone try and hot-wire a 1962 P.O.S."

Loki frowned. "What does that mean?"

"Piece. Of…"

"Oh."

"Yep." *Click, tap, click.*

"Odd you should make such an apposite comparison."

Scratch allowed himself a tiny grin. "Having trouble getting it up, up and away?" He clicked on the site counter to get an idea of the day's take of suckers in search of true love. Huh. Didn't seem to want to load. The hourglass of doom taunted him, hovering in the middle of his screen.

"I appear to be… stuck," Loki admitted.

"Yeah? Join the club."

"I cannot change shape, you simpleton!"

"Bummer." *Click, click.*

"Well?"

"Well, what? You think I can do something about your issues? Find a therapist."

The angel laid a solid, surprisingly warm hand on Scratch's shoulder, squeezing with gentle insistence.

"I," Scratch gritted, "do not help people. Why aren't you getting this? You want someone who'll give a hand to a friend in need? Dig around the sofa for a quarter and call someone who cares."

The hourglass mocked him. "Piece of junk!" Scratch smacked the side of his monitor. "Work!"

"Scratch." The angel's voice was quiet. "I should tell you something."

"Unless you're serious about one for the road? You have nothing I want to hear."

Firm lips grazed the side of Scratch's throat. A tongue flickered out to draw a wet, nasty pattern on his skin. "Actually," the angel murmured, "I was, and am."

Scratch stopped in his tracks. He tried to speak, had to swallow a knot of utter *huh*? and finally came out with, "Say what now?"

"I'll show you mine if you show me yours."

"You're serious?"

Nod.

"Huh." Scratch rubbed the back of his neck. "Enjoy a quality snit, or get fucked a second time in the same century. Choices, choices." He sighed. "Fine, I'm easy. Way too easy. I'll play along—if you tell me who sent you. Although, I'm pretty sure I can guess. Loki? You up to talking speed yet?"

"After a fashion," Loki grated. Sounded painful. "Let me be the first to assure you I did not send this most peculiar angel to you. I merely spotted him on his way, and thought to make use of him."

Scratch heard Loki staggering closer, step by unsteady step. "However, I would also like to inform you that I had absolutely nothing to do with what happened once he arrived."

"And you just doodled Freyja's love runes because you were what, bored?" Scratch stared very, very intently at the rotating hourglass. He drummed his fingers on his mouse pad.

"No. I had intended to infect you both with unholy lust." Loki sounded sour as raw persimmons. "I had thought my ploy successful, but in the angel's first lunge at your person, he ran through the spell and knocked it all to buggery. Literally. The magic died. He kept on going. So did you, as a matter of fact."

Scratch snapped. He spun around his chair, staring. "Wait a second. You mean it wasn't a trick?"

Loki looked as sour as he'd sounded. "At least not one of mine," he admitted, rubbing his bruised neck. "If someone else is playing games, I know not who, nor why."

"You're... telling the truth." Scratch shook his head to clear it. "Son of a... you're telling the truth." He laughed without a trace of humor. "Never thought I'd see the day."

"Yes, well, that makes two of us." Loki glowered. "If you don't mind, I would enjoy hearing a few answers to my own questions. How did you infect *me*, Scratch?"

Scratch frowned. "Come again?"

"If I could, rest assured I would."

"Huh?"

Loki rolled his eyes and turned to face Scratch, pelvis front. Pelvis with attachments showing a definite interest in something. Apparently, himself. "I am not gay," he said angrily.

"That looks kind of gay to me." Scratch reached out to finger Loki's swollen cock. "Hey, little guy. You want to play?"

"I beg your pardon!"

"Okay, medium guy."

"Scratch!" Loki snarled. "Intriguing as certain parts of my anatomy find your inappropriate sense of humor, as well as your offer, I must point out something you seem to have overlooked."

"It's obviously not a cure for impotence."

"The door, you horn-brain!" Loki shouted. "The door to your antechamber! Look! It's gone, Scratch. Gone without a trace. Melted into the walls."

Scratch sat up straight, staring. "I'll be damned all over again," he said after a moment. The door *had* vanished. "Got a bad feeling about this, guys."

"Your insight astounds me."

Scratch stood up and waded toward where the entrance used to be. He ran his hands over the area, finding nothing but peeling paint and smooth rock. "Things just got a lot more interesting," he said absently.

A quiet *ding*! sounded from behind him. A sound Scratch knew by heart. One he usually liked to hear. The sweet sound of a web page finished loading. Yet for some reason, he knew—just knew—maybe because of the way his day had been going so far—when he turned around to look, he wasn't going to like what he saw.

He took a peek.

"Sucks to be right," he said, almost resigned, as he watched the PMS meters of "good match" versus "mismatch" reversing in size and success rate. The negatives went down like a popped balloon while the successes went up like a cock at the sight of Mr. February.

"And somehow I'm not surprised to see this," he said. "Neither one of you had anything to do with wacky website shenanigans? Before you even try to start, don't lie to me, okay? I know you now, and I can tell if you lie."

The angel and Loki shook their heads in tandem. Scratch took in a deep breath and rubbed his hand across his face. "To summarize, then: we're stuck, we're alone, and my mis-match-making system just went tits up in a big way."

"So it would appear."

The angel nodded.

"I could get mad. You think it'd help? Nah, don't answer the question. I already know." Scratch held up a hand, then turned it palm up, reaching out. "We'll figure something sooner or later. Beat your sword into a jackhammer if we've got to. In the meantime…"

He glanced over his shoulder. "You two want to try that one for the road thing and see if a road opens up?"

The angel glanced at Loki. Loki glanced at Scratch. Scratch glanced at the angel. In defiance of physics, they glanced at each other simultaneously.

The angel grinned, nodding.

Loki shrugged. "I'm in."

"Works for me." Scratch turned around, his smile maniacal and his cock going up like a flag on a pole. "I thought I'd never ask. Spread 'em, boys. The Devil's goin' down to George's."

Chapter Seven

There's just a certain something men bring to sex. Sex with women? Not to be taken lightly. Females of the species invested all kinds of... feelings... in five minutes' worth of making slippery noises.

For one thing, they'd rather it lasted longer than your basic five minutes. But not *too* long now, and hey, don't lean on her hair, get beard burn on her boobs, or, Heaven forefend, leave any hickeys, bite marks, scratches, or any kind of sign a man had been there. Her orgasm came first, last, and most important of all.

A guy intent on pleasing his woman—hurray for him, sure—but face it, after he got done being Mr. Enlightened, Sensitive Gentleman, his own climax was more or less an afterthought. A sad, lonely spurt of semen safely confined within a condom. Ladies didn't want to get messier than their preference or ruin the sheets, and usually weren't looking to get pregnant.

So women were great, no doubt about it. Hats off to the double X. Still, they had the ability to turn a guy's basic need to get in, get off and get out into a serious exercise in concentration and control. Kind of like being faced with a chalkboard full of calculus equations when you'd been hoping for some dirty graffiti.

Depending on how well a guy controlled himself when horniness replaced other higher brain functions, he could either have a good time or end up banished to an inevitably uncomfortable couch.

Overall and after a few-odd million years, the so-called "gentler" gender tended to give Scratch a migraine. He respected their inherent evil, but there were things even the Devil didn't tangle with.

Hence his current tussle with the angel and Loki, of all people—beings—entities—whatever. Loki said he wasn't gay, sure, fine, but Scratch had plucked a few stories off the grapevine before, and it didn't look like the old god's cock minded the idea of a good, dirty mano-a-mano session. Scratch figured underneath the bluster, Loki was like himself: tri-sexual. Try anything once, repeating as needed if he had a good time.

As for the angel, his flaming sword probably had all layers of phallic meaning.

Not that Scratch cared. It looked like he was about to get off in a big way, which meant time to stop thinking and start grappling. From the looks on his soon-to-be partners' faces, they agreed. And faster would be better, yeah?

Scratch grinned at the two male-shaped beings one last time — and pounced.

Vive la games!

* * *

When he had been given his unusual attributes and a tacitly implied lack-of-being-forbidden to go forth and make use of them, the angel had not quite known what to do. He supposed the ability to achieve an erection and come to human-type climax was a sort of Heavenly paycheck for the work he did.

There were certainly worse means of compensation. However, he had quickly learned sex with women, his first experiments, were not terribly to his taste. Women were lovely, smelled sweet, and had deliciously soft curves, rounded breasts, plus dips and swells fit to drive a male mad.

He had very much enjoyed his first few encounters.

Then time passed, as was its habit, and the angel found himself completely bewildered by the gender's rapid transmutation. Women no longer looked like women. They lost all their softness in a never-ending quest to streamline themselves into a size 2. Breasts shrank from generous pillows to tiny bumps in the road often re-augmented by horribly distasteful, hard silicone fillings.

The angel shuddered. The feel of a man-made breast made the flesh of his fingers crawl. What had happened to make females so unhappy with their natural shapes? Why force and squeeze themselves into fleeting ideals of fashion's fancy? It made no sense to him.

Therefore, being a logical sort, he had turned to men to see how he fared with his own chosen gender.

Much, much better. Some problems remained, of course, but the angel generally did not need to worry about hurting them, and if anything had been surgically altered, it certainly didn't come up during bed sport.

Scratch wondered why he didn't speak. He had learned the wisdom of silence after answering, honestly, the question, "Do these pants make my ass look fat?"

After the bruises healed, he had decided keeping his mouth shut to be the wiser part of valor. Also homosexuality. Men might be oversensitive about the size of the swords they packed, but they would never hurl a high-heel at your head with devastating accuracy if you dared to be honest.

Well, most men. Drag queens were a different story.

But why was he wasting time on thought? Scratch, that most unlikely of bed partners, and Loki, perhaps more unlikely still, were very clearly ready to "get it on."

Far be it from him to object.

The angel did what he did best: got down to work.

* * *

I must say, it's been some good years since I have found myself in this particular situation.

Surprisingly, I find I've missed it.

Loki squirmed a bit, both from the pressure in his loins and the knowing glitter in Scratch's eyes. Gay? Certainly not. He merely considered himself the open-minded sort. A being of his nature, more often than otherwise free to walk all the worlds as he so chose, had taken advantage of many sexual offers in his day. Some male, some female, some which could only be classified as "other" or "none of the above." He'd found a new set of kinks for each gender on every landmass and in each dimension he'd explored. Anything from tentacles to hanging upside down during fellatio rituals had caught his fancy in the past.

Orgies were nothing new. It had merely been... a while. Longer still since the chance of clashing with beings easily his equal in power and might, not to mention libido. The thought crossed and re-crossed Loki's mind that he should be careful before diving into this particular pool.

But only for a moment.

There was simply too much fun in the offing to turn back. He suspected he might walk away with permanent damage, possibly on favored parts of his anatomy, but he also felt more than certain almost anything would be worth it.

Time to dance.

* * *

The pause that refreshed came to an abrupt end as the three men pounced upon one another.

Truly a sight to behold, if one had the nerve. Sinewy arms twining about those bulging with muscle. Legs tangling together in a three-way pretzel fit to give Escher nightmares. Deep, wet, dirty kisses that were more clashing of mouth against mouth against mouth than expressions of affection. But then, affection was not so much the order of the day or hour.

Three cocks, ranging from long and elegant to shorter and thicker to alarmingly yet enticingly massive bashed against hips and bellies, leaving behind sticky trails that smeared from one to another until they mixed in a seriously blasphemous cocktail. No pun intended.

And in reference to tails, hands wasted no time on gentle, preliminary petting. They went straight for the gold mine, diving between ass cheeks to probe at tight rings of muscle. Testing to see how well they stretched. How far up and at what angle a man needed to crook his finger to hit another's happy spot and be rewarded with yelps of pleasure.

They lost track, quickly, of who was who was who. Did it matter? In their opinion, no. All three were more than happy to be caught up in a maelstrom of wandering hands, eager cocks, and strength that matched and challenged their own. When their legs gave out beneath them, they collapsed to the floor with hoots of laughter and picked up right where they'd left off.

The earth above took notice of what was going on in its guts and shook for fear. Milk soured, hailstorms rained down on California beachfronts, and mockingbirds began to chirp an uncannily accurate rendition of "Jailhouse Rock."

Monks prayed. Nuns wept. Priests headed for their church's stashes of communion wine.

Scratch, the angel, and Loki continued to fuck with merry abandon. Hard-swollen cocks thrust into eager asses, hips pumping in a ragged rhythm no one bothered to finesse. Nails scored along backs and teeth sank deeply into skin and muscle. There was pain and there was pleasure, rising to such great heights they could no longer tell who was who or doing what.

It didn't matter. This? This was the best that sex ever got. Ever.

For immortals, it meant considerably more than it might to mayfly humankind. Had a considerably further-flung effect as well.

This particular orgy made the earth move.

When they climaxed, the sun eclipsed ever so briefly. Someone, or something, tolerated the shenanigans, possibly even approved of them, but for all that had to wink away from the sight of three male faces twisting in orgasm.

Some things simply aren't pretty even in pornography. It doesn't mean they aren't the best times of your life, no matter how many years that might span. Be that as it may, though, there was nothing creepier than the expression a man made while shooting his load. Or funnier. Again, it all depended on your point of view.

* * *

"Whoa," Scratch said from where he'd sprawled out, all but boneless, on the floor. He'd pillowed his head on an overstuffed, well-aged binder. Possibly a user's guide from the early 1980's. "Not bad, my friends. Not bad at all."

The angel sighed, a definitely happy sound, tucking his arms behind his head.

Loki mumbled something incoherent, but well-pleased.

"You want to go again?" Scratch asked.

Loki raised his head wearily, peering out through tangles of sweat-soaked hair. "You cannot be serious."

"Criminy, calm down. I didn't mean right now." Scratch petted his satiated cock like a puppy. "Good boy. Sometime later. You know, after you guys find a way out. I'm just saying I wouldn't mind you finding your way back down here from time to time."

Loki raised one eyebrow. "I have no soul to barter for what you offer."

"Did I ask for it? Sheesh. You take one guy up on a mountain, try to make a deal, and suddenly you're the creepy dude who walks around in a dirty raincoat asking people if they want a piece of candy." Scratch shook his head in disgust. "I get plenty of souls who end up here no assistance needed, thanks. Nah. Best I'm hoping for — and it's a whole lot better than a soul — is another mind-blowing party like this."

The angel sighed again. Almost purred.

"I think he might be agreeable," Loki commented.

"For him? It was as good as a speech. Kind of wrapped up *thanks, I had a great time, sure, we'll do this again soon* all in one, don't you think?"

"Peculiarly enough, I do."

"'Them's the words I likes to hear. Even if they aren't, you know, actual words. On his part." Scratch chuckled to himself. He gazed at the ceiling then, his expression slowly falling into somber lines. "Does always seem to be the way, though, huh?"

"What would that be?" Loki's hand, which could be amazingly creative when he put in decent time and effort, crept over to lay itself atop Scratch's arm. He rubbed the pad of his thumb against sweat-dampened skin. "You sound displeased."

"Who, me? Nah. Trust me, I am beyond satisfied."

"What happens to be the problem, then?"

"Nag, nag, nag."

"Indulge me."

"Meh… it's my mind coming back together after you two blew it to smithereens." Scratch bit his lip. "I just meant, this is life for me. I find something good? It isn't something that can stay, or wants to stay for long. Soon as we crack open a hole in the wall, you two are gonna be on your way, and me? Stuck here until the universe turns the lights out and hangs up its Closed For Business sign."

"Would you like a handkerchief to mop up your tears of woe?"

"Stick a cork in it, Loki."

"Rather stick a cock in it," the angel murmured.

"Stop *doing* that!" Loki and Scratch both shouted. They shared twin looks of annoyance and *what-can-you-do?* as the angel laughed.

Loki paused in thought. "Do you suppose we could really beat his sword into a jackhammer?"

"If you've got a decent toolkit, you can upgrade a turtle to a rabbit."

"Kindly refrain from violating metaphors quite so horribly in future." Loki frowned. "If that's what you just did. I'm trying to parse the sentence, and it's already begun to make my head ache."

"Yep. Still number one with a bullet." Scratch allowed himself a moment's pleasure, soaking up the last drops of afterglow, then raised up with a sigh. "Okay. No sense putting off the inevitable. You two need to be on your way and I have to figure out just what the Heaven went wrong with my PMS." He raised a finger. "Do *not* crack wise the way I can *feel* you wanting to. Okay?"

"Who, me?"

Scratch shot Loki a look that tried to be a glare, but didn't quite succeed. "Shut up, would you? If it's even physically possible."

Loki twinkled at him, smug and annoying. Back to his usual self.

Scratch grinned, shook his head, idly scratched his stomach, and padded, still naked, over to his main terminal. He dropped into the chair with his usual thud—paused until the main reason naked computing had never caught on eased into a dull ache— then gritted his teeth and reached for the mouse.

"This doesn't look so bad," he muttered after a few moments' navigation. "I think I see what whoever did."

"Can you fix it?"

"Who do you think you're talking to?" Scratch clicked busily away. "Old god, I invented computers. Developed HTML in the back of meaty mortal minds. Inspired pop-up advertising. Embedded subliminal cocaine in instant message systems. There's nothing I can't do with one of these infernal machines, pun fully intended."

"Mmm."

"Want to translate that for me?" Scratch asked absently, scanning line after line of source code.

He heard Loki roll up to balance himself on one forearm. "I simply wonder if you haven't bitten off more than you can chew. Adaptation and mutation are notoriously difficult to combat."

"So?"

"So—do you think yourself man enough to do battle with anyone able to hew into one of *your* systems?"

"Hack, moron. The word is 'hack.' And trust me when I say there's no hacker out there I can't whip into a crying momma's boy."

He paused. Winced. "Crap."

"I do suspect you shouldn't have spoken those words aloud," Loki agreed.

Scratch attempted a nervous laugh. "Hey take it easy. What could go wrong? I..."

The lights overhead fizzled and spat out sudden showers of sparks. Each and every one of Scratch's monitors filled with animated rodents doing the Hamster dance to a teeth-grating MIDI set on a five-second loop. The room filled with the scent of bitter almonds and burning roses.

A peal of laughter, soft at first, rose until it choked the air. Light, sweet, scarier than—well, Hell—and worst of all? Female. Definitely female.

Someone, somewhere, began to clap daintily.

"That's not good," the angel muttered.

"No," Loki said, voice tight. "I do believe I know who's behind this now."

Scratch whirled on him, shouting above the laughter. "You say what?"

Loki ignored the Devil. He stood and shook his fist at the air. "Sigyn! Sigyn, explain yourself at once!"

The dancing hamsters vanished. A hundred images of a small, plain woman with sparkling eyes blipped up in their place.

Looking at her smile, Scratch wondered why anyone ever thought his grin was creepy. "Loki, is that who I think…"

"I'll be damned," the angel muttered.

"It's a little late for that," the woman said. She folded her hands smugly as a Siamese crossing its forepaws. "Greetings, Lucifer Morningstar, and you, Wanderer of the World. Oh, and yes, I mustn't forget you, Loki. It's been quite a long time since we met. Still, I have thought about you from time to time."

The woman's glance turned sly. More than sly. More like pure, candy-coated evil fit to make any man's testicles try to crawl up and hide inside his belly.

"Loki," she crooned, trailing the name over her tongue. "How have you been, husband?"

Chapter Eight

Scratch decided this would be a good time to take stock of his options.

Running? No door plus eternal damnation equaled the impossibility of escape.

Hiding? A better idea. If he angled himself just right, he could stand behind the hulking mass of the angel— "Wanderer of the World," was it? Figured. Why couldn't angels actually be named Clarence, Joe, or Fred? Always had to be something elegiac with the intention of making people go "ooh" and "ahh." Nepethar, Taramasalata, or Bending Branches of Eternal Beatitude. Some such crap.

And people sometimes asked him why he'd ditched "Lucifer Morningstar" for "Scratch." Please. It was possible to be too pretentious for the Devil.

Crap, rambling again. Back to the plan in progress. Run — no. Hide — maybe. Gotta do something. Because, frankly? Looking at the pure white, candy-coated poison of Sigyn's smile, Scratch remembered once more and all too clearly why he'd given up on the females of most species.

Deadlier than the male? Oh, you betcha.

And Hell had no fury like...

"Sigyn." Loki took three measured paces forward, arms folded across his chest. Scratch glanced at him in curiosity. His gait and expression were thunderous as Thor, but the arms told Scratch that Loki had much fear of this lissome lady. Lady? Minor goddess? Not so minor? He forgot what Sigyn had once been— goddess or woman?—but it looked like she'd had some upgrades since then.

Scary ones.

Yeah... hiding sounded good. Real good. Ever so casually, Scratch began to kick-scoot his computer chair behind Mt. Holy.

Sigyn arched an eyebrow. The wheels on Scratch's chair froze, locking into place. When he gave a desperate nudge, they screeched in protest. A screw snapped off and went *ping!* against a far wall.

"Lucifer, you wouldn't be trying to hide from me, would you?" Sigyn dipped her head charmingly and gave him a supermodel smile that sent goose bumps chasing each other up and down his spine. "I really do need to talk to all three of you. Be a good boy and sit right there for a while, why don't you?"

She pointed one French-manicured nail at Scratch. A wave of paralysis slammed into him with tidal force, locking his physical form into a bizarre mannequin rictus with one hand raised and mouth half-parted.

The angel snickered.

"Now, whatever could be so funny, Wanderer?" Sigyn leaned forward. "You wouldn't be laughing at me, would you?"

The angel hesitated. He glanced back and forth between Sigyn and Scratch, took a peek at Loki, and gave his head a decisive shake.

"What was that, Wanderer?" Sigyn waved a playful finger at him. Terrifying.

"No, ma'am," the angel said, running the words together in his rush to get them out: *nome.*

"That's the spirit. While I do sometimes enjoy a strong, silent type, I think I'd like to hear you answer me out loud when I question you. I'm sure you don't mind, do you?"

"Nome."

"See, Loki?" Sigyn gave her ex-husband an arch look. "Things are so much easier when men know their place. Which is to say, right where we women want you to be." She laughed, tinkling silver bells of terror. Like being delicately stabbed with a hundred needles. "A few centuries in a cavern holding a venom bowl does give a lady time to think. To reach certain conclusions she might not have otherwise. To—"

"Go barking insane?" Loki asked.

Sigyn rolled her eyes and made a dismissive gesture. Loki's legs folded beneath him. The *whap!* with which his posterior connected to the floor made both devil and angel wince. Loki turned a whiter shade of pale, but score one for Team XY, as he managed not to yelp or whimper. Score two when he dredged his glare back up after the first moment's surprise.

Minus three points when he opened his mouth and nothing came out but the sounds of a mongrel dog with a broken larynx trying to growl. "Mmm. Not terribly attractive, but it'll do." Sigyn turned to the angel. "Two down. Will you behave yourself?"

"Yessim."

Scratch took a long mental step back, decided it was insane for three grown men, let alone the immortal variety, to be so very afraid of one small woman, and briefly pondered trying to stage a rebellion.

His gonads contracted. Eyes crossing, Scratch decided staying put sounded better and better.

Sigyn smiled. "And they say men can't learn. Actually, I say as much myself. Often." She buffed her nails against her bodice, peered at them, and nodded in satisfaction. "All it takes, though, is a little threat aimed at their favorite toys, and they fall in line like lambs. Delightful."

The three men froze. To an icier degree.

Sigyn laughed. "Now, now, don't you fret. I'm a reasonable woman. A thoroughly modern Millie. I don't believe in violence unless I'm pushed. You won't push me, now, will you?"

Scratch, Loki, and the angel answered immediately: "Nome!"

"Good, good boys." Sigyn dropped the charm—at last—and sat up straight, all business. Scratch had a brief, uncomfortable split vision of her needing only half-glasses on a chain to be the librarian of everyone's worst nightmares, Chairwoman of the Only Board That Mattered. "Let's speak plainly. I expect you are wondering why I've brought you all here."

You brought us here? Scratch boggled. *You? Did you — the angel — the door — my website! My PMS website! I'll be damned a fifth time!*

Sigyn tapped her temple with one elegant nail. "Well done, Lucifer. It isn't so hard to think with your big head if you just try." She folded her hands, not demurely. More like she was preparing a ninjitsu move and planned to hit them all where it really, really hurt.

Scratch couldn't decide which frightened him more: the thought of another physical assault or more of her smug yammering.

"I'll be quick, boys, no need to fret. Once I've said what I came to say, I'll let you go." She drew a symbol across one breast. "Cross my heart, hope to die, stick red-hot needles through all your eyes."

The men shuddered.

"Bullet points: yes, Scratch, I am the one who's hacked into your PMS website. Honestly. Do you think I could let a nasty, petty joke like this go unchecked? So many innocent men, women, and other types out there, hungry for love, and you were getting your jollies by causing them pain? I do understand that's more or less your job description, but there is a line you just can't cross before you cross me." Her eyes sparkled. "A tip? I wouldn't use titles of books from the Old Testament for passwords. It was a snap to break through your firewalls." She frowned. "Yes? You have something to say?"

Scratch's lips flapped loose. "How? I mean — who told you? What — where — "

Sigyn sighed. "I knew I'd regret permitting you speech. Lucifer, it doesn't matter how I found out. As it happens, one of my new acolytes spilled the burned beans, but what does that signify? I would have found out sooner or later. Before you ask, I also hired the Wanderer of the World to come and put you temporarily out of commission. You can't be killed, of course, but in your preferred guise of a male, with your proclivities and those of the Wanderer's? Sex does nicely to keep you distracted."

"You set me up!" the angel blurted.

"And you fell for it, both of you, like little dominoes." Sigyn flicked the air with finger and thumb. "That had Scratch taken care of. Loki, though... I must say, husband..."

"Ex!" Loki managed to bark.

"Ex-husband, yes. You haven't lost your knack for playing the wild card. Always popping up where you're least expected and where I don't want you. I could have sent you scampering along, but really... I did owe you a bit of payback for those centuries in the cavern." Her eyes twinkled with frightening good humor. "You never did research your spell-work. Freyja's runes, when cast, affect everyone in the viewing area. *Everyone.*"

"But... after," Scratch said. "Why?"

Sigyn giggled. "Don't look at me. You took it from there all on your own, boys. And my, did you ever take it. It was quite a show. Not exactly technical perfection, besides being a bit rough and tumble for my taste, but there's just something so very... *warming*... about seeing two or more men have at the oldest game." She fanned herself. "In fact, I liked the performance so much I'll give the players a gift."

Somehow, Scratch doubted he would enjoy whatever Sigyn had in mind. Still, no choice, huh? Women!

"Now, now, Lucifer, be nice."

"*Nice* isn't my thing, Sigyn."

She made a moue with her lips. "I know. Pity. You can catch so many more flies with honey than vinegar. But, enough. I don't have the time it would take to hammer a bit of respect out of you."

"Healthy respect here, ma'am," the angel piped up.

"Pussy-whipped," Loki grumbled.

Scratch stared at them both, slowly shaking his head.

Sigyn, for her part, arched a perfectly plucked eyebrow. "I'm sure. Scratch, the Paranormal Mates Society matchmaking service is no longer yours to command. I've taken over, and I'll see it goes into the hands of someone who'll handle the concept *efficiently.*

"Wanderer, you are free to go."

"Loki?" Sigyn tapped her chin. "By rights, I should leave you where you stand, unable to transform or leave this particular Hell for a few odd millennia. I would, if a far better punishment hadn't occurred to me. I'll give you the *choice* to stay or go."

"Bitch!"

"Yes, I am." Sigyn glowed with pride. "Everything I know, I learned from you, darling." She paused, then burst into laughter. "No, sorry, I can't say that with a straight face."

Her image began to fade. "Neither can I stay and chat all day, boys. So much to do!"

"Wait!" Scratch surprised himself by blurting. "What are you? I mean—I'm the Devil, I punish the damned. Quid pro quo. Who do you—"

Sigyn's glow took on a painful edge. "Me? I've made myself the goddess of women's wildest dreams, silly. I bring fantasy to life. And I do an excellent job of it, if I do say so myself." She winked. "Bye, now—have fun!"

Her laughter echoed through Scratch's antechamber long after the visual faded, eerie chimes tinkling on loop.

The angel shook his head, reached out with one massive arm, and hit "play" on Scratch's MP3 player. Eighties metal blasted out.

All three men sighed in relief. Tension melted from their bones, and testicles carefully peeked out to see if it was safe again. Shuddering, each male in the room surreptitiously checked to see if their packages were intact.

"Men," Scratch said after a long moment, "never underestimate the power of a seriously pissed-off woman."

The angel nodded emphatically. Loki sneered. About what Scratch had expected, really.

He reached for a paper carton of three-day-old lo mein noodles, sniffed them, and shrugged. Picking up a pair of chopsticks from the mess on the table, he dug in. "So," he said, mouth full. "What now?"

Loki shook his head. "I must confess I've no idea. Sigyn is... she... er. Well. Would you mind, terribly, if I did remain down here for a while? Perhaps a century or so?"

"Hiding out?" Scratch shrugged. "Fine by me. Just no pranks that involve crossing wires or pushing buttons to see what they do, and you're more or less welcome to stick around. I'll even teach you how to whip up a computer virus. Update your pranks to the day and age."

"Virus?"

"Trust me, you'll love it. Practical jokes get no better than strategic placement of embarrassing pop-up ads." Scratch ate another bite of lo mein. "What about you, flyboy? Wanderer?"

The angel looked at Scratch, at Loki, then back at Scratch. He lifted his hands helplessly.

"Yeah. I hear you." Scratch took aim with one chopstick and sent it whizzing past the angel's ear. "Thanks for telling us about the whole Sigyn set-up so we'd have time to mount a defense. Really nice of you."

The angel's cheeks reddened. He looked down, shuffling one huge foot through some wads of paper. After a moment, he shrugged again.

Oddly enough, that really did say everything that needed to be said. It'd take a stronger man, god, or portion of the Host to stand up to a woman who'd just discovered her inner Albright.

Scratch finished his leftovers, dropped the box carelessly toward a trashcan, missed, and yawned, stretching his arms high above his head. "So," he said, semi-casually.

"So," Loki echoed, examining Scratch with a sideways curiosity.

The angel peeked up at both of them.

"You guys want to have that one for the road after all?" Scratch asked.

The angel sighed. Loki groaned. "I thought you'd never ask," they said together, and launched themselves at him. Scratch went down beneath the double-teamed assault, half-smothered but happy.

His last thought before he traipsed off to happy orgasm land was, *Good luck with the PMS, Sigyn. Really good luck. Ten to one you come crying back to me the first time a customer yells at you.*

But hey, in the meantime? I have better things to do. Two of them.

And I think I'll get started taking care of my new business right now...

Willa Okati

Willa Okati is made of many things: imagination, passion for manlove, creativity and sheer bloody-minded determination to keep writing, getting out all the stories in her head.

The only problem with that clever plan is that as she writes, more story ideas pop up...

She's getting into ménage these days, and finding that it's really peachy to write female leads — but these leading ladies have always gotta have their two men (who are into each other as well as her). That makes for extra-special spicy good times!

You can reach Willa at willaokati@gmail.com, visit her at her website (www.willaokati.com) or join her Yahoo! Group for updates at http://groups.yahoo.com/group/willa_okati.

May the force be with ya'll!

Paranormal Mates Society: Finders Keepers

Lacey Savage

Chapter One

"Mirror, mirror, on the wall... who's the fairest of them all?"

Claudia Foster stifled a groan and tugged the thin scrap of cloth tighter over the polished surface of the bronze-gilded mirror. "Can't you be quiet for longer than two minutes? I have work to do."

The mirror went on as though she hadn't spoken. Its voice practically dripped with honeyed, well-practiced flattery. "Why, you are, your majesty. You're the fairest woman in all the land."

"Shut up!" Gripping one edge of the mirror, she shook it briefly, hoping to threaten it into submission.

The mirror wouldn't let itself be so easily silenced. "Mirror, mirror—"

"Enough!" She wrapped the cloth securely around the garrulous object before shoving it into her backpack. It fit snugly between a thin-leafed tome Claudia hadn't had a chance to peruse and a wooden jewelry box she believed had been carved more than eight-hundred years earlier. She also thought the plain-looking container had the ability to turn ordinary metal trinkets into gold, but that was another experiment that would have to wait... at least until after she got rid of the mirror.

The backpack muffled the low baritone, but Claudia could still hear the incessant buzzing of its continued chatter. She took a quick glance around, then beamed a smile at three men huddled at a nearby table. They glared her way and spoke in hushed, urgent voices. She could feel the weight of their accusing stares and the disapproval radiating from them. Worse yet, she didn't even need her talent to do it.

Sighing, Claudia flipped her laptop open. Although she'd been in Cairo for three months and frequented the Desert Wind coffee shop a few times a week, the regular patrons still hadn't gotten used to the presence of an unescorted woman in their midst. At least they'd stopped hitting on her, though she'd preferred that kind of attention to the hostile glares being thrown at her these days. Flattery and charm she could deal with, especially since her half-telepath abilities came in handy when trying to distinguish real interest from macho bluster.

Of course, it probably didn't help that she talked to more than her share of inanimate objects. She'd hoped the men simply thought she talked to herself, but right then, Claudia didn't know which was worse.

A few button clicks later, Claudia's laptop boasted a solid Internet connection through the wireless hotspot provided by the Desert Wind coffee shop. Located in an open-air square ringed by merchants selling everything from coffee beans to handcrafted knick-knacks, the Desert Wind mirrored a hundred other such establishments sprinkled along Cairo's busy streets. Still, this place drew her like no other.

She told herself she kept coming back because they served the best *sahlab* in the region. The sweet, thick, milk concoction did wonders for her state of mind after a long day of digging through archeological sites in the desert. Somewhere deep inside, though, she knew better. She kept coming back because of *him*.

"You're early."

The familiar voice startled her. Claudia jerked her gaze up from the laptop screen to stare into a pair of dark eyes. Flecks of tarnished gold danced within the depths of those bottomless orbs, yet she couldn't hide a twinge of disappointment.

"Expecting someone else?" Ra'ees Bayar asked as he slid his muscled frame into the chair across from her.

"Of course not." *Hoping* was entirely different than *expecting*, wasn't it?

Ra'ees crossed his arms over his chest and watched her with a bemused expression. "Whatever you say. That dreamy stare certainly wasn't intended for me."

"Dreamy?" Claudia frowned. She didn't do dreamy, infatuated, love-struck or any of a thousand other romantic notions. Especially not while she was working. "That's impossible."

Ra'ees grinned, flashing white teeth against his tanned face. "Whatever you say. Do you have it?"

Claudia returned the smile. "Did you doubt I would?"

"Never."

She narrowed her eyes, trying to read him. Being the offspring of a clairvoyant mother and a telepathic father had its advantages, but it had a great deal more disadvantages. She'd inherited a little of both talents, which meant she wasn't very good at either. Now, squinting at Ra'ees, Claudia wished for the thousandth time she could have had one gift or the other. *Jack of all trades, master of none. That's me.*

Forcing a smile onto her features, she dug into her backpack and gripped the mirror. Keeping her palm plastered to what she hoped was its mouth, she pulled the object out of the bag and slid it across the smooth surface of the table.

"It's authentic?"

"Now you're insulting me."

Ra'ees held up his hands. "Just asking."

"You can find out for yourself, just not here. I haven't been able to get it to be quiet for longer than a few minutes. The damn thing craves attention."

Ra'ees raised an eyebrow but didn't try to remove the cloth covering, having apparently decided she was serious. "What about the lamp?"

Claudia's chin jutted out as she prepared for yet another argument. "I told you, these things take time. I have a few leads on the Aladdin lamp, but nothing concrete yet."

"It's been three months."

"I know how long it's been." She blew out a breath before continuing. "And I also know how much you're paying me, though you're obviously getting your money's worth. I've brought you more than a few priceless artifacts since we began working together."

As she braced herself for the onslaught of argumentative banter she knew was coming, Claudia instinctively slid her hand inside the pocket of her jeans. She found the lighter and twirled it between thumb and forefinger, a nervous habit she'd picked up years ago, back when she still smoked. It had been almost a decade since she'd lit a cigarette, but the lighter remained. "I'll find the lamp, Ra'ees. I swear it."

Ra'ees surprised her by nodding. "I know you will."

She gaped at him while he brought two fingers to his mouth and blew a long, high-pitched whistle between them. A moment later, the jingling of tiny bells filled the square and a camel rounded the corner, heading straight for their table. None of the patrons as much as flinched when the beast made its way through the coffee shop to kneel beside its master. Murmuring soft words in Arabic, Ra'ees slid the mirror into a leather pouch strapped to the camel's back.

"I see you brought your faithful companion," Claudia said when she'd sufficiently recovered. Ra'ees wanted the Aladdin lamp more than he wanted any other artifact she'd been able to bring him. They'd bickered about her inability to find it for months.

"Kalil goes everywhere with me. Don't you, Kalil?"

The camel blew out a great snort in agreement.

Claudia couldn't contain her laugh. Catching a waiter's eye, she motioned him forward. "Another *sahlab*, please. Want anything?"

The taste of copper flooded her mouth, thick and metallic, threatening to gag her. It slid over her tongue and down her throat in a streaming gush. She swallowed rapidly, though she knew her mouth was empty. Moonlight peeked from around a cloud, sending a silver beam down to highlight the golden flecks dancing in Ra'ees's eyes. In a flash, she saw him as he really was, canines extended, claws protruding from massive paws, silky gray fur covering his body.

The image dissipated suddenly, taking the taste of blood with it. The coppery essence receded as swiftly as the rushing tide, leaving in its wake nothing but the taste of the sweet, lightly flavored milk concoction she'd been drinking all evening.

"Nothing for me, thank you," Ra'ees replied.

The waiter frowned, though whether because Claudia had ordered before Ra'ees or because he'd noticed her reaction, she couldn't be sure. She waited until he was out of earshot before leaning forward. "Tell me," she said at last, "why does a werewolf need a magic lamp?"

If she'd shocked him, he didn't show it, nor could she sense anything through her talent. She swore inwardly. At times like these, she'd have done anything to know what people were actually thinking. Her occasional flashes of insight had proven tremendously useful, but nothing could replace the real telepathic ability her father had.

"Tell me," Ra'ees said, his tone mocking hers. "Why does a beautiful woman like you need a membership to a dating site?"

Claudia scowled. She glanced at the screen, where the Paranormal Mates Society slogan flickered brightly. *Paranormal Mates Society — Where finding the love of your life is supernatural, super easy.* She flipped the lid of her laptop closed. She wasn't ready to divulge that part of her investigation for the elusive lamp, even to Ra'ees who was footing the bill. "None of your business."

"Ditto."

She was about to say something else when sexual awareness flooded her core, swift and relentless. It dampened her panties instantly, making her inner walls clench in anticipation. Her nipples tightened and brushed against her cotton blouse, the soft texture sending a moan rushing to her throat. She swallowed hard, fighting to keep some semblance of control on her raging libido before it became painfully obvious to anyone who glanced her way that in a mere flash she'd become hornier than a virgin on prom night.

"Are you all right?"

"I'm fine."

She saw him then, striding into the square like he owned the place. *Mr. Big.* Not the most creative nickname, she acknowledged, but since she didn't know his name she'd had to come up with something. It suited him perfectly. Standing at over 6'5" and built like a Greek god, the waves of authority and pure masculine confidence streaming off him took her breath away.

He faced the opposite direction but she had a clear view of the thick, wavy hair brushing his broad shoulders, his sleekly muscled back, tapered waist and loose silk pants that seemed to practically drip off his hips and mold to his muscled thighs. The flowing material brushed his ass, giving her the slightest glimpse of taut buttocks. The sight took her breath away. Her pussy clenched, protesting its empty state. Claudia could even picture his cock, thick and engorged as it made its way inside her, filling her until she dug her fingernails into his flesh and screamed—

"Claudia?"

Heat rushed to her face. She made a show of rummaging through her backpack, hoping her long hair would cover the blush staining her cheeks. The desire in her eyes would be a dead giveaway, so she kept her gaze averted. "I'll call you when I learn anything, okay? As soon as I have the lamp, you'll be the first to know."

She held her breath, waiting for Ra'ees to leave. Her stomach tightened and she pressed her thighs together, hoping to quench the incessant ache that had settled there.

"I'll be waiting."

She nodded and clenched her hands into fists to stifle an unbidden groan. If the man had this kind of effect on her when he stood fifteen feet away, what would happen if he actually touched her? A ripple of anticipation flowed through her veins, sending wild, hungry sensations to every nerve ending.

The jingling bells signaled Ra'ees departure and Claudia released a breath she didn't know she'd been holding. Unwilling to risk another glance in the newcomer's direction, she pulled her laptop forward and flipped it open again. She'd come here to get some work done, and she'd be damned if she allowed Mr. Big to keep her from it.

She knew when he sat, and where. She felt his presence in every caress of the wind on her skin, and she shifted her chair slightly so she could peer over the top of her laptop and catch a glimpse of his full lips, dark eyes and chiseled cheekbones.

Forcing herself to look away took every last ounce of willpower she possessed. She could sneak another glance later. After her body had stopped teetering on the edge of a full-blown orgasm.

Willing her hands to stop shaking, she tapped the keyboard lightly and brought up her personal mailbox on the Paranormal Mates Society website. From the moment she'd agreed to look for the Aladdin lamp, she'd known the answers to her search lay here, on this site. She just didn't know why... or with whom.

She quickly scanned the dozen or so emails she'd received overnight, allowing her senses to guide her. There were a couple of intriguing offers from men who, under different circumstances, she might have enjoyed meeting. After deciding none of her would-be suitors was the one she sought, she navigated to the new profiles section to browse through the members who'd recently filled out membership forms.

One profile, in particular, caught her attention.

Yeti—9 feet, 3 inches and solid as a glacier—seeks non-Yeti companion for a change of pace, possible LTR. Must enjoy body-sledding, ice fishing, ice cream, and bear hugs. No fragile creatures need apply—this alpha male prefers a substantial woman who can appreciate his rough-and-tumble nature. Serious inquiries only to: longtallfurry@paranormalmatessociety.com.

No picture, which was a real shame. A slight flutter tingled in her belly, but she knew it was the remnants of the overwhelming desire she felt for Mr. Big. No, LongTallFurry wasn't for her. But she had no doubt he'd find the creature of his dreams — or she'd find him. It was the twenty-first century, after all. Paranormal beings deserved their happily ever after just as much as everyone else.

Except Claudia herself, of course. She'd only joined the Paranormal Mates Society to find the lamp. She held no illusions about finding her life mate or any such nonsense. People who were meant to be together would find each other the old-fashioned way just as her parents had, without the help of modern technology.

Glancing slyly at Mr. Big from beneath lowered lashes brought another stream of panty-wetting cream dripping from her pussy. Damn. She wasn't going to get any work done at this rate. He had a laptop open in front of him as well, though while Claudia's computer was a small, lightweight white plastic model, his was as solid and awe-inspiring as the man himself. Brushed silver and as wide as the table, it drew almost as much attention as the bare-chested Mr. Big.

Being half-naked in Cairo wasn't so much a choice as it was a requirement, especially in the middle of July. At least, if you were male. Claudia had to make sure she wore long pants and shirts with sleeves that reached at least past her elbows. Mr. Big obviously didn't have the same requirements placed on him by society. His broad, muscular chest glistened in the light spilling from a nearby street lamp. The neon glow highlighted his chiseled cheekbones and aristocratic nose and shone off the golden armbands encasing both his wrists.

He looked up then and their eyes met, the force of his gaze sending Claudia's heart hammering hard against her ribcage. Her tongue darted out to moisten her suddenly dry lips. He grinned at her, a predatory smile, pure male. Her stomach flipped over. Tearing her gaze away, she forced herself to focus on her laptop.

What's wrong with me?

She didn't get involved with men while she still had a job to do. It wasn't only entirely unethical, it was simply unprofessional. Maybe once she found the lamp she could simply walk up to Mr.

Big and introduce herself, but until then, her fantasies needed to stay firmly in her mind, where they belonged.

Taking another sip of her drink, Claudia tried to concentrate on her task while forcing herself to keep from looking at him again. Was he staring in her direction? Did she have the same effect on him as he had on her?

She shook her head. Of course not. She knew what she looked like, and while she was attractive enough in a female Indiana Jones kind of way, her looks weren't enough to attract a man like him. Heck, he probably had an entire harem waiting for him back home.

The thought made her grit her teeth, and she banged on the laptop keyboard harder than needed, bringing up profile after profile of every kind of creature imaginable. There were vampires, werewolves, satyrs and full-blown telepaths, yet none elicited more than a half-hearted scan of their profile. None of these men had the lamp.

Resigning herself to another night of fruitless searching, she drained the rest of her drink and prepared to disconnect from the Internet when the last new member profile flashed across her screen.

GrantingWishes was his username, and he'd joined only a few minutes earlier. He'd barely have had time to fill out a user questionnaire. Claudia's senses were instantly focused and alert. Excitement thrummed through her veins. Her fingertips hovered over the keyboard, an image of the lamp taking shape clearly in her mind's eye. It was there when she scrolled down the page and scanned his profile, but disappeared when she moved on to another member's information.

A shiver ran down her spine. This was it. She'd found him.

Tall, dark and smoldering genie seeks easygoing, confident woman for moonlit strolls in the desert, stimulating conversation and sexy delights. Gold fetish and a fondness for antiquities a definite bonus. Five thousand years is a long time to go without female companionship, so while one-night stands may be considered on an individual basis, I'm looking for a long-term relationship. Serious inquiries only to Granting@paranormalmatessociety.com. Let me make all your wishes come true.

No picture accompanied his profile, but as he'd only just joined Claudia wasn't surprised. Besides, she didn't give a rat's ass what he looked like. The only thing that mattered was whether or not he had the lamp.

Without a second's hesitation, she clicked on his email address and composed a quick message, then settled in to wait. Tilting her head, she snuck another peek at Mr. Big's strong hands tapping out a steady rhythm on his metal keyboard. She could hear the tap-tap-tap of the keys, and her pussy clenched and pulsed with the beat.

Oh yeah. As long as Mr. Big wasn't going anywhere, she could wait all night.

* * *

The woman sitting two tables away from Xander had to be a gift from every God he'd ever believed in, and he wasn't about to refuse it.

He'd seen her for the first time at the Desert Wind last month, then he'd noticed her again two weeks ago and she'd even been here last night. Each time she came near, Xander's senses flared, instantly on edge. He could smell her perfume, flowery yet with a spicy scent that rushed straight down to his groin.

Then there were her eyes. She had a way of looking at him that made him want to avert his gaze, as though she could see right into his soul. A woman like that could detect every flaw, every tiny secret hidden deep in a man's heart. Definitely not the kind of woman Xander needed to get involved with.

Yet he couldn't help but stare. She was mesmerizing. From the way her long brown hair hung straight, brushing her high cheekbones, to the way her long legs seemed to go on forever, every breathtaking inch of her screamed with sensual promise.

Five thousand years of genie experiences, granting wishes and watching others receive their deepest desires, hadn't prepared Xander for a woman like her. But he was mortal now, and with a human body came human cravings, needs he hadn't known he couldn't control.

His cock pulsed, throbbed and grew eager just from watching her. Grateful for the loose pants, he brought his hand beneath the tabletop discreetly and adjusted himself, suppressing a shiver at the feel of silk gliding against the tender tip of his shaft.

The waiter approached his table and Xander pulled back his hand. "Can I get you anything else?"

Yes. That woman there, naked, her legs spread wide before me. I want to feast on her juices until every other man in this courtyard has a hard-on that could break glass, and then I want to take her home with me and finish what we started. "No, nothing. Thanks."

The waiter nodded politely and moved on. At the next table, a bony old man with liver-spotted skin and long skeletal fingers puffed on a *shisha*, a water pipe. The aromatic smoke enveloped Xander, tugging at his composure. He felt his knees go weak, his legs begin to revert to the shape that suited him much more than this constrictive mortal body.

Smoke. Fog. Mist. His natural shape had been called many things, but to him it was simply... bliss. Even now, having been freed from a life of servitude, Xander's ability to change shape remained. As before, though, he needed a vessel that could hold him. A lamp, a candle, anything would do, really, as long as it held the possibility of a flame to which he could bond. The flame didn't have to be lit, but the promise of that feral, fiery energy was enough to allow him to float into a euphoric state. He'd tried to explain the feeling once to a human, but he hadn't been able to find the words. The closest he could come to describing the unbelievable pleasure was to say it felt like being just on the edge of orgasmic release, with all that entailed: the joy, anticipation, ecstasy and rapture, and overall a sense of rightness, of belonging.

His friend hadn't understood. Then again, Xander didn't think he understood humans any more than humans understood genies, at least not when his new body caused him so much trouble. If he wasn't hungry, he was tired. If his neck didn't hurt from sleeping in an uncomfortable position, his feet ached from shoes that were too tight. If he wasn't concerned about the odor of his breath he was worried his hair might start to fall out, or he'd get heavy around the middle, or become afflicted by one of any hundred of diseases mortals suffered from. And if all that wasn't enough, he was constantly, insatiably, horny.

As a genie, lust reared its head only once every few hundred years, and even then another of his kind could easily satisfy those rare desires. It was the way of things, all written down in the Genie Code of Conduct. Genies served humans, granting their deepest longings, but the djinns' own appetites wouldn't interfere with their duties. Xander had heard stories of genies who weren't like most of the species, genies who craved the same ecstasy and carnal pleasures mortals did. Luckily, he hadn't been one of them, or he wasn't sure he could have survived five millennia of watching humans engaged in every erotic act imaginable. At least, not without losing his mind.

Smoke drifted up to the sky from the nearby table, but otherwise the night was clear. The moon wandered behind elusive clouds. Pale light shone from the streetlamps and Xander had an unobstructed view of the gorgeous brunette. She seemed engrossed in her work, though he'd seen the way she watched him when she thought he wasn't looking. The lustful longing glimmering in her wide eyes sent signals even a blind man couldn't have missed.

He leaned back in his chair and considered flipping his laptop closed, gathering his computer and his drink and joining her. The man she'd been with earlier had left, vacating his seat. Judging by the hungry looks some of the men threw her way, the chair wouldn't be empty long.

The metallic ping of an incoming message stopped him in mid-rise. Heaving a sigh, he settled back into his chair and opened the flashing envelope at the bottom of the screen.

A real genie! Having never met one before, I was beginning to think your kind nothing more than myth. Imagine my surprise when I saw your profile. I'm also glad to see how much we have in common. Antiques are a specialty of mine, though of particular interest at the moment are lamps and other such objects. Perhaps you'd be willing to answer a few questions about yours sometime? I'm not sure what kind of paranormal being you were hoping for, but I'm afraid I'm rather bland. Half-telepath, half-clairvoyant, and damn good at both. I promise not to read your mind if you promise not to grant any wishes without my express permission. ;-) Maybe we can meet sometime? You didn't specify your location, but let me assure you, it's not an issue. Money's no object when it comes to the possibility of true love, don't you agree?

ThinkPink29

Xander's lip twitched with amusement. Life moved at an entirely different speed in the twenty-first century. He'd only filled out a membership form to the Paranormal Mates Society website less than fifteen minutes ago and he already had a prospective mate to consider. Perhaps joining the dating site hadn't been such a bad idea after all.

He liked the casual tone of the email, though the mention of his lamp made him clench his jaw. Still, he couldn't very well overlook a possible mate because she asked about the one thing everyone eventually asked about, could he? Ever since the Aladdin story gained in popularity, that's all anyone wanted to know about. And if word ever got out he'd actually inhabited that same lamp for longer than the history of mankind, well, answering a question or two would be the least of his worries.

He looked up from the screen just in time to see the brunette bring her drink to her lips. Her luscious mouth parted, revealing perfect white teeth. She pressed her lips to the gleaming surface of the slender flute and his cock stiffened even further. Wind ruffled her hair. She met his gaze boldly over the rim of her glass, inclining her head slightly in acknowledgement. He grinned broadly. She returned the smile, but a hint of color rushed to her face and she lowered her gaze, returning to her work.

For a long moment he hesitated, debating whether to answer the email he'd received. The woman didn't look up again and he sighed, deciding he'd let ThinkPink29's profile determine whether she'd be a good match.

He scrolled past the section on education and previous relationships, paused briefly to skim through the sexual preferences part of the questionnaire, and continued on until he came to her picture. The thumbnail image was small, too small for him to make out anything other than long brown hair and a luscious set of full, red lips. He clicked on the image to enlarge it, and his breath caught in his throat.

Even when composed of pixels on a computer screen, the gorgeous brunette he'd been eyeing all night was still the sexiest woman he'd ever seen. In her profile photo, she wore a tight, bubble-gum pink off-the shoulder top that hugged her full breasts and shoved them upward, like a ripe, inviting delicacy ready to be savored. Her big brown eyes stared at him with that same intensity he'd noticed earlier. *Half-telepath, half-clairvoyant, and damn good at both.* Did that mean she'd been reading his mind all this time?

Every muscle in his body tensed and his cock throbbed harder; the idea of her knowing just how badly he'd wanted to fuck her for the past hour arousing him even further. Did she know she'd contacted him? Or had her email just been a fortunate coincidence?

If she hadn't set out to deliberately get to know him better, then she'd simply been cruising for a date on an online website. Money was no object, she'd said. Just how far was she willing to go for a midnight fuck? Jealousy settled like lead in his stomach. Without a second thought, he clicked the instant messenger button. ThinkPink29 was online.

GrantingWishes: Do you know what most women wish for?

He clicked the Send button, his gaze never leaving the brunette. Her eyebrows shot up in surprise as her computer beeped, signaling his message. Xander leaned back in his chair and waited.

ThinkPink29: A man who puts the toilet seat down?

Despite the annoyance blazing in his veins, he chuckled. At least she had a sense of humor. That was good. Very good.

GrantingWishes: Close, but no. Believe it or not, most women's desires are simple. A man with a big cock, who knows how to use it.

Her eyes widened as she stared at her laptop's screen but her luscious mouth broke into a grin. She hesitated for only a moment before replying.

ThinkPink29: And I suppose you're the answer to every woman's fantasy, huh?
GrantingWishes: Not *every* woman's. Just yours.

She frowned, her brows furrowing over her dark eyes. She rubbed the bridge of her nose and took a sip of her drink before returning her fingers to the keyboard.

ThinkPink29: Funny. You didn't list arrogance as a personality trait.
GrantingWishes: You're trying to tell me you didn't sign up for the same reason everyone else did?
ThinkPink29: I assume you're talking about sex.
GrantingWishes: What else is there?

ThinkPink29: I thought your profile said you were interested in a long-term, serious relationship.
GrantingWishes: It also said one-night stands would be considered on an individual basis.
ThinkPink29: I'm flattered.

He glanced up to make sure she was still smiling. She was, though the rush of color had spread to both cheeks, making her look flustered and even more breathtaking. Her nipples beaded beneath her cotton shirt, making him realize he wanted her more than he'd ever wanted another woman in his entire existence. His already stretched cock swelled even further as his balls tightened in their sac and Xander tapped out another message.

GrantingWishes: Prove it. Have sex with me. Right here, right now.

Chapter Two

Claudia's heart thumped, slow and steady, matching the rhythmic pulse between her legs. If she'd been having a normal conversation with GrantingWishes, she'd have asked him to repeat himself. As it was, the words remained plastered on the screen, in full view of anyone who might glance over her shoulder. The cursor blinked again, mocking her inability to come up with a clever retort.

Taking another sip of her drink, she allowed the cool liquid to glide down her throat, but the usually soothing beverage did nothing to steady her trembling fingers when she returned them to the keyboard.

Claudia hadn't joined the Paranormal Mates Society to find a mate. And despite what this arrogant, lamp-owning genie thought, she hadn't joined to find a willing sex partner either.

She wanted the lamp. That was the only reason she was here, and so far her heightened abilities hadn't led her astray. Now that she knew his handle, it shouldn't be too difficult to figure out his identity, even if he didn't make it easy for her. But no matter what, she wouldn't have cybersex with a stranger. That hadn't been part of the deal, and Ra'ees wasn't paying her nearly enough to come up with racy comments that she could use to turn on a guy who likely lived half-way across the world. Besides, he was probably overweight and balding. And much too arrogant. Definitely not her type. She glanced up, where Mr. Big seemed enthralled by something on his own laptop screen.

No. This genie, whoever he was, would definitely not be right for her. She'd already found a man who was everything she wanted. Too bad she couldn't just march up to him and tell him that. Yet.

Fortunately, she could tell GrantingWishes exactly what she thought of him and his stupid suggestion. She poised her fingertips over the keys, but before she could even begin to tap out a reply, her stomach muscles clenched, sending a wave of heat streaming through her body. Her pussy fluttered, clenching and unclenching, wetting her panties so they stuck to her slit. She wriggled on her seat, but that only helped to bunch up the material of her jeans tighter over her pussy, and what had begun as a slight flutter grew to pulsing proportions.

Her nipples beaded, brushing against her cotton top. She clenched her hands into fists, the reply forgotten. Pressing her thighs together, she tried to squelch the overwhelming need assaulting her from all sides. Phantom fingers glided over her breasts, tweaking her nipples, palming the underside of her full curves. The touch moved lower, over her stomach, dipping below the waistband of her jeans. An invisible finger slid between her folds.

Claudia stumbled to her feet, sending her chair scraping against the pavement. She bumped the table and her drink went flying, spilling the rest of its contents before shattering on the ground. Gripping the edge of the table, Claudia sucked in a long breath between clenched teeth.

Where had that come from?

The waiter reached her side in an instant. After assuring him she was okay, she sat down and flipped her laptop closed, needing a moment to think. Across from her, Mr. Big looked as frustrated as she felt. She watched him for a moment, allowing her breathing to return to normal.

Whose thoughts had she picked up? She knew they hadn't been her own, but the overpowering sensation told her whoever was thinking about her that way was close. Too close. She darted a nervous glance around the square. Most of the usual patrons had begun to leave, but a few tables were still occupied. After the commotion surrounding her broken glass had died down, none of the men seemed to be watching her with any more interest than they'd shown before.

Which only left one possibility. Her laptop.

It wouldn't be the first time she'd felt something that strongly through an Internet connection. Her paranormal talents seemed to hone in on technology, to use the energy it provided. That explained why she knew she'd find the lamp through the Paranormal Mates Society website. Unfortunately, it did nothing to explain the headlong path to the impending orgasm she'd hurtled toward a minute ago.

Taking a deep, steadying breath, she opened her laptop and glanced at the corner of the screen. GrantingWishes was still online. His last message remained plastered on the screen, continuing to await her reply.

Over the years, she'd learned to trust her abilities, but right now, she really wished she had a firmer grip on them.

ThinkPink29: OK.
GrantingWishes: OK?
ThinkPink29: Yes, OK, whatever. Let's do it.
GrantingWishes: That's not exactly the enthusiastic response I was hoping for.
ThinkPink29: Sometimes a woman needs a little more foreplay than you've offered. I can't get in the mood on a whim, you know.
GrantingWishes: Now why do I find that hard to believe?

Claudia's cheeks heated and she squirmed on her metal chair. Her pussy gushed, reminding her that although those might have been someone else's thoughts, they'd felt real enough to her body.

ThinkPink29: Because you're arrogant. I thought we'd already been over this.
GrantingWishes: OK, then, you call the shots. What do you want to know?

Claudia leaned back in her chair and grasped her lower lip between her teeth. This was her chance to fluster him a little.

ThinkPink29: What does your cock look like?

She waited for what seemed like an unusually long time, her body continuing to hum with awareness and arousal. Had she judged him too quickly? Could this genie be anywhere near as hot as Mr. Big looked right now? The object of her desire quirked his full lips in a heart-stopping smile, then looked right up her. Claudia swallowed hard, the beep of the laptop announcing a reply.

GrantingWishes: It's thick, long and curved, guaranteed to hit the G-spot precisely.

A clear image of his cock flashed through her mind. Jutting out from a nest of dark curls, his rod was just as he'd described. Dark veins ran along the underside of the shaft, while a bead of pre-cum glistened on the tip. She trembled, squeezing her thighs together. The seam of her jeans rubbed against her clit. She did it again, pressing her hips upward, relishing the coarse friction of the cloth scraping her clit.

It took all her willpower to type out a reply that wouldn't let him know just how turned on she was.

ThinkPink29: Now you're starting to sound like a late-night infomercial.
GrantingWishes: Would you like a demonstration?
ThinkPink29: I'm intrigued; I'll give you that much. OK, then. Demonstrate.
GrantingWishes: Picture the tip of my cock poised to enter your pussy. The swollen, reddening head is prodding your slit, nudging the entrance. My hands are on your breasts, pinching your nipples. I lower my head to swipe at your breast with my tongue. You shudder beneath me as my cock plunges inside you, your pussy tightening around

me, gripping me like a clenched fist. You like that, don't you, baby?

The images returned, stronger than the first time. A strong, masculine body pressed down on hers, lean and muscular. Hair sprinkled a broad chest, and she brushed her hand along the span of flat abs, then moved lower, letting her fingers splay over the coarse curls surrounding a solid cock.

A moment later, the cock filled her, just as he promised, huge and hard, stretching her inner walls. She met the rhythmic motion of his thrusts with the upward rolling of her hips. Every time his cock plunged in, the curved tip hit her G-spot, sending her thoughts reeling. The sound of their bodies slamming together and the wet slurp of his cock pounding her pussy filled her ears.

His thumb found her clit. Claudia's body ached, tensed and trembled. Fire burned in her veins as the orgasm that had been building all night finally burst forth. She couldn't stop it, even as reality came crashing back around her, mortification replacing the intense pleasure. Her pussy spasmed, releasing even more cream over her panties, her jeans, the chair. She bit down on her lower lip, hard. Hot tears flooded her eyes from the effort.

Her moan lodged in her throat.

Mr. Big was walking toward her. She struggled to think, to come up with some witty remark about what she'd been doing with her legs crossed and pressed hard together, her body almost doubled over on itself as she trembled and came.

He stopped beside her table, his laptop in one hand, the other outstretched toward her, palm up.

She gripped it before she could stop to consider what she was doing. He tugged gently and lifted her to her feet. His breath was warm against her cheek. The smell of her arousal was everywhere.

"If we're going to continue this demonstration," he said, his voice low and throaty, "we really should do it in private."

* * *

Though he knew it wasn't exactly gentlemanly of him, Xander couldn't help gloating. "So, you came just from an instant messenger conversation, huh?"

Claudia hadn't said a word since they'd walked out of the café five minutes earlier, but now she glared at him. "It wasn't just that, and you know it."

He quirked an eyebrow, feigning innocence. "I have no idea what you're talking about." In truth, he suspected his vivid fantasies had made their way to her mind. Her Paranormal Mates Society profile had stated she was part telepath and part clairvoyant, but he hadn't known just how powerful her abilities were until he saw the flush creeping up her cheeks, her nipples pressing against the fabric of her shirt, her lips parted in ecstasy.

"So, what? Now you're going to try to convince me you'd be much better in person?"

"I would be."

Her laugh sounded more like a disbelieving snort. "Then why do you need to join a dating site? Wouldn't a man with the kind of sexual prowess you claim to possess have women falling at his feet?"

Xander grinned. "What makes you think I don't?"

Claudia halted in mid-stride. Darkness enveloped the city like a shroud. Here, on the outskirts of Cairo, the street was quiet. Aside from a few men returning to their homes in solitude, Xander and Claudia were the only ones still out at this hour. Golden light spilled out onto the street from a narrow window, bathing Claudia's face in its luminescent glow. She frowned, staring at him intently. "You're lying."

"Is that what your psychic abilities tell you?"

Her face reddened and she averted her gaze. "I'm not psychic. I'm part telepath. There's a difference."

"If you can read my mind, I'm afraid you have me at a major disadvantage."

"That's not entirely how it works." She brushed a long lock of brown hair behind her ear. "At least, not always."

She shifted from foot to foot, still not meeting his eyes. Five thousand years of dealing with women had taught Xander a thing or two, and he suspected Claudia didn't want to talk about her abilities. He touched her elbow lightly and resumed walking in the same direction they'd been heading. His place was only another few blocks away.

"So, tell me about you," she said at last. "How does a genie end up strolling through the streets of Cairo? Shouldn't you be in a lamp somewhere, obeying a master's every whim?"

He hid his grimace behind a smile. If Claudia didn't want to talk about her psychic talents, he certainly didn't want to talk about his lamp. But at least she was talking to him now. That was a small victory.

"I'm an ex-genie. My years of servitude are over."

"Really? What happens to your lamp when you no longer use it to grant wishes?"

"Tell you what," he said, sliding his hand down to grip hers. For a moment, he thought she'd pull away. She didn't. "You answer one of my questions and I'll answer one of yours. Fair?"

Her eyes narrowed as she looked up at him, her gaze measuring, assessing. He wondered if she was reading his mind again. Almost unbidden, an image of her naked, wrists and ankles tied to his bedpost, flashed before his eyes. He sucked in a breath between clenched teeth and tried to clear the sensual vision as quickly as possible, knowing she'd lash out at him if she realized what he was thinking.

Claudia's gaze remained focused on his, but her expression gave no indication she'd picked up on the fantasy running rampant through his thoughts. "Why?"

"Because I think the dating site was an omen. And now it's my turn."

She laughed. "An omen?"

His grip tightened on her hand. "No fair cheating. You've had your question."

She shrugged nonchalantly, but her expression remained guarded. "Shoot."

"Did you know it was my profile you were contacting on the Paranormal Mates Society, or was it just coincidence that I happened to be sitting across from you?"

Her lips curved into a half-smile. Xander wished she'd laugh, really laugh, just once. He wanted to see her face light up with pleasure as it had for that brief moment in the café when she'd let her inhibitions slip while she came in front of all those people. His cock stirred at the memory of her flushed skin, her parted, moist lips, her ragged breathing.

"Coincidence," she admitted. "But a welcome one. And you? Did you know it was me?"

"Guilty as charged."

"So you deliberately set out to humiliate me."

She might as well have poured ice water down his veins. His libido screamed in protest as he stopped walking and tore his hand away from hers. "I did no such thing. You just looked so damn sexy sitting there by yourself. All hot, smoldering woman. I couldn't resist having a little fun."

"I'm glad I could amuse you."

He gritted his teeth, wishing he could read her mind this time. Did she honestly think that little of him?

Claudia crossed her arms in front of her chest, as though to shield herself from him. Gone was the woman who only twenty minutes ago had given in to her primal urges in a public place. Now she looked as though she'd rather be anywhere else but here with him, as if she feared he'd hurt her given half a chance.

Standing there, only an arm's length away, she seemed small, delicate, almost fragile, though he suspected that impression was deceptive. "My turn to ask a question," he said when he could trust himself to speak through unclenched teeth. "Why did you come with me?"

Emotions flittered over her face, so apparent he didn't have to be a mind reader to recognize her inner turmoil. She hesitated for much too long, every second delivering another crushing blow to his already bruised ego.

"To hell with this." He took hold of her shoulders and pulled her to him. If she thought he had so little self-control, he'd prove her right. He brought his mouth down on hers, hard. She tasted like *sahlab* and arousal. Her flavor flooded his senses, driving all logical thought from his mind.

She fought him, her hands balling into fists, slamming against his chest while his mouth crushed hers. He barely felt her struggles. His fingers dug into her shoulders, keeping her hostage, his tongue fighting with her lips, demanding entry.

She cried out against his mouth and then suddenly, unexpectedly, she yielded. Her lips parted for him, her tongue swept over his, tentatively at first, then with more insistence. Her fists unclenched and she laid her palms flat against his chest. The feel of her skin against his bare chest nearly drove him out of his mind. His cock twitched, hard as a rock against her belly while his tongue thrust in and out of her mouth, imitating movements he fiercely yearned to duplicate with his cock.

His hands roamed down her back, cupping her ass, bringing her even closer to him as if trying to absorb her body into his. Her slender form molded to his much larger frame. He couldn't get enough of her. Her scent was everywhere, surrounding him, claiming him. His thoughts spun with the feel of her.

"My place is just around the corner," he whispered breathlessly when they parted. "Come with me."

"I... can't." He took small pleasure from the fact that her words were wrung from her lips, her voice as fevered as his.

"Why?"

"You wouldn't be good for me."

He caressed the swell of her ass, kneading the firm globes with his palms. She shuddered against his chest. She wanted him as much as he wanted her, so why was she refusing what was obviously happening between them?

She started to pull away, drawing out of his arms. The loss of her body heat hit him with physical force. He had to think fast, and act faster. "Don't go. I have something to show you."

She lifted an eyebrow, clearly expecting him to once again proclaim his superior sexual abilities and try to convince her that way.

"You seemed interested in my lamp earlier. I have an entire collection you're welcome to take a look at."

Her eyes widened, desire sparkling in her intense dark gaze. "All right," she said, slipping her hand back into his. Her skin was warm, the contact sending a delicious shiver down his spine.

He stifled a sigh and used the heel of his other palm to push down on his rigid shaft. His chest constricted at the knowledge that inanimate objects were more interesting to Claudia than he was. He'd joined the Paranormal Mates Society to find a mate. Instead, he'd found a woman with a lamp fetish.

It figured.

Once a genie, always a genie. Other people's wishes always came true before his own.

Chapter Three

Claudia stared at Xander, amazed. "You live *here?*"

"You expected the inside of a lamp?" He motioned her inside the wide, blue-marble tiled hall and closed the double-doors behind her.

Claudia was too stunned to speak. She didn't know what she'd expected, but the two-story square mansion was definitely not it. From the outside, it had looked like a restored ancient ruin, its sandstone walls looming against the dark backdrop of the night sky. On the inside, though, the place glittered without being gaudy. Instead, the dark marble floors and rich colors gave the place a masculine look that made Claudia think of power, charm and elegance.

"Are you a sheik of some sort?" she asked as she followed him into a round room off the main hall. Silver-gilded walls and beautiful paintings contrasted with dark mahogany furniture. Her heels sunk into the plush burgundy carpet with every step.

Xander laughed. "Hardly. But five thousand years of servitude entitles a genie to some fringe benefits."

Claudia raised an eyebrow. "Like a retirement plan?"

"Something like that." He walked over to a cabinet and pulled its doors open, revealing rows of delicate crystal bottles. Claudia's heart quickened. Every container looked to be an antique. "Drink?"

She licked her dry lips. "Brandy, if you have it."

"Coming up." He chose an exquisite bottle with a long neck and lifted the stopper, sniffing the contents before pouring some into a decanter. The dark liquid swirled inside the crystal glass.

Claudia reached for the drink. Her fingers brushed Xander's, and a rush of heat pulsed through her veins, settling low in her stomach. It was all she could do not to moan. Through the haze of lust clouding her vision, she snatched her hand away, spilling brandy all over the carpet.

"Oh! I'm so sorry." She thrust the glass at Xander, then knelt and ran her hands over the stain. The liquid had seeped in to the lush fabric, darkening it. The scent of alcohol stung her noise.

Xander touched her shoulder and she fought another shiver of desire. "Don't worry about it. One of the housekeepers will clean it up later."

"You have housekeepers?" She rubbed at the stain with her bare hand, grateful for something to do that didn't involve touching Xander. The man oozed raw sexuality. Around him, she couldn't keep her powers in check. Her thoughts twirled and twisted, conjuring up image after image of sweaty bodies, tangled bed sheets and Xander's luscious cock. His fantasies pushed out all coherent thoughts from her mind until there was only pure raw desire, only him.

She had to get out of here.

"A couple. Does that surprise you?"

"Sure. Didn't you watch *I Dream of Jeannie*? All she had to do was wiggle her nose and her entire house was clean from top to bottom."

This time Xander tugged on her arm, and Claudia couldn't help rising. Nor could she stifle the heat that pooled between her legs, or squelch the cream that smeared her panties. *Fuck.* This was not going as planned. When Xander had invited her over here, she thought it would be easy: get in, get the lamp and get out. Now her body hummed, hovering on the brink of orgasm, and the man hadn't done more than touch her arm. This was *not* good.

He grinned, showing perfect white teeth. Claudia's stomach flip-flopped. "That was *Bewitched*, and she was a witch, not a genie. There's a big difference."

"Right. I'm not really up to speed with the whole paranormal being thing. I'm more familiar with talking artifacts." She cleared her throat, trying not to glance at the strong fingers that still gripped her elbow. "Did you say you had a lamp collection?"

Xander sighed, releasing her arm. "Yeah, but none of them talk, if that's what you're after."

Claudia waved a hand in the air, feigning nonchalance. "Oh, that's okay. I'd really like to see them, though."

Xander hesitated, and for a moment Claudia feared he'd say no. Then he shook his head and indicated the direction they'd come. "Go back out into the hallway. It's the second door on your left."

She was almost at the door before she realized he hadn't made a move to follow. She cast a curious glance over her shoulder. "Aren't you coming?"

He watched her intently, his dark eyes smoldering with sexual awareness. His hands were deep in his pockets and he shifted, thrusting his hips forward as he rocked on the balls of his feet. The movement stretched the silky material over the apparent bulge between his thighs. "Apparently not."

The knowledge that he barely held his lust for her in check shouldn't have surprised her, but hearing him admit it did. She'd been able to read just about every carnal thought he'd had about her, and worse, she was just as aroused as he. Her gaze traveled over his broad shoulders, the black curls sprinkling his chest, his trim hips and flat abdomen.

It would be so easy to give in. She could cross the distance between them in only a few steps. His kiss still tingled on her lips. He'd respond instantly if she dropped to her knees before him and tugged on the loose pants until they dropped down to his ankles, freeing his cock.

Business before pleasure.

Ever since they'd stepped outside the coffee shop, Claudia had repeated the phrase in her head like a mantra. She didn't fuck on the job, no matter how tempting the prospect. Ra'ees wasn't paying her to get laid, but he was paying her—and very well—to find the stupid lamp.

With any luck, Xander would be willing to part with the lamp for the right price. As she'd stated in her bio, money was no object. If the transaction went smoothly and she had what she'd come for, she could fuck Xander until he begged for mercy. But not until then.

It took every ounce of willpower for Claudia to pretend she had no idea what Xander's cryptic comment meant. She spun on her heel and headed out into the hallway, stopping before the door he'd indicated.

She tried the handle, mildly surprised to find it unlocked. This room resembled the one she'd just left, but it was square instead of round. In one corner, a fire had been lit in a cozy-looking fireplace. A shelf only a few inches wide spanned the entire perimeter of the room. Along its surface, lamps of all shapes and sizes sent light from the sparkling chandelier above glinting off their polished veneers.

Claudia's chest tightened. Here, in this room, she'd find the Aladdin lamp and return it to Ra'ees. Then she'd be free to indulge in any pleasurable activity Xander's mind managed to conjure.

"I see you found what you came for." Xander's voice echoed from the doorway. Claudia didn't have to turn around to know he was frowning. That's all he'd done since she mentioned the lamp.

"Not yet," she admitted, moving closer to the first lamp on the ledge. Its tarnished copper surface shone dully, and she moved on to the next, this one made of stained glass. Her gaze traveled along the length of the shelf, resting on each item in turn. There were glazed lamps, bronze lamps, lamp fillers, lamps made of stone, even molds of lamps, but none looked like the artifact she sought.

The lamp she'd seen when she'd come across Xander's profile had been relatively basic; golden, with an elongated spout and volutes along its outer rim. The handle, though, she'd recognize anywhere. It sprung wings from either side, the design delicately crested.

"It's not here," she said, her breath catching in her throat. She turned quickly and slammed into Xander's hard chest.

She didn't get a chance to say anything else. His arms enveloped her, crushing her breasts against him. She moaned, letting her head loll back and closing her eyes as he laid a trail of warm kisses along the side of her neck. He paused to dip his tongue into the sensitive hollow of her throat, then continued lower, stopping to nibble at the taut peak of her nipple while his thumb and forefinger closed in around the other.

Claudia shuddered against him. His thoughts burst through her mind, so vivid they threatened to overwhelm them both. She saw herself as he imagined her, naked and bound by the wrists and ankles with a satin sheath to the headboard and footboard of a massive bed. The image should have shocked or even revolted her, but it only served to arouse her further. She wanted him to take her, fuck her senseless until they both came in a fevered rush.

His hands roamed over her body, gripping her waist while his tongue laved her bud through the material of her shirt. The sound of a zipper being lowered filled the room. Belatedly, she realized it had been hers. His fingers dipped beneath the waistband of her panties, finding her slick folds. He couldn't see her pussy but he pictured it, pink and glistening as his fingers played within the wet depths.

"We can't..." she whispered, but her protests sounded feeble even to her own ears. Xander ignored her. His thumb stroked her clit, sending her knees bucking. She leaned back against the lamp shelf, grateful for the support.

Her body tensed and she gripped Xander's head, pulling his mouth closer to her breast. He seemed to know just what she wanted, nibbling and sucking harder, his fingers thrusting deep inside her tight channel.

The images his fantasy conjured drove her over the edge as he stroked her to climax. Clamping her mouth shut to prevent a scream, Claudia came silently, powerfully, with Xander's mouth on her breast and his fingers deep in her pussy.

When her body ceased spasming, Xander withdrew his hand and raised his head, meeting her gaze. Guilt hit her, hard. She shouldn't have let him believe there could be more than that heated, fevered encounter between them. His lust assaulted her, tugging at her thoughts. She knew his cock throbbed, eager to fuck her, needing to finish what they'd started. She'd spent weeks dreaming about Mr. Big. Now that he was here, ready and willing to fuck her, she had to be crazy to turn him down.

But although her cunt throbbed in protest, her ethics still wouldn't allow it. She had to find the stupid lamp first, and deliver what she'd promised. It was risky, though. If Xander wasn't willing to part with the lamp voluntarily, she still had to acquire it. Then the only sex she'd be having with him would be of the fantasy variety.

"I'm sorry," she whispered, running her hand through his thick, wavy hair. "I… I need to ask you to show me something."

He grinned, sending another wave of remorse to her belly. "Right. I did promise you a long, thick, curved cock."

"Yeah, well, that's not it."

He frowned, the lust dimming from his dark eyes. He straightened, putting some distance between them. "What, then?"

Her words tumbled out before she could reconsider. "I know you have the Aladdin lamp. Now I need to know where it is."

Xander's features tightened, a muscle jumping in his jaw. The raw sexual energy that had filled the room only moments ago dimmed and disappeared. She didn't need her talents to know all that pent-up frustration had been replaced by pure, unbridled anger.

Claudia tried to ignore the quelling look he gave her, but she couldn't shut out his words. When he spoke, the force of his fury invaded her senses, setting her abilities on edge. "I thought going through the Paranormal Mates Society would mean meeting a woman who doesn't want me for my fucking lamp."

Rage flooded Claudia, thrumming through her veins. She had to dig her fingernails into her palms to keep from letting his fury become her own. "I don't just want you for your lamp. Weeks ago, I—"

"Let me make this very clear for you," he said as though she hadn't spoken. "You're too late. I don't have the lamp. Another woman beat you to it."

Xander watched the color drain from Claudia's face. Even now, knowing that she'd used him, he wanted nothing more than to grab her, carry her up the stairs and tie her to his bed. Or maybe the desire was so strong *because* she'd used him. He didn't want to think about that.

"You can't be serious." Her soft, sensuous voice was barely above a whisper.

"You bet your ass I'm serious. It's becoming very clear to me that women are after one thing, and one thing only. To trick men into doing their bidding. Once they have what they've come for, they leave. It's that simple. Women are exploitive and manipulative."

Claudia pulled up her jeans and zipped them up, revealing just a hint of her perfect, flat stomach. Xander looked away. "I thought all women wanted a big cock. Now they all want to use men? Do you always change your mind so quickly?"

"What makes you think I've changed my mind? It's the same thing."

Claudia threw up her hands. "That's one of the most ridiculous things I've ever heard. And for the record, I didn't come here for your cock."

"Of course not," Xander said between clenched teeth. "You came for my lamp."

She opened her mouth as though to protest, then seemed to think better of it. She stormed out of the room, her heels tapping loudly on the marble floor. At the front doors, she stopped and turned around. Hands planted firmly on her hips, she glared at him. "Has anyone ever told you you've got trust issues?"

"Has anyone ever told you you're not so good at this psychic thing? If you were, you'd have known I didn't have the lamp."

Claudia's eyes widened as if he'd slapped her. She yanked on the knob, then fumbled with the lock for a moment before finally releasing the mechanism and rushing outside. The door slammed hard behind her.

Xander felt like shit.

Ten minutes later, he stood under a hot stream of water pouring from his silver-plated showerhead. Of all the luxuries that came with being mortal, the ability to bathe was his favorite. He couldn't get enough of the feel of water flowing over his skin. Baths, whirlpool hot tubs, stand-up showers, it didn't matter. As long as it was hot and wet, he was willing.

That thought made him groan. Blood pounded in his cock again, flooding his shaft with the incessant need Claudia had stirred in his groin. What was wrong with him? Five millennia of watching people fuck should have cured him of any lust-inducing desire that might have reared its head, but now he was convinced mortal drives were slowly but surely going to kill him. He hadn't fucked anyone since he'd been freed from his lamp. He'd wanted a mate, someone he cared about, to be his first.

He stroked his palm over his cock, realizing how crazy that sounded. No one in the twenty-first century waited for true love before fucking. That was as old fashioned as… well, as he was. And still, he'd signed up with the Paranormal Mates Society because he figured that was his best chance at finding someone who'd understand his past.

Steam built up around him, caressing his overheated skin. He glanced at the bronze lamp sitting on the edge of the bathtub, waiting for him. It wasn't his first choice, but he no longer had access to the Aladdin lamp, so this had to do.

Need stirred low in his stomach. His cock throbbed. His gaze darted from the lamp promising relief to his hand clutching his cock, stroking his shaft. An image of Claudia's full lips flooded his thoughts. He wanted to thrust his cock between them, to fuck her mouth until he spilled his seed down her throat.

He stopped, panting hard, hand clamped firmly around the base of his cock. It was no use thinking of Claudia. He'd never see her again. Pre-cum dripped down his shaft. His hand glided back up over his dick, his fingers clenching around the head. He made quick, twisting motions up and down his shaft until his balls tightened and he felt the stir of impending orgasm.

His muscles taut with the onslaught of his release, Xander could no longer fight the images flooding his mind. The pink top hugging Claudia's voluptuous breasts. The way her wet pussy clenched around his fingers. Her mouth parted, her lips moist and glistening, swollen from his kisses.

He came, suddenly and violently, his cum squirting over the shower walls. It dripped down the white tile and as he watched, the water streaming from the showerhead washed the creamy mess away.

Still breathing hard, he rinsed his spent cock and then let the warm, comforting mist take him. Though the Genie Code dictated that he could only spend two hours a day in his natural form, those two hours would be pure bliss tonight. He'd change shape, and for as long as he could, he'd think of nothing, feel nothing, *be* nothing.

He shifted, letting his body adjust to his new weightless form. The mist within him swirled, slipping through the spout of his last sanctuary, knowing even thoughts of Claudia's full tits and her maddening, cock-hardening smile couldn't reach him there.

Chapter Four

Annoyance surged through Claudia's veins as she stared at her laptop screen for the hundredth time that night. She moved the mouse cursor and clicked on the Get Mail button, tapping her fingernails impatiently on the desktop while her mail system queried the server.

You have no new messages.

She leaned back in the tacky beech wood armchair that passed for high-class furnishings at the Queen's Own Hotel and Casino. The penthouse suite had been her home away from home ever since Ra'ees hired her to find the lamp. At first, she'd found the gold-gilded mirrors and cream-colored wallpaper inviting in a kitschy sort of way. Now she just wanted to go home.

A week had passed since Claudia's disastrous encounter with Xander. She'd gone back to the hotel room that night convinced he'd email or try to contact her again, but when he didn't, she went out to look for the lamp on her own. Seven days of searching every ancient site she could think of and contacting every antique collector in Cairo had gotten her absolutely nowhere.

Worse yet, her abilities weren't helping. Her telepathic talents no longer flared when she logged in to the Paranormal Mates Society. Over the past week, she'd read every profile, concentrating on anyone who might have ties with either Egypt or Xander, but only managed to find paranormal being after paranormal being, each seemingly hornier than the last. Even that wouldn't have been so bad, if she could allow herself the indulgence. But while she was on Ra'ees's payroll, playtime was entirely out of the question.

The screen flickered and beeped, jolting Claudia upright. Her heart drummed an insistent rhythm in her chest. *Xander?*

Warning: Laptop battery is low. Automatic shutdown in ten minutes. Please save your work.

Claudia released a breath she hadn't realized she'd been holding, then slammed the laptop closed. This wasn't working. She'd lost contact with the only person who knew anything about the lamp. She needed to march right back to his place, ring the doorbell and ask — politely — who took the lamp and where.

Like hell.

Without hesitating, she picked up the phone and dialed an international number. She paced from the window overlooking the city to the bathroom door and back as she waited for someone to pick up.

"I need help," she said when the melodious familiar voice answered.

"Well, well. It's good to hear your voice, too. How long has it been?"

Despite herself, Claudia smiled. "Too long."

She'd met Danara when she worked on a dig in Santorini. The site had only recently been discovered, and Claudia had been hired to find a particular mural and release the Goddess imprisoned within. She never would have been able to gain access to the site if not for Danara. The mermaid had more than one trick up her tail.

"What is it this time?" Danara asked. "No, wait, let me guess. You're in trouble with the Order of the Knights of Aragorn again because you returned for the singing sword? Or does the Vatican want you back for questioning for the third time?"

"Very funny." Claudia cradled the phone to her ear and sat on the edge of the king-sized bed to pull off her high-heeled shoes. "The Knights can keep the sword. It's a fake. And the Vatican thinks I'm bad for business, so they informed their guards

I'm not to be allowed within twenty miles of the place. But that's not why I'm calling."

"No?" Danara sounded intrigued. "Why are you calling, then?"

"Can't a woman call a mermaid for a friendly chat every now and again without having an ulterior motive?"

Danara's silvery laugh rang in Claudia's ear. "I'd believe that, if not for the fact that you opened this conversation with a plea for help. So spill it. What kind of trouble have you gotten yourself into now?"

An image of Xander's broad, powerful muscles, his chiseled abs, the promise of that thick, curved cock hit Claudia like an unexpected heat wave. She swallowed hard. "Man trouble."

"Ah. The worst kind."

Five minutes later, she'd spilled out the entire story, from the first time she saw Xander in the Desert Wind coffee shop to the door slamming behind her as she stormed out of his house.

"Well?" Claudia asked when Danara hadn't said anything. "What do you think?"

"I think you're being stubborn."

Claudia sighed. "Who asked you, anyway?"

"I believe you did. But if you'd rather go to your client and tell him you know someone who knows where the lamp is but you refuse to ask him… well, you go right ahead."

"I'll have to sleep with him, you know."

"Ra'ees?"

A picture of the handsome werewolf formed unbidden in Claudia's mind. "No, though that wouldn't be so bad, either. Xander."

"Ah. So that would be bad then."

"Yes. No." She moved the receiver from one shoulder to the other and fell back on the bed. The feather-soft mattress felt great beneath her weary muscles. "I don't know."

"What did you say this site was called?"

"The Paranormal Mates Society. Why? Are you interested?"

"Umm… My sister might be."

Claudia sat up, grinning. "Oh, no, you don't. You're not fooling me. If you're thinking of joining, I think it's a great idea. Just go to www.paranormalmatessociety.com and fill out a quick questionnaire."

"And you vouch for these people?"

"Can you think of a better place to meet someone as screwed up as we are?"

"Hey! Speak for yourself." Danara tried to sound affronted, but her light tone betrayed her words. "So, what are you going to do about Xander?"

"I thought I'd find the lamp, get it to Ra'ees, then show up at Xander's doorstep and pretend nothing happened. So far, it's not working as I'd planned."

"Nothing ever does."

"Yeah. Thanks for reminding me."

"What are friends for?" Danara hesitated for a moment. "There's more, isn't there? Something else is bothering you."

Claudia licked her dry lips. "His profile is still up on the site. I thought after we'd met, he wouldn't feel the need to keep looking."

"I hate to point out the obvious, but you only went after him after he mentioned the lamp. His ego's probably bruised. And you left him with a hard-on the size of a baseball bat. A man has needs, you know."

Jealousy pricked through Claudia's defenses. Had she really pushed Xander into another woman's arms? "Now you're starting to sound like all my ex-boyfriends. Men aren't monogamous creatures. You know that as well as I do."

"When did you become so cynical?"

"Probably about the time the griffon cheated on the Goddess."

For a minute, they were both silent. Claudia knew Danara remembered the story as well as she did. When they'd met in Santorini, Claudia managed to rescue the Goddess trapped in the mural, but she'd also freed her lover. It turned out they were both there because of his indiscretion. A griffon by day, human by night, he'd betrayed the Goddess with another woman. Angered and hurt by the betrayal, the Goddess doomed them both to an eternity trapped in stone. At least, until Claudia broke the spell.

"Not all men are like him," Danara said, her voice barely above a whisper.

Claudia closed her eyes. "Do you really believe that?"

"I do. And somewhere deep inside, you do too."

"Maybe," Claudia grudgingly admitted. "Check out the Paranormal Mates Society, okay? You might find a man worthy of you."

Danara laughed. "Take your own advice, will you? Email Xander. Tell him you're sorry for running out. See what he says."

"Good advice." It really was. Yet Claudia knew she wouldn't take it.

She hung up, promising to call more often. Then she put her shoes back on and left the hotel room.

* * *

The Queen's Own Hotel and Casino loomed over Cairo. Having only recently been built, it boasted the designation of tallest structure in the city.

Leaning against a streetlamp across from the lobby, Xander wasn't impressed by the fact that the penthouse crested the sixty-story mark, or the knowledge that any of the hotel's guests could likely single-handedly purchase half the city without blinking an eye.

What did astonish him, however, was knowing that Claudia had stayed at the Queen's Own Hotel and Casino for the past two months; and in the penthouse suite, no less. That kind of luxury would have cost a small fortune by anyone's standards. Fortunately for Claudia, she wasn't footing the bill.

Xander clenched his teeth, his gaze fixed on the hotel guests pivoting through the revolving doors. It had been relatively easy to find information on the elusive treasure hunter. Within a matter of hours, he had Claudia's entire life history at his fingertips, which included some details he'd have been happier not knowing—like the fact that Ra'ees Bayar, a notorious businessman whose dealings weren't always as legal as the Egyptian government would have liked, was funding her entire trip to Egypt.

Who Claudia chose to do business with shouldn't have mattered, but the *type* of business she was doing gnawed at his insides.

He hadn't been able to get her out of his mind over the past week. Ever since the night she stormed out of his house, he found himself flipping open his laptop at all hours of the day and night just to stare at her profile. Part of him wished she'd remove it. Thinking of her in another man's arms made him bite his lower lip until he tasted blood. But another part of him, the part of him that had him stroking his cock until he spilled his seed all over his stomach, wanted her picture accessible to him any time. All the time.

He crossed his arms over his chest and continued to wait. She had to leave the penthouse sooner or later. His human friends would have told him he was obsessed, but he wasn't ready to chalk up the feelings stirring in his veins to such a negative emotion. Sure, he wanted her, craved her, hungered for her every waking moment. But it was more than that. She'd managed to get under his skin like no woman before her, and he refused to attribute that simply to unbridled lust.

As if to challenge that very thought, Claudia appeared in the entrance of the lobby. She waited behind an older couple, then stepped through the revolving doors. Xander's breath caught in his throat. His cock was instantly hard, throbbing at the sight of her. She wore a low-cut black and white striped top that would have looked unflattering on any woman who didn't have her lean figure, her full breasts. Blue jeans encased her long legs, tighter than proper attire for women the Middle East dictated, and sexy as hell. Strappy, high-heeled sandals completed the ensemble.

As before, her hair was unbound. Reaching almost to the middle of her back, the straight dark locks reflected the streetlight, giving her a sparkling, eye-catching, cock-tingling quality.

Xander swore low under his breath. There was only one place she was going dressed like that, and it wasn't to the mosque.

He'd planned to wait until she left the hotel, then pretend he just happened to be walking by and it was sheer coincidence they'd run into each other like this. He'd figured they'd both have a laugh over how they seemed to meet in the oddest places, and then they'd take it from there.

Yet now, seeing her like this, knowing she was probably going to meet Ra'ees, sent an irrational surge of jealousy thrumming through his veins. Xander held his breath, waiting to see if she'd ask one of the bellhops to call her a taxi. She didn't. Grateful for at least that much good luck, he watched her turn right onto the main road, then he fell into step about fifty paces behind her.

Xander gritted his teeth and clenched his hands into fists at his sides. His fingernails dug into his palms. As usual, his well thought out plan had gone to hell, fast. Following Claudia, he realized he had absolutely no idea what he was doing. If she was in fact going to see Ra'ees, what could he do about it? Stand outside, leaning against a tree trunk and watch their silhouettes through the window as they fucked each other senseless?

Images flooded his thoughts, each more unwelcome than the last. He knew from experience how uninhibited Claudia could be when aroused, how eager to come. He could picture her, pressing her lips to Ra'ees's chest, her hand stroking his cock. Then she'd trail her tongue lower over his abdomen until she sunk to her knees. She'd take his cock deep in her mouth with quick, expert motions. She'd close her eyes in ecstasy as the taste flooded her throat and his hips ground against her mouth, his cock thrusting in and out of her luscious lips.

Xander's rod hardened even further as anger continued to build inside his chest. She took another turn, this time onto an empty side road. His footsteps made a loud crunching noise on the unpaved, pebbled street. He forced himself to remain even further behind.

Not that Claudia would care, even if she knew he followed her. Like him, she probably only had one thing on her mind. He imagined her strolling in to Ra'ees's bedroom as though she belonged there. She'd strip the moment she crossed the threshold, pulling off her top and baring her full, firm breasts before she closed the door.

The mental picture of her taut, straining nipples slicked by another man's tongue sent a groan to his throat. His balls ached with need. Deep, primal desire settled in his groin. The knowledge that Claudia was eagerly, willingly going to fuck someone else was too much to bear.

He quickened his step to catch up with her. The hell with spying. He'd take her right here, right now, if that's what he had to do. She was *his*.

Though his footsteps made enough noise to alert her to his proximity, Claudia didn't quicken her step. He caught up to her easily and reached out to touch her shoulder, but she spun around at the last moment, meeting his gaze.

"Just as I said," she murmured.

Before he could speak, Claudia cupped his balls in the palm of her hand, stroking him through the thin material of his pants. Her scent filled him, sweetly fragrant and intensely arousing. "You have trust issues."

Chapter Five

Claudia waited for Xander to retaliate with another clever retort, but the brusque rebuttal she expected never came. The full moon overhead bathed his profile in silvery light and dark shadows, giving him a rough, dangerous edge. She could see his brows were drawn over his dark eyes, but his expression told her nothing.

His emotions, on the other hand, assaulted her from all sides, wrapping her body in an intense, furious arousal. Beneath the edgy lust lay something else, an emotion she could only describe as jealousy and… fear? No, something else… discomfort, perhaps. He didn't know how to deal with the onslaught of emotions any more than she did. The fierce craving puzzled him, but the extreme possessiveness he felt toward her perturbed him much more than he cared to admit, even to himself.

"You were right, you know," she said at last. He hadn't made a move to touch her, and now she noticed his hands fisted at his sides.

"About what?" He snapped the words out as though just speaking to her took effort.

"I'm not very good at this telepath thing. Or at the clairvoyant thing, for that matter."

For a moment, his lips turned upward into a smug smirk that disappeared as quickly as it materialized. "Why are you telling me this?"

"Because maybe, just maybe, you can admit that I was right too."

Instead of answering, he covered her mouth with his. The kiss was wet, hot, primal, sending a rush of moisture to her pussy. She moaned against his lips, struggling between pushing him away and giving in to everything he offered. His fingers roamed down her back, cupping her ass, pulling her close to him. His erection throbbed against her belly, thick and insistent.

His tongue teased her lips, not forcing them apart until she opened for him. Another groan found its way out of her throat. Xander's thoughts poured into her mind in a rush, intensifying her own need for him.

"Oh," she breathed when he finally pulled away. "Oh."

His smile was genuine, though guarded. She wasn't the only one fighting an internal battle tonight, but neither of them would be satisfied in any way until she had that lamp.

Xander pushed a strand of hair behind her ear. "I'm sorry I followed you."

Claudia's pulse quickened. "Why did you?" She'd known he walked behind her from the moment she left the hotel. She should have been angry or scared, but his presence had the opposite effect. It made her feel safe, somehow, knowing he was there, just a few steps behind.

"I…" He looked away, thrusting his hands into his pockets. "It's stupid."

A vivid image of herself on her knees, naked, flashed before Claudia's eyes. She knelt in front of Ra'ees, his rod hovering just at the entrance to her slightly parted lips. Her eyes were wide, shining with barely contained lust as she gripped the solid shaft he offered and flicked the tip of her tongue over the head of his aroused cock. She saw Xander too. He stood in a corner, his jaw clenched, his brow furrowed, his erection tenting his pants.

Suddenly, she understood. "Oh," she repeated, then shook her head. "No. That's not where I was going. Why would you think that?"

His sigh of relief was audible, though he tried to cover it with a well-timed cough. He didn't fool her for a minute.

"You're not the only one who can find things people would rather keep hidden," he said. "The only difference between us is that I don't use people to get what I want."

Her stomach clenched at the raw tenderness in those words. "I'd never use you… not on purpose." She looked away, guilt washing over her like a tidal wave. Then the rest of his meaning sunk in. "You looked me up."

"I did," he admitted.

She jabbed a finger into his solid, bare chest, then wished she hadn't. Arousal drifted off him in waves, making her head spin. "The hotel shouldn't have been that hard, but Ra'ees is too good at covering his tracks for you to have figured out he was paying for all my expenses."

"I'm better than you give me credit for." The arrogant smirk returned, and with it, so did the image of his cock, long and curved, perfectly shaped to deliver a mind-blowing orgasm with no more than a well-placed thrust.

Claudia tried to keep her voice flat. "If this is going to go anywhere, you need to trust me."

"Is this going anywhere?"

"Don't ignore the issue. Are you willing to give me the benefit of the doubt now and then? I don't want to have to look over my shoulder every moment of every day." Inspiration struck like lightening. "I get myself into dangerous situations sometimes. I don't want to have to look out for you too."

She was rewarded by the sight of his jaw dropping. "You're a woman."

"And that's another thing. These old-fashioned values of yours have got to go."

He pinched the bridge of his nose as if trying—and failing—to keep a headache at bay. "We're not even together yet, and you're already trying to change me."

"You wanted a mate. That's what mates do."

He growled, stepping closer to her. His arms enveloped her, pressing her to him. Her curves molded to his hard muscles and she had to bite her lip to keep herself from moaning. Again.

"What else do mates do?" His voice was low and rough in her ear.

"They tell each other the truth," she murmured, burying her face in the side of his neck. He smelled like musk and mint and sex.

His hand caressed her ass, squeezing slightly. "I've never lied to you."

"Where's the lamp, Xander?" Claudia held her breath as he hesitated, convinced she'd just blown it. If he'd only tell her where to find the lamp, they could both have what they wanted. People had their cake and ate it every day, right? Why couldn't she?

"I'll take you to the lamp."

Claudia's mouth gaped open. Had she heard right? Had her tempting, mouthwatering, delectable cake just dropped in her lap? "You will?"

"Yes. If—"

"Ah. I knew there was an 'if.'"

He pressed his index finger against her lips, silencing her. "You have to grant me one wish."

Since he wouldn't let her speak, Claudia cocked an eyebrow and tilted her head in inquiry.

Xander lowered his head until his warm breath fanned her face and his dark gaze bore into hers. "I want to be inside you."

His words made her insides melt. The tip of her tongue swept over his finger and she felt him shudder at her touch.

"Wish granted," she whispered.

* * *

Xander could no longer fool himself. He'd wanted Claudia since the first moment he'd seen her, though he'd tried to convince himself it was just mortal lust, as if what he felt was... normal.

It wasn't normal. It was raw, savage, insistent, overwhelming. His desire for her swam through his veins, blinding him to everything else. The only light penetrating the dark alley came from the silvery moon and the starlit night. He couldn't see Claudia as well as he wanted to, but he could make out her features in the inky blackness, her pale skin, her lush, inviting curves.

He ran his fingertip over the silky skin of her throat, feeling the wild pulse beating there. "Are you afraid of me?" he asked slowly, wishing he could see her eyes.

She shook her head. "I'm afraid of me. I'm afraid of what I feel when I'm with you. But I'm not afraid of you." A strand of glossy hair tinged blue by the moonlight fell over her brow. Xander swept it away, then touched his lips to hers.

He'd intended to be gentle, to show her she had nothing to fear, but the hunger took over before he could stop it. He thrust his tongue between her lips and felt her open to him, her hot, wet mouth drawing him in until he thought he'd lose whatever weak control he still had over his sanity.

As a genie, he'd heard rumors of lust so overwhelming it could make a man do baffling, mystifying things to be with the woman he wanted. Xander had granted his share of bizarre wishes, but he'd been able to maintain his objectivity and regard those people as the hopeless, lovesick beings they were.

Now he was one of them. He should have been troubled by the knowledge, but he couldn't bring himself to care.

He slid his hand down her hips and inside the apex of her thighs. The tight jeans she wore denied him access to the one place he wanted to touch more than anything. He couldn't feel her heat, her warmth, but he craved it as he craved his natural shape. He tugged on the button holding her waistband closed, then pulled on the zipper.

Claudia wiggled, helping him ease the garment over her hips. She wore satin panties beneath. Her jeans hung down around her knees, and he couldn't hold back long enough to take them off entirely. He returned his fingers to her slit. This time, he was rewarded by the damp feel of the crotch and Claudia's low, guttural moan.

"Yes," she murmured. "Xander."

He dropped to his knees before her, his hand never leaving her cunt. "Say my name again."

"Xander." She gasped as he rubbed the wet center, molding the thin material to her slick folds.

"Again."

"Xander." Her voice was louder this time. Though the street was deserted, there were houses not too far from where they stood, and a large parking lot just a block away.

His name on her tongue was the most erotic thing Xander had ever heard. It took all his self-control not to come right there, in his pants, with his hand on her pussy.

To distract himself, he tugged on the waistband of her panties. The triangle of hair covering her mound glittered with her cream in the pale moonlight. Her scent was intoxicating, spicy and mouthwatering. He wanted to taste her, to sample, nip and savor her, to feel her essence flowing down his throat until she was a part of him.

Claudia gripped his head, pulling him in closer to her pink, swollen folds. "Lick me," she whispered, her voice hoarse.

He didn't need a second invitation. He covered her mound with his mouth possessively, insistently, then slid his tongue in the moist heat. Her thighs trembled and her knees buckled. He felt her grip tighten on his hair, her hands fisting close to his scalp, tugging on the strands. If it hurt, he didn't feel it.

He gripped her ass, squeezing the firm flesh as he thrust his tongue inside her slit. She had the ideal ass, round and well curved. His palms closed over her flawless cheeks. She was perfect for him. Built for him.

His senses reeled from the impact of that thought and the flavor of her cream flooding his mouth. She panted, her low, guttural moans flooding the still night air. In the distance, a dog barked and a car honked, but Xander's senses were only attuned to her. The rest of the city noises faded into the background, where they belonged.

He found her clit with the tip of his tongue and swiped it with a quick darting motion. Her hips pushed her mound against his face, her movements as fevered as his own.

"Oh, yes. Yes." She repeated the words over and over, just loud enough for him to hear. "More."

His cock throbbed. His sac ached, ready to burst from wanting to be buried balls-deep inside her tight, inviting cunt. His tongue delved deeper, searching for that spot that would make her come on his tongue. He felt her muscles tense a moment before her release flooded his mouth. She whispered his name as she came, making his throat tighten and his gut clench. If he wasn't already on his knees, the unfamiliar emotion would have brought him there.

Staggering to his feet, he held her labia open with the fingers of his right hand and untied the cord holding his silk pants together at the waist with his left. They fell around his ankles and his cock thrust out, his erection jutting forward, already searching for her slick, wet channel.

"I want you so bad," he murmured, nibbling on her neck and inhaling the sweet scent of her hair.

"You can have me."

He wanted to push her up against a wall, a car, anything, but the street looked abandoned. Trees lined the sidewalks, small and fragile looking. They'd have to do.

Tugging on her hand, he led her to one of the nearby trees. She didn't protest, but wrapped her arm around his neck and pulled his mouth down to hers. Her tongue thrust against his, wet and willing. Her fingers entwined with his, parting her folds, leading his cock to her slick passage.

"Fuck me," she whispered in his ear. "Hard."

He didn't know how hard he could go with the trunk at her back flimsy enough to break with a vigorous thrust, but he wasn't about to disappoint her.

He gripped her thighs and lifted her off the ground. She wrapped her legs around his waist, her cunt clenching around his shaft as she impaled herself on his erection. He groaned as her muscles tightened around him, already threatening to milk him dry; and they hadn't even begun.

He gritted his teeth, willing his self-control to hold. Her cream ran down his shaft and over his groin to drip down his thighs. She rocked back and forth, her hips shifting her pussy over his cock in tight increments that left him panting, his fingers digging into her ass.

She felt so good, so right fucking him. He bit his lower lip and closed his eyes, but she wouldn't let him have even that small respite.

"Look at me."

He did, and what he found in her gaze took his breath away. He expected lust, desire, even need, but her smile and the way she glanced at him as her cunt squeezed and gripped his shaft made him stumble. She nearly fell out of his arms.

"I'm sorry," he said, tightening his hold.

The tip of her tongue darted out between her full lips. "I'm not."

"That's not what I meant."

She opened her mouth to reply but he thrust his hips forward, hard, slamming her back against the trunk. She gasped, her words lost on a fevered sigh.

Her nipples were hard, brushing against his chest as her breasts heaved with her ragged breaths. He wanted to bite down on the tempting nubbins, to palm her breasts while he fucked her, but like many other things, that would have to wait. He wanted to do everything to her, again and again and again until he had no more to give, and even then, he wanted to continue until she screamed for mercy.

Her head lolled back and her fingers dug into his chest, biting into his skin. He groaned, his balls clenching and tightening, knowing he couldn't hold back much longer. Releasing his tight grip on her for just a moment, he slapped her ass, not hard but enough to make her head snap back and her eyes widen.

"Look at me." He repeated her words, slapping her again. She shuddered and gripped him tighter, her motions on his cock frenzied. Then she stilled and came with a low hiss, bringing him over the edge with her.

His cock jerked and he spilled his seed deep in her pussy, holding her motionless on his twitching rod. He felt his release seep down his shaft, and knew it would escape down her thighs the moment he withdrew from her slick folds. Only he didn't want to withdraw. He wanted to hold her like this for eternity.

She laid her head on his chest and he leaned her against the tree, supporting them both. Her heartbeat thrummed insistently. The smell of sex permeated the air, teasing his softening cock back to semi-hardness.

He ground his hips against hers and she stirred against him. She nipped his earlobe, then wrapped her lips around the bite mark. He sighed. Mortality was worth every moment of torture for this. He'd always thought shifting to his natural shape was pure bliss, with orgasm coming a distant second.

Standing here, his cock buried inside Claudia, he knew he'd been wrong for the past five thousand years. There was nothing better than this.

He wanted to tell her how he felt, but he couldn't put the emotion clogging his throat into words. How could he explain that she made him feel something he thought was impossible?

Her breath tickled his ear. Maybe she'd speak first, confess she felt the same way. Hope rose in his chest, quickening his breathing. Was it possible this had been more than mind-blowing sex for her too?

He waited. When she spoke at last, her words cut deeper than any mortal weapon. They turned his blood to ice.

"Where's the lamp, Xander?"

Chapter Six

Xander slid Claudia off his cock and placed her on her feet before stepping away and pulling up his pants. Guilt stirred inside her. She could see how much her words had hurt him, but she'd been wrong to let things between them go so far in the first place.

In ten years of working as a treasure hunter, she'd never let pleasure interfere with business. If any of her clients ever found out that she spent her time fucking when she should be searching, her cozy paycheck and the reputation she'd worked so hard to build would be gone in a flash.

It was too much to risk, even for him.

"Where's the lamp, Xander?" she repeated while she zipped up her jeans. She ran a hand through her long hair, trying to smooth it.

He turned, moonlight flashing in his eyes. She felt his barely contained anger along with his disappointment. In her? Probably. He'd expected more than she could give.

"I told you I'd take you to it." His words were low, his voice menacing in its intensity. "I got what I wanted. You will too."

Remorse churned in her gut. She'd wanted him just as much as she wanted the lamp; perhaps even more. His need for her had been palpable. She could feel it rolling off his skin in heavy waves, his passion and possessiveness engulfing her, calling to her. She'd never been so aware of anyone else's thoughts before, and in truth, the knowledge that he could get so far under her skin scared her. But he hadn't forced her into sex. She was every bit as responsible for their impulsive lovemaking as he was.

Admitting that, though, was more than she was ready to do. At least not until the lamp was safely where it belonged. With Ra'ees.

Claudia smoothed her hands down the front of her shirt. "I'm ready."

Xander scowled. "Of course you are."

She decided to let that remark go without comment and fell into step beside him as he turned back the way they'd come. It was past midnight. Here, on the outskirts of the city, the streets were dark at this hour, with only a few people returning home from their late-night liaisons disturbing the quiet of the night.

As they moved further into the heart of Cairo, the city came alive with sounds of modern technology. Cars honked, merchants peddled their wares at all hours of the day and night and streetlights flickered, bathing the pavement in their cool glow.

They'd been walking for almost an hour. Claudia's feet ached. Had she known they'd be taking the scenic tour of the city, she'd have worn something other than the high-heeled strappy sandals she'd chosen earlier that evening.

They crossed the street and turned onto another side road. Even in the heart of the city, the pavement was coarse and pebbled with small rocks. Pain shot up Claudia's calf as her heel twisted in a crack in the rough road. "Would it have killed us to take a cab?"

Xander didn't even bother to glance her way. He hadn't said two words since they'd left the alley, and it seemed he wasn't about to start now. His silence bothered her, though not nearly as much as not being able to read his thoughts. She'd had no problem delving into his mind when he was thinking about fucking her, or when he'd imagined her with another man. He was obviously not thinking about either of those things now, and not knowing the direction his thoughts had taken set her nerves on edge.

The narrow street was lined with shops, each smaller and more unassuming than the last. The storefronts didn't have the elegance of downtown boutiques, or the expensive flair of the specialty shops claiming they carried everything from Cleopatra's real wig to Nefertiti's scepter. Still, they looked more appealing and inviting than any of the places tourists favored.

Xander stopped before a wooden door and knocked softly. Claudia shifted from one foot to the other. Her hand went instinctively to her pocket, finding the lighter she kept there and turning it over. The nervous habit helped soothe her frazzled nerves. Footsteps echoed from the other side of the door and Xander whispered something in a language she didn't understand.

She was about to ask what he'd said when the door swung inward, letting the soft glow of warm light spill onto the sidewalk. A woman stood in the doorway, her skin wrinkled and spotted with age. Her white hair stuck out of a haphazard bun arranged at the back of her head.

She smiled when she saw Xander. "I didn't expect to see you again."

"If it's any consolation, Isis, I didn't expect to be back, either."

Isis? Like the Goddess?

Claudia peered at the woman curiously, but their host gave no indication that she was anything but ordinary. Opening the door wider, the woman allowed them to step through.

Inside, the shop seemed as steeped in time as Isis herself. The aroma of sweet herbs drifted through the air. A thick layer of dust coated shelves upon shelves that held every kind of object imaginable, from the mundane to the extraordinary.

Claudia's breath caught in her throat. She recognized finely crafted statuettes of ancient Egyptian Gods, various amulets, letters written on blocks of stone and even a mummy leaning up against a wall at the back of the room. Her thoughts spun with the relevance of the find. Every one of these objects was *real*.

"I had no idea…" she murmured.

An inviting fire blazed in an old-fashioned hearth. The woman indicated a chair near the flames. "Sit. I'll be right back with the object you seek."

Claudia glanced at Xander, but his gaze was shadowed as he looked into the fire. He leaned against the mantel, his arms crossed over his chest. Firelight gleamed off his skin, drawing

Claudia's attention to his finely muscled chest, his rippled abs and the dark path of hair disappearing beneath his waistband. Her pussy tightened with feminine recognition.

Unnerved by the unexpected arousal, Claudia did as Isis bid and sat in the plush chair. It molded to her, offering comfort in a room shrouded in ancient secrets. She allowed herself to lean her head back and close her eyes for a moment.

An image of the lamp came unbidden to her mind. She could see it clearly, polished wings gleaming golden in the sunlight. Mist drifted from its elongated tip, taking shape slowly. A man emerged from its depths, dark hair falling over his eyes, his mouth turned down in grim determination.

Claudia blinked her eyes open. "The lamp *was* yours, wasn't it?"

Xander's dark gaze rested on her like a touch, sending a wave of sensation through her already aroused nerve endings. She fought the urge to squirm in her chair. "It was."

"Then why is it here?"

He sighed deeply and turned back to the fire. For a long moment, Claudia was sure he wouldn't answer. When he spoke at last, his voice was so low she could barely hear his words. "The Genie Code of Conduct, established thousands of years ago, governs the way our race lives. It's simple, really. For five thousand years, we live a life of servitude, granting three wishes to any human who commands us. After that, we're free to live the rest of our lives as mortals, as long as we stick to the Code."

Claudia's brow furrowed. "I don't understand. If you're no longer forced to serve, then why do you have to follow rules?"

Xander shrugged. "We never stop being genies. Not really. We can still shapeshift and rest within a lamp, but if we do it for longer than two hours a day, the will of the lamp binds us to it, returning us to an eternity of granting wishes and living vicariously through others."

"The will of the lamp?"

Xander turned back to her and nodded. "We're drawn to ancient vessels. We seek them out, crave them like we do human contact. It's in our nature."

"That still doesn't explain why you no longer have the lamp."

Xander scowled. "Although we can take temporary shelter in any vessel with the promise of flame, very few lamps have the power to bind us. There are more genies than there are lamps we can permanently inhabit. We can't be mortal until our term of servitude is up, and we can't serve unless we have a vessel. Do you see?"

She didn't, entirely. "What happens to genies without a lamp?"

"They drift, aimlessly, until they find one that's no longer occupied."

"And that's what happened to your lamp," she guessed. "Another genie took it over when you vacated it."

"The Genie Code decrees that a genie cannot be in possession of an inhabited lamp. We must send it out into the world as quickly as possible, so the genie inside can fulfill his destiny, and eventually be released."

"And live as a mortal for the rest of his life," Claudia finished.

"Yes. As long as the genie doesn't break any of the sacred rules, such as returning to his natural state for longer than two hours or asking to have a wish granted by another genie."

Claudia's head throbbed. Being a genie sounded a lot more complicated than she'd thought.

"Here it is," Isis announced as she entered the room through the back door. Claudia's mouth went dry as the woman offered the lamp freely. She glanced at Xander, but he'd already turned back to the fireplace.

Her heart beating an insistent rhythm against her chest, Claudia took the lamp and reverently ran her fingertips over the ancient object. It seemed to pulse beneath her hand, its power unmistakable. Taking a deep breath, she rubbed the spot just below the outstretched wings.

At first, nothing happened. Then, as Claudia watched, mist began to drift from the spout. It wafted out in heavy puffs, amassing around Claudia's ankles, then gathered into the unmistakable shape of a woman. Slender and shapely, with a mass of blonde curls that tumbled to her knees, the genie was utterly breathtaking. She wore nothing but what looked to be a skimpy gold bikini and a belly chain that hung provocatively over her hips.

The genie's gaze swept the room, settling on Xander. "You! The Genie Order will never allow you to own me."

His shoulders slumped, and he looked weary and exhausted. Claudia yearned to cross the distance between them and draw him into her arms, smooth away the creases in his brow. "I'm not your new master, Ambrosia." He pointed at Claudia. "She is."

The genie turned to Claudia, scorn clear in her brilliant blue eyes. "A woman. Figures."

Despite her relief at having found the lamp, annoyance skimmed down Claudia's skin. "You have a problem with women too?"

"I'm so tired of granting stupid wishes to stupid women!" Ambrosia stomped her foot. A puff of dust rose from the ancient carpet. "Make me pretty; give me a hundred pairs of shoes; let my hair be infinitely shiny. Why can't anyone ever ask for anything *fun*?"

Claudia tilted her head and frowned at the genie. "What kind of fun would you like to have?"

"Well…" Ambrosia cast a sly look beneath her long lashes at Xander. "You wouldn't happen to want to watch him fuck me, would you?"

Claudia's eyes widened. The mere thought of Xander with this blonde bombshell sent a wave of jealousy coiling in her stomach. "No."

The genie pouted. "Would you like me to strip? Masturbate for you? Shift into a man and fuck you senseless?"

With each wild idea, Claudia grew more impatient. She lifted up a hand to stop the onslaught of wild sexual fantasies. "Enough. What I want you to do right now is get back in the lamp, okay?"

"Figures." Ambrosia blew out a long breath. "Let me know when you've decided which shoes, purses and other stupid accessories you want to own." She disappeared in a stream of smoke.

"How much do I owe you?" Claudia asked Isis when the genie was tucked safely back in the lamp.

The old woman waved a hand dismissively. "It was only mine for safekeeping. It's not for sale."

Claudia smiled. "I'm grateful."

"Let's go." Xander stormed through the doorway into the street. Claudia followed him, feeling his anxiety, his need to be away from this place. Or from her. She couldn't tell which, and the knowledge was disturbing.

"There's one last thing I need to do," she told him as they headed back to the main street.

"Whatever." He flagged a cab, not waiting for her to continue. "You have the lamp. Go to Ra'ees."

His fury slammed into her. Wild sexual images flooded her mind, all of her with Ra'ees.

"No! It's not like that." She struggled to explain, but the words wouldn't come out fast enough. She couldn't betray a client's trust, even now. "I'll come to you tomorrow. I promise."

Claudia knew Xander was convinced she wasn't telling the truth. Disappointment and anger vied with one another inside him as he struggled to control his temper and banish the unwanted images. Still they came, each more intense than the last. Ra'ees fucking her from behind, his cock slamming deep into her ass, her breasts swaying with each thrust, her screams filling the air.

She inhaled sharply, feeling as if he'd just hit her in the stomach. "You promised to trust me." Claudia was dismayed to realize her voice shook. Tears stung the back of her throat. "You promised."

He slammed the cab door, then rolled down his window. "And you promised not to use me to get what you want. I guess we both lied."

Chapter Seven

Ra'ees loomed over Claudia, his dark shadow falling over the lamp in her hand. "It took you long enough."

They stood in his multi-room, walnut-paneled office. Bookshelves lined three walls from floor to ceiling, while a full-sized window took up the fourth. The view of the city at night was spectacular, but Claudia had no interest in it tonight.

She smiled sweetly, trying not to let her aggravation show. She'd given up a lot to get the lamp for Ra'ees, perhaps too much. "I never said finding it would be fast, or easy. Besides, I've given you enough artifacts to tide you over until this precious little relic was safely in your furry paws."

Ra'ees scowled, showing even white teeth. "If you ever mention that little-known fact to anyone—"

"Yeah, yeah. Threaten me all you want. Unlike most people, I'm not afraid of the big, bad wolf." She thrust the lamp into his hands. "Take it. It's given me enough trouble."

His frown disappeared as he slid his hands over the smooth surface of the lamp. "I've waited so long for this."

"And patience is definitely not one of your virtues." She grinned at the look in his eyes, hungry and excited at once, like a kid at Christmas. "Well, what are you waiting for? Rub the damn thing, summon the genie, and let me get out of here."

She needed to leave, to see Xander. The more time she spent away from him, the more she felt the desperation, the need clawing away at her. She had to explain to him she hadn't used him as he thought, that she'd worked too hard and for much too long to throw her career away on… what? A fling? Love?

Claudia watched, impatiently, as Ra'ess rubbed the lamp. Nothing happened. "Give it a minute," she suggested, but there was no sign of the mist, no flash of all-encompassing smoke ready to seep from its tip.

"Are you sure this is the right lamp?"

"Of course I'm sure." She grabbed for the object and rubbed her palm along the base. The lamp glowed, the golden sheen intensifying as Ambrosia made her way out.

"You beckoned, Mistress?" The words were sweet and submissive, but there was a mockery in the genie's tone Claudia couldn't miss.

"Yeah, I did. I want you to do as this man commands. He's your master now."

Ambrosia's gaze swept over Ra'ees, her eyes widening appreciatively. Ra'ees's smile mirrored hers, filled with longing and barely-contained lust.

"You've really outdone yourself this time, Claudia. I mean, I knew you were good, but this…" He indicated in the genie's direction. "… is more than I'd hoped for."

"I'm a 'she,' not a 'this,'" Ambrosia said, taking a step closer to Ra'ees. She ran her fingertips over his jaw, drawing her thumb over his lower lip. "But for you, I'll be anything you want."

Ra'ees sucked in a breath at her touch, and Claudia noticed the bulge forming in his pants. "Look, I'm really happy for you both." She picked up her purse from the walnut credenza. "Do you think I could leave now?"

"No." It was Ambrosia who answered, startling Claudia.

"What do you mean, 'no'?"

"I mean, you can't release me until you've had at least one wish. Once I grant you that, you can forfeit the others. But not before. You can ask for whatever you want, as long as it's not an emotion. I can't make people fall in love, or stop hating you, or suddenly start admiring you. Everything else is fair game, though." She looked at Ra'ees apologetically. "Look, I'd much rather tend to your needs, but the Genie Code forbids it."

"I'm so sick and tired of hearing about this damn Code." Claudia gritted her teeth. "Fine. I wish…"

What?

She could have anything she wanted. More money than she'd know what to do with in a lifetime, a mansion filled with all the artifacts in the known world, a wardrobe full of designer clothes. The possibilities were overwhelming.

Her pulse quickened. There was only one thing she craved more than any other, and it wasn't an object the Genie could just grant. She wanted Xander. She ached for the touch of his strong fingers, the arrogant grin, the sound of his voice.

She wanted him to want her as much as she wanted him, to need her as much as she needed him.

"I wish to know where Xander is right this very moment." The words spilled out before she could stop them. "You can do that, right?"

The genie gave her a haughty smile. "Of course." She closed her eyes, pursed her lips, lifted a finger in the air and whispered something Claudia couldn't understand. It sounded like the same language Xander had used earlier that day, but she couldn't be sure.

Heat pulsed between Claudia legs, sudden and insistent, warming her pussy with a relentless ache. Her nipples tightened at the intrusion as phantom fingers brushed her slit. The sensation spread between her thighs and she knew she was blushing furiously, but she couldn't stop it any more than she could stop the growing mist spreading from the pocket of her jeans.

Her mouth gaped open as the smoke gathered and shaped itself into a solid form, all muscle, sinew and pure male sex appeal.

"It seems Xander just couldn't wait to get back in your pants," Ambrosia supplied helpfully between giggles.

Claudia had the sudden urge to leap over the credenza and smack that smirk right off her face. "Ra'ees, I need a minute. Take your lamp and go play."

Xander's eyebrows lifted. A smile tugged at the corners of his mouth. "So you're really that feisty with everyone, huh? I thought it was just me."

"Don't flatter yourself." She turned to Ra'ees, who hadn't moved. "Go. Now. Please," she added, for good measure. Ra'ees looked like he wanted to argue but Ambrosia grabbed his elbow and steered him out through a side door. Relief flooded Claudia.

"How is this possible?" she asked Xander through gritted teeth. "How could you have followed me without me knowing?"

"Technically, I didn't follow you." He ran a hand through his hair. At least he had the decency to look uncomfortable. "You took me with you."

"How?" she repeated. She could feel his desire. It tore at her defenses, threatening to break them down, but she refused to give in until she understood why he was here.

He pointed at her pocket. "Your lighter."

She pulled out the small object. She'd had it for years. Black with a picture of a camel on one side, it was out of lighter fluid and no longer worked.

"The flint's still there, as is the promise of flame. It served as a perfect container for my shape."

"Why?" Her heart pounded, matching the throbbing in her head. "Wait, don't answer that. I know why."

Xander nodded, looking grim. "I needed to see for myself. I really thought you were… that you and Ra'ees…"

She knew what he thought. She'd known all along. Xander took a step toward her and brushed his warm fingers over her cheek. She struggled with the emotions warring within her, some of them his. "I can't do this with you if you're going to follow me everywhere."

He lowered his head until his lips were inches from her own. "I'm sorry," he whispered.

She felt what that admission had cost him. He wasn't used to apologizing to anyone, for anything. He'd spent so long knowing the next person who'd summon him would only need him for a short while. Then, when he'd done all he'd been asked to do, he'd be discarded like yesterday's trash. Five thousand years of being tossed away when you were no longer considered useful would make anyone think twice about placing his trust in another human.

Since the day she'd met Xander, Claudia had done nothing to disprove his opinion of people. She'd pursued him relentlessly, but always for the wrong reason. When she should have been striving to earn his trust, she'd only pushed him further away.

Claudia's anger lifted. Shame and guilt replaced it, along with something else, an emotion more powerful than all the others. Her chest constricted. Her stomach churned. Sweat coated her palms.

After the way she'd treated him, it was a miracle he'd wanted to follow her at all.

She opened her mind to him, allowing his desire to fill her, to merge with her own and flow through her veins, pooling between her legs. Heat encompassed her from all sides. "You wouldn't be here if you didn't love me."

His low growl sent a tremor down her spine. "Do you love me?"

She licked her lips. When she answered, her voice was barely above a whisper. "Yes. But I asked you first."

Xander nuzzled her neck, raking his teeth along the side of her throat. "You know I do."

"Prove it."

She expected kissing, fondling, slow, sensual teasing. He surprised her by unfastening her jeans and yanking them down in one swift motion.

She suppressed a gasp as his breath tickled her wet folds, but he denied her even that pleasure. His mouth moved down the inside of her thigh at slow, torturous speed. He paused to lick the back of her knee, his hands sliding along her legs, setting all her nerve endings on fire.

She fidgeted, thrust her hips out, all but begging him to taste her. He'd done it so well in the alley, his mouth sweeping over her cunt with an expert's touch, his tongue bringing her to the height of ecstasy before taking her over the edge.

"Xander," she murmured. "I won't use you. I'll never ask you to do anything you don't want to do. But oh… If you don't fuck me right now, I can't be held responsible for my actions."

His low, throaty laugh sent a wave of longing coiling low in her belly. Her pussy clenched in on itself. When he rose to his full height, his pants were gone, having been discarded beside her jeans. His cock thrust out from a nest of curls, long and curved, just as he'd promised.

She stared, marveling at the beautiful blue veins snaking up its length, the deeply flushed tip, the bead of wetness dripping from the slit. "You're incredible," she whispered.

He lifted her off her feet in an easy motion and set her on the edge of the credenza, parting her knees. She watched as he placed the tip of his cock at her entrance, nudging her channel open a little at a time until she thought she'd go mad with anticipation.

At last, his cock filled her, stretching her inner walls. She clung to his shoulders, pulling him to her, inhaling his scent. He thrust against her and she wrapped her legs around his waist, feeling his body heat, letting his thoughts enter her mind.

This time, the images he conjured were all about them. He lowered his head and nibbled at her breasts, twirling the tip of his tongue around an aroused nipple as his cock slid in and out of her pussy. She whimpered. The exquisite pleasure of his teeth scraping against her aroused skin bordered on pain.

He brought his fingers between them, caressing her clit with a gentle yet insistent rhythm. She squirmed against him, knowing she was close; felt him tense, knowing he was closer.

His thoughts flowed in her mind, tugging the last of her defenses down. Nothing stood in their way now. Business was finished, but they weren't. Not by a long shot.

Claudia's inner muscles rippled around his shaft and Xander stilled his thrusts, his gaze boring into hers. "Mine," he growled between clenched teeth as his orgasm gripped him, sending her over the edge with him. She came hard, the climax making her entire body shudder with unrestrained pleasure.

"Yours," she agreed when she could trust herself to speak. His heartbeat drummed against her chest. His forehead rested against hers. Sweat coated their bodies and the smell of sex drifted through the office. "Always."

Epilogue

Xander gripped his cock, running his palm over the hard length. "It's past three in the morning. Come to bed."

Sitting at the old-fashioned desk in the hotel room, Claudia smiled and tapped a few buttons on her laptop. Like him, she was naked. Unlike him, though, she could work when all he could think about was finally tying her to the bedposts and fucking her until they woke up every other guest in the hotel and the concierge had to toss them out on the street.

"Just another five minutes. I have to finish this testimonial."

Xander groaned. "Are you still working on that?"

"The Paranormal Mates Society has been so good to us. It's the least we can do."

"Can't you do it tomorrow?"

"I've put it off for two weeks."

"Well, my cock hasn't had any attention in the last two hours. Shouldn't your priorities lie between my legs?"

Her silvery laugh filled the room, filled his heart. He'd never tire of making her smile. "I think your cock will survive."

Heaving a weary sigh he didn't feel, Xander's feet slid into the plush carpet. He walked over to where Claudia sat, reached down and tweaked her nipple. She rewarded him with a low moan.

"My, my," Xander whispered. "Such powerful words for such a horny woman."

She glared at him, but her lips quirked upward. The blue electronic light of the laptop screen flittered over her features, making her dark eyes look almost black. "Do you want to write this? One of us has to."

"I'll write it. If..."

"There's that 'if' again. Can't you ever do something without wanting something in return?"

"Hey, I spent five thousand years doing things for others. Don't you think I've earned the right to have some of my wishes granted?"

She stood up and motioned to the seat. He slid down into it, sending her a clear image of what he wanted done in return for writing the testimonial. Claudia's nipples beaded further and a dark patch of color stained her cheeks. "Oh." Her tongue flicked over her full lower lip. "It's a deal."

Xander's cock twitched in anticipation. He'd known she'd agree, but hearing her say it made him even harder. As he poised his fingertips over the keyboard, Claudia crawled under the desk and pushed his thighs apart. Her warm mouth enveloped the tip of his cock.

He read the words already flashing on the screen.

Although I wasn't looking for a mate, fate, with the help of the Paranormal Mates Society, found him for me anyway. We had a rocky start, filled with ulterior motives (mine) and more sexy thoughts than anyone should have (his), but when you're meant to be together, obstacles don't mean a thing.

The cursor flickered, waiting for him to type the rest of the testimonial. Claudia's tongue swept over the base of his shaft. She palmed his balls, squeezing gently. All logical thought flew from his mind. "Uh... maybe this wasn't such a good idea."

She released his cock with a loud pop. "Oh, no you don't. Finish it, or I'm not finishing you."

His cock pulsed in protest. He wanted to come in her hot, wet mouth, to feel his seed squirting down her throat. His rod dripped with her saliva. Her every breath was sheer, delicious agony.

"Don't stop," he murmured, forcing himself to type. His cock slid between her lips as soon as he started tapping on the keys.

It took a few tries, and a lot of backspacing and deleting of typos, but a few minutes later he had the end of the draft written. Claudia's mouth never stopped working. She took him deep, until he felt the tip of his shaft hit the back of her throat. Her mouth was hot, wet, impossibly tight, and she made soft moaning sounds that drove him to the brink of delicious agony. He couldn't hold back any longer.

Xander came with the words on the screen flickering across his mind.

Although sex isn't the basis for our relationship, it sure is a wonderful benefit. Without the Paranormal Mates Society, we never would have found the release we were both so desperately searching for. And now if you'll forgive me, I have to cut this short. My cock has earned some of that release and needs (desperately) to take it.

Sincerely,
Xander (and Claudia)

Lacey Savage

Award-winning author Lacey Savage loves to write about her dreams—or more specifically, she loves to breathe life into her steamy fantasies (and she's got plenty!). She pens erotic tales of true love and mythical destiny, peopled with strong alpha heroes and feisty heroines. A hopeless romantic, Lacey loves writing about the intimate, sensual side of relationships. She currently resides in Austin, Texas, with her loving husband and their mischievous cat. You can learn more about Lacey by visiting her website at www.laceysavage.com, and can reach her at lacey.savage@yahoo.com.

Paranormal Mates Society: Long Tall Furry

Rachel Bo

Chapter One
Ancient History

Sinna stared into the dark, swirling waters of the Amazon River. After a moment's concentration, her human skin dried and split, sloughing off into a neat pile on the muddy bank. Immediately, an army of ants swarmed over it. She smiled to herself, knowing that within minutes, the telltale remainder would be gone.

With a satisfied hiss, she slithered into the raging waters and swam against the swift current. The river's caress rippled soothingly across her heated flesh. When she reached the Amazon Abyss, she flexed powerfully, rocketing down into the deep trench, shivering deliciously as the unreleased heat of the past three days dissipated in the river's chill embrace, marking her path with warm bubbles that spiraled lazily upward.

Hugging the steep side, she swam unerringly to a cave mouth about sixty meters down. A subtle flexion of her muscular tail sent her arrowing through the opening, down a short tunnel and up into a quiet pool. Slipping out of the water, she curled up gratefully on the cool sandbank, intending to rest.

"Sinna! How was your trip?" A lilting duet shattered the welcome silence.

Sinna whipped her head around, gaze narrowing as she regarded her unexpected guests. Stasi and Ssara, the youngest and most annoying of her sisters.

Great.

And in human form, as well, which meant that in order to be polite, she must also change. Sighing, she uncoiled, hissing as she shrank, her beautiful scarlet scales replaced by fragile human skin. Crystalline droplets glittered on her now jet-hued flesh for a moment, and then evaporated, surrounding her with a halo of fog briefly before even that disappeared. Sinna rotated her head to loosen the kinks she already felt arising, and then strode over to where her sisters sat near the center of the brightly illuminated cavern, typing blithely at the computer keyboard.

"The trip went well. Evan loved the new textiles." She stared at the computer screen.

"Welcome to Paranormal Mates Society!" flashed brightly at the top. "Where finding the love of your life is supernatural, super easy."

"*What* are you two doing?"

Stasi grinned. "You know how you said you're bored with one-night stands, and how you want to find someone you can have a meaningful relationship with? Well, Ssara and I decided to help you out."

Sinna's flesh prickled as irritation kicked the temperature of her already feverish body up a notch. "Help me out how?"

"Paranormal Mates Society." Stasi grinned. "It's an on-line dating service for, shall we say, the 'unique' among us." Her eyebrows arched suggestively.

Beside her, Ssara giggled. "You should see some of these profiles. *Randy centaur, hung like a horse.* Can you say cliché? But this one sounds intriguing. *Double the pleasure. Wacky werewolf twins seek sexy supernatural for fun, games.*"

Sinna shook her head. "Then *you* join the club."

Stasi's grin faded. "Aww. Come *on*, Sinna." She shared a glance with her twin. "We're... concerned about you."

Sinna started to utter a sharp retort, but the look in her sisters' eyes brought her up short. Oh, hell. They thought she was going to pull an Aunt Seleste. "Look, you two, I'm not ready to jump into a volcano just yet."

They relaxed, but never one to give up easily, Stasi nodded her head toward the screen. "Then why not give it a try?"

Sinna suppressed the urge to grab them both by their necks and toss them back into the river. How dare they come here and invade her privacy? She shuddered, forcing her breath to slow. That was the heat talking. She had to get a grip on herself. *Curse that ancient Brazilian hag, anyway!* "I told you, I'm tired of playing games. I don't want to live forever if that existence is just an endless procession of brief encounters with callous, macho jerks who are already thinking about the next lay."

"Exactly!" Ssara gestured toward the keyboard. "At least take a look. This is a *paranormal* dating site, Sinna. Surely there's someone out there who's compatible with you, someone you can share your secret with." She tilted her head, batting her eyelashes. "Why not give this a chance? If you don't, you might be missing your one opportunity to spend the rest of your life in eternal wedded bliss." She and Stasi glanced at each other and giggled.

"Out!" Sinna hissed, six foot three inches of ebony fury towering over them, intimidating even in her nakedness. Especially since her youngest sisters had chosen particularly petite, waif-like appearances for their human façades.

The twins shrank back, then flushed. Stasi squared her shoulders and stuck her nose in the air haughtily. Shoving the chair back, she stood. "Come on, Ssara." She held out a hand to her sister. "She won't do it." Her eyes flashed with anger even as they sidled warily past her. "She hasn't got the guts!"

Quick as a flash, Sinna lunged, but the pair were already sloughing their skins and plunged hastily into the river. She stood there, hands clenched, until a slight shifting of her feet warned her that the gray sand upon which she stood was beginning to melt.

Sighing, Sinna kicked her sisters' skins into the dark waters and watched for a moment as a pair of blind tubesnouts tugged the remains underwater for a rich meal, then turned and stalked back to the computer, collapsing heavily into the contoured basalt seat of the steel chair before it.

She shouldn't have allowed herself to become so angry. Relatively speaking, even though they were nearing fifty, Stasi and Ssara were still young. Rolling the chair forward on its onyx wheels, she placed her elbows on the desk and rubbed at her temples.

She still found it hard to believe, at times, that something that had occurred thousands of years ago could still affect so many lives today. Oh, wars, famine, natural disasters, it seemed right that they would have repercussions throughout history, but the curse of an Amazonian *bruja*?

Sinna's many-great-grandmother had definitely crossed the wrong witch. After apprenticing to the woman for decades and never having her power sealed, which would allow her to become a full-fledged *bruja* in her own right, she challenged Saya to a magical duel.

There'd been more to it than simply thinking her mentor was unjustly holding her back. Asuri was a power-hungry woman, according to the oral history, wanting to take Saya's place as the head of their matriarchal society.

And of course there was a man involved. An important, handsome, virile young man whom Asuri couldn't believe didn't love her. She swore that the *bruja* had tied him to her with a spell, and believed her rival's death would set him free. According to legend, however, he had loved Saya since childhood, long before her gifts manifested, and before she became the queen of their clan.

Saya hadn't wasted any time. Immediately following the challenge, she stripped Asuri of her powers before the woman could utter the first syllable of a shielding, and uttered a curse that doomed her progeny forever.

In retrospect, the curse seemed extreme, but those had been harsh times and the Amazons a brutal society. Still, after thousands of years, in Sinna's circles their "little problem," as everyone insisted on referring to it, remained known as the mother of all curses.

It really was an intricate piece of work. Calling on the powers of earth and fire, the *bruja* anointed her enemy with the blood of the Brazilian fire serpent. From that day forward, Asuri would exist in two forms, that of a human and that of the fearsome fire serpent. The serpent would embody the heat and rage that had driven a good woman to the edge of darkness. First, since the fires of professional jealousy had poisoned her mind, she would forever burn with physical heat, needing constantly to seek ways to dissipate that heat. Second, since she had allowed the flames of physical desire to stoke that jealousy to the point of mortal challenge, she would forever blaze with undeniable need, a hunger that must be sated or drive her mad. To top it all off, Saya decided not only to bind the curse to every female of the line, but appealed to the goddess that every child born of the line *be* female.

Apparently, Saya and the goddess were tight, because that's exactly how things had been for nearly three thousand years now.

The biggest problem was that the fires within them could never be quenched. Neither of them. In human form, the physical heat built up relentlessly, yet could only be alleviated in shifted form. Sinna had found that she could last approximately three days as a human before she had to shift and slither into a tub, river, or pool to dissipate the buildup. Sexual desire, on the other hand, occurred in both forms and had to be addressed as soon as possible, or embarrassing things happened. And there was no predicting when it might strike.

Despite her anguish, Sinna smiled at her pun, though the situation really wasn't funny. Once, she'd been so overwhelmed in the midst of a meeting with a client that she'd excused herself, asking his assistant to show her to the ladies' room, then tugged the poor man inside and locked the door behind them, taking him right there on the leather couch in the upscale anteroom. He'd enjoyed it, of course, but she had to nearly break his arm during their next meeting when he kept trying to slip his hand between her legs beneath the table.

Sinna wriggled against the hard seat, trying to get comfortable. She could sit in normal chairs when necessary, but had to be hyper-aware, constantly having to move so that the transferred heat from her body had a chance to dissipate before fabric, leather or plastic melted or burst into flames. She preferred the items in her own home to be fireproof, so that she could relax her vigilance. As a matter of fact, she'd made her living not only with her fresh new prints, but with an innovative production process that resulted in fabrics that were ninety-nine percent heat resistant. Everyone in the family now wore clothing made from fabric designed by her company. Sometimes, though, fireproofing also meant sacrificing comfort.

Sighing, she glanced up at the screen. A pair of grinning werewolves with mischievous green eyes stared out at her from the monitor.

Double the pleasure, huh?

Intrigued despite herself, she studied their bright eyes a moment more. Fun and games?

Sinna shook her head. Nah. She'd played all the games; now she wanted something permanent. Something loving.

Idly, she clicked the Next icon. This time, a lone werewolf dominated the screen.

I'm thirty-seven, in excellent physical health, attractive and I'm a werewolf. I love women of all shapes and sizes, but I'm particularly attracted to a fuller figured lady. I'm here on a whim, searching for my lifemate because I can't seem to find her anywhere else. My future mate must love to take long runs beneath the light of the moon, have a strong sense of family honor, enjoy watching baseball from time to time and be willing to take it nice and slow if we dip our toes into the relationship pool. Read my in-depth profile and let's see if we have something in common, then, e-mail me.

Sinna studied him for a moment. She was certainly a fuller figured woman, and he was definitely attractive, and apparently in the market for a more serious relationship than the mischievous twins. Maybe she should… but, no. She read the last line. "Only other werewolves need apply."

She closed the popup and found herself on a page filled with thumbnails of twenty or more men with "Wild Thang, I think I love you—Hairy Critters (werewolves and more!)" emblazoned across the top. On this page full of color, her gaze was drawn immediately to only one.

A shaggy white mane tumbled down to broad, very bronze shoulders. His sharp, rugged features instantly appealed to her. Most of the men in the pictures smiled, some open and friendly, others a bit shyly, but this one appeared quite serious. Prominent eyebrow ridges covered with shaggy white hair should have left his eyes in shadow, instead, the most enticing, ice-blue gaze she'd ever seen seemed to peer into her very soul. She experienced the most startling sense of… connection.

Her finger seemed to move of its own accord, moving the mouse so that the blinking arrow hovered above his picture. After a moment's hesitation, she double-clicked the thumbnail.

His features were even more arresting enlarged. His body fairly glowed with health. Tight black pants emphasized the bulging curve of his thighs, hugged his narrow waist. His highly muscular upper torso brought to mind some ancient ancestor of Conan. His lips… mmm.

Sinna shifted uneasily in her chair as a flicker of desire licked in her belly. She turned her attention to his bio.

Yeti, 9 feet 3 inches tall and solid as a glacier, seeks non-Yeti companion for a change of pace, possible LTR. Must enjoy body sledding, ice fishing, ice cream, and bear hugs. No fragile creatures need apply, this alpha male prefers a substantial woman who can appreciate his rough-and-tumble nature. Serious inquiries only to: longtallfurry□@paranormalmatessociety.com.

A Yeti? Sinna leaned forward. She hadn't realized they actually existed. Then again, she'd pretty much shunned paranormal society, since her condition wasn't exactly hereditary in the normal sense and it was literally a curse, not a blessing.

She gazed into those piercing blue eyes again. He wasn't exactly her type. With his tight black pants, bulging muscles and bare chest, he seemed more fairy-tale barbarian than twenty-first-century man. Yet, his eyes gleamed with intelligence, and burned with a chill intensity that just might rival the hottest of the fires that raged within her.

Well, she was certainly a substantial woman, bear hugs sounded fabulous, and she had no idea what body sledding was, but wouldn't mind finding out. Grabbing a pen, she jotted down his e-mail address and backed out to the site's home page.

Welcome to Paranormal Mates Society, where finding the love of your life is supernatural, super easy.

Tired of squeamish humans passing you over because blood is your beverage of choice? Do you long to indulge in intimate moonlit jaunts with a potential Pet Smart Companion? Are your fins fed up with the goldfish bowl of dating? Did the devil make you give up on ever finding your soul mate? Long to soar to the heavens with the match of your dreams?

Fill out our in-depth entry form. Browse thousands of profiles from paranormals just like you! Make new friends — find the immortal man or woman of your dreams with just one easy click.

Sinna frowned. A little hard sell, perhaps, but... she skipped down to the description of membership packages. They had three and six month packages available for a fee, but there was also a Purgatory membership at no cost, which would allow her to send and receive up to five e-mails per day and up to two vibes per day. Vibes turned out to be a button you clicked to send a non-text message indicating interest.

Well, if she contacted this guy and it didn't work out, she didn't plan to remain a member, so all she really needed was the Purgatory membership.

Unfortunately, she couldn't join until she'd filled out the entry form. She clicked rapidly through the form, a check here, a no there. For Hobbies, she just typed "varied," and for Your Ideal

Date, she put "surprise me." That was kind of like cheating, but frankly, she only planned to give this site one try.

And she couldn't even believe she was doing *that*.

But those bright blue eyes beckoned her throughout the process, and so she continued until the site welcomed 2hot2handle as the newest member of Paranormal Mates Society.

The "vibe" sounded cute, but she wasn't really the cutesy type, and he didn't seem to be, either. Better to approach him directly.

"Long Tall Furry," she typed. "Brazilian fire serpent, anything but fragile, also interested in change of pace. Eager to discover whether opposites attract." She tapped a fingernail against her bottom lip, thinking a moment, then resumed typing. "Not big on small talk, let's get right down to business. If interested, please respond to arrange a face-to-face as soon as possible."

She clicked Send immediately, knowing that if she stopped to fully consider what she was doing, she'd most likely delete the message and trash this whole idea. A smile tugged at her lips as the message reduced to a miniature envelope appropriately sealed with a kiss, then whisked off-screen. Stepping away from the computer, she strode to the edge of the pool that was her entrance and exit to the river. As water swirled around her ankles, she sloughed her skin, the blunt mouths of tubesnouts bumping gently against her ruby scales in their quest for dinner as she slithered deeper. Her tongue flicked in the air. The embers of desire smoldering within her now blazed with undeniable urgency. As hypocritical as it seemed for someone who desperately wanted a meaningful relationship, after sending the message that might bring that very wish to fruition, the first thing she had to do was find someone to fuck.

Chapter Two
Change of Pace

Goss stared at the computer monitor, reading the newest message for the third time, then shook his head. The woman must be nuts. A Yeti and a fire serpent? Not only opposites, but antithetic. It couldn't possibly work.

She was bossy, too. "Let's get right down to business. Arrange a face-to-face as soon as possible." She sounded like one of those power-professionals, used to bowling over people to get what they wanted. Definitely not for him. Heck, that's why he was looking *outside* the Yeti community for a mate. The Himalayan females were brassy and cold, and used to calling the shots. Goss didn't necessarily want a weak-kneed simperer for a lover, but he did want someone who would not only allow him to take the lead, but welcome the experience.

And she hadn't even bothered to include a photo. He'd checked the site, finding only a text link for 2hot2handle's bio, with no thumbnail. He tried to keep an open mind, but a nagging voice in the back of his head kept wondering what someone who was afraid to post a picture might look like.

As his finger poised over the delete key, he felt a surge of doubt. So many women had responded to his posting, and yet none of them were interested in the real him, the Yeti side of his nature. Their e-mails mentioned only his looks, as if nothing else mattered to them. When he mentioned in the first getting-to-know-you e-mails that he preferred to spend his time shifted, the majority of them backed off immediately. A few had requested a photo of him in his Yeti form, and he hadn't heard from them since. One had actually agreed to come and meet him, until she found out that he lived in a very remote, very cold mountain in the Himalayas.

This woman seemed attracted to him for his very nature. "Also interested in change of pace. Eager to discover whether opposites attract."

Maybe that was it. Maybe people at the extremes, even for paranormal society, had to go outside the box, try something completely outrageous. "All right, 2hot," he murmured as he began typing. "Let's see what you've got."

2hot2handle. Thank you for your letter. I have to admit that I questioned the wisdom of two such polar opposites attempting to build a relationship. However, I find myself very curious about you.

Before arranging a face-to-face, I'd like to know a little more about you. Things that aren't in your profile. Where do you live? Do you have brothers and sisters? What do you do? What made you turn to a dating service?

Of course, it's only fair that I answer those questions myself, as well. So, here goes: I'm a customized computer software developer, primarily in the fields of computer-aided drafting, interior design, and landscaping. I work mostly from home, though I do travel occasionally to meet potential clients and to demonstrate the final versions of my software. Being a Yeti, it's in my nature to be somewhat of a loner, though I do enjoy the company of friends and family on a regular basis. When at home, I prefer to spend the majority of my time shifted, as the Yeti rather than the human seems to me to be my true form.

I live in a very cold, very remote cavern complex in the heart of a mountain in the Himalayas. I have never been married and have no children, though I would certainly consider fathering a den with the right person.

I decided to try a dating service because I am looking for something different. Yeti women tend to be very strong-willed and rather abrasive. It's not that I want someone who *isn't* strong-willed. What I really want is someone who knows their limits and will not hesitate to speak out if I step over the line, but who would nevertheless welcome a strong partner in her life, someone to whom she can hand over the reins after a long, hard day and relax. From your letter, I'm not sure this is something you would desire. What do you think?

He paused and read the letter through. Should he tell her he'd like to see a photo? No. Not yet, anyway. Heck, since he'd been tied up with business and had just gotten around to checking this particular mailbox, the woman's original e-mail was about two weeks old. She might have moved on already. No need to ask for a picture until he knew whether she was still available. Nodding to himself, he resumed typing.

I hope to hear back from you soon.

Sincerely, Long Tall Furry

He clicked the Send button, rolling his eyes as the message dwindled to a tiny envelope sealed with a kiss. A woman must have developed the site. A man would never be so hokey. He chuckled. A man would probably have it morphed into a football, then lobbed out of sight.

He sighed and stretched, his spine releasing a volley of sharp cracks. Now for the hard part. Waiting for a reply.

"You've got mail."

Sinna rolled over on her granite bed and groaned.

"You've got mail."

She reached out and slapped a hand on her clock radio's snooze button.

"You've got mail."

"Whu—" Sinna opened one eye and realized it wasn't the radio that was determined to annoy her this morning. Instead, an icon on her computer screen blinked insistently, accompanied by a nauseatingly cheerful voice.

"You've got mail."

"Yeah, yeah, I know." Sinna slid off the granite slab and stumbled over to the computer. Sitting down in the chair, she rubbed the sleep from her eyes with one hand as she opened her mail with the other.

"Holy crap!" There it was, in black and white. A reply from Long Tall Furry. After two weeks of waiting, she'd pretty much given up all hope for a reply.

The rapid beating of her heart and the lump in her throat surprised her. Was she really that desperate, that an e-mail from a complete stranger would have her body reacting like that of a silly schoolgirl?

Apparently so, because as she read the note, her pulse increased dramatically.

It wasn't going to be as easy as she had hoped. No arrangements for a face-to-face. He wanted to know more about her first.

She frowned. She couldn't blame him, but something inside her was so afraid that she'd somehow type the wrong thing, drive him off before they even got to know one another. She was much better in person. She'd never been good at writing.

Still, she'd come this far, she might as well follow the thing through to its conclusion.

Long Tall Furry. I'm so pleased to have received your letter. I have to confess that I'm much better with words in person. I've never been a great writer, but I'll do my best.

I'm a textile designer, developing new weaves, new fabrics, new prints, even new colors. I know you're a program developer, but in order to write code for successful design programs, I would imagine you must know a lot about design itself, so it sounds like we at least have that in common.

I am also a loner. Well… sometimes, anyway. It's hard to explain. Or… well, I guess I should be honest. I don't *want* to explain until I know you a little better. But, I think that our lifestyles would be very compatible.

I have eleven sisters, no brothers. Again, I'm forced to be honest about something that might scare you away… I'm not sure I ever want children. There's a reason for that, but again, I'm not quite ready to share it.

I live in the heart of Brazil, near the Amazon Abyss. Wait, you're a paranormal, so I guess I can tell you, I live *in* the Abyss, also in a cavern complex.

I think I might prefer spending more of my time in shifted form, if I found a permanent mate I could be completely honest with. For now, I do spend more time in human form.

She examined her feelings for a long time before she continued.

I may have come across as a little overbearing in my original e-mail. Bear in mind that I was extremely nervous at the time and just wanted to get the note over with and sent. I admit that I'm used to being in control. Since I run my own business, I am naturally the one in charge. However, after some consideration, I find the idea of letting someone else take the lead once the day is through very appealing. I'm willing to give it a try, if you're inclined to take a chance on me.

It never would have occurred to me to try an online dating service. I never imagined there would be one for people like you and me. I have two meddling sisters, though, and they basically coerced me into signing up.

She read what she had written and sighed.

Actually, they dared me to sign up and I ran them off, but after they left I thought about it and... oh, what the heck. The truth is, I wasn't going to do it, but I clicked a few buttons randomly and for some reason, your eyes drew me in. When I read your post, I just felt I had to take a chance.

Oil and water don't mix, but maybe fire and ice *will*. I'm six foot three inches in my human form. Basically, I'm a broad-shouldered, muscular, black-skinned woman. The kind people describe as statuesque, majestic, imposing, but never beautiful. Just being honest here. Think ancient Amazon. I keep my tight curls cut short in a close cap. You know, I didn't even realize until the site asked for it that I don't have any photos of myself, or I would send you one. If you like, I'll ask one of my sisters to take a picture and scan it in.

I guess I'll stop there and give you a chance to consider what I've said so far. I'm looking forward to hearing from you again. Sincerely, 2hot2handle

Sinna clicked the Send button and sighed. Her temperature had risen several degrees as she typed, in more ways than one. Never one to indulge in self-pity, she shocked herself by allowing a tear to slip from the corner of her eye. Damn Saya! The curse hurt more now than it ever had. Before, she'd never been ashamed of what she did, knowing that it wasn't something she could prevent. Now, trying to build a relationship with a single individual, she experienced a fire of another sort.

Sinna doubled over in pain. Gasping, she shifted quickly to her serpent form. She had no choice but to go to the city and find a man for the night. But another tear dimpled the surface of the pool just before she slipped in. The burning shame eating at her heart was almost enough to dwarf the fire in her belly.

Almost.

Chapter Three
Face-to-Face

A chime sounded, and Goss glanced at the bottom of the screen. He had mail. He saved his work and shut down the program. This would be a good time to take a break, anyway.

Even though no one was there to watch, he still attempted to act nonchalant as he double-clicked on the icon to open the letter. He told himself that it didn't matter. Yet his throat tightened and his pulse raced nervously as he read 2hot's response.

She sounded much more at ease in this e-mail. He was delighted to see that they did have things in common. And she had no photos of herself. Obviously not vain.

She said she was willing to let him be in control, or give it a try, anyway. She'd been very honest, which he found deliciously refreshing.

Without stopping to think about it, for fear he'd lose his nerve, he typed rapidly.

2hot2handle. Thank you so much for your reply. Upon reflection, I find myself not only willing, but eager to take a chance on you. It won't be necessary to send a picture. Instead, I'd like to send you a first-class ticket, round-trip, so that we can have that face-to-face you mentioned. Can you get away for, say, a couple of weeks?

He considered saying more, but every thought seemed to lead to a long discussion of the "Life and Times of Goss Kemini," and he wasn't ready for that yet. After reading the note through, he realized that it really said all he wanted to say. At this point, he simply had a strong desire to meet this woman.

Respectfully awaiting your reply,

Long Tall Furry

The smooch-sealed packet sailed away, and Goss stood and walked to the weight room. He had to do something to take his mind off the waiting.

* * *

Sinna believed her heart actually skipped a beat as she read Furry's reply. He wanted to meet her! She couldn't believe it. Should she go?

As if in response, a wildfire seemed to ignite in her pelvis. Not again! She typed a quick answer and then stared at the screen, hardly believing what she'd said.

* * *

Goss was amazed to hear the computer chiming only ten minutes later. He settled the weights to the floor with a grunt and lumbered into his office. He opened the mail program.

I can book a flight now and be there tomorrow. Would that be too soon? You don't have to pay for it, but if you insist, you can reimburse me when I get there.

He got the distinct impression she'd answered the minute she received his note. She hadn't even given the customary greeting and sign-off! Eager, or *desperate*? Goss didn't know what to think. But hey, he'd gotten himself into this. He might as well see it through.

2hot. Wowed by your quick response. More intrigued than ever. Will have to insist on reimbursing you. You will need to fly in to Pokhara, then take a private plane to Jomsom.

Simply give the authorities in Pokhara your name once you've arrived and I will arrange with my friend Alek to fetch you for the short hop to Jomsom. I will then provide transportation to my home. Just let me know when and to which terminal in Pokhara you'll be arriving, so that I can notify Alek.

LongTall

* * *

Sinna stepped into the terminal and glanced around. Her gaze immediately fell on the one individual who towered over the rest. In his human form, Long Tall was not nine foot three inches, of course, but he was still almost half a foot taller than she, so about six foot nine, she reasoned. His white hair couldn't be missed either. Swallowing past the bundle of nerves lodged in her throat, she strode quickly toward him.

Goss scanned the people crowding the small building that passed for an airport terminal in Jomsom. Instinctively, his gaze latched onto a tall black woman striding purposefully in his direction, and his breath caught.

Majestic, yes. And statuesque. And he could see how she might seem imposing to the average non-shifter.

To him, she was absolutely beautiful.

She stopped a few feet away, eyeing him a bit apprehensively. Goss allowed himself to drink her in. From the top of her ebony head to the tip of her scarlet heels, she was everything he could want in a woman. Strong without appearing masculine, shapely without looking like a faint breeze might blow her away. As a matter of fact, he realized he'd never known what a "substantial" woman was, until this moment.

Her lids swept down, long lashes tickling her cheeks as her dark skin flushed a sort of midnight purple at his regard. Goss shook himself and reached out a hand. "I'm Goss Kemini, and... I'm *very* glad to meet you." To his surprise, his voice came out thick and husky. A woman had never had this type of effect on him before.

2hot looked up and set down her suitcase, then grasped his hand. "I'm Sinna. Sinna Anjel."

Despite her size and obvious strength, her hand trembled in his grip. Goss bit back a frown and broke the contact. "Let me get your bag."

He led her skillfully through a group of milling tourists to the parking lot. He tossed her bag in the back of his hardy sport utility vehicle and assisted her into the passenger seat. Starting the engine, he swung smoothly onto the main thoroughfare and began the long drive home.

For the three hours it took to drive to the small town at the base of the mountain that was his home, they barely spoke. Sinna sat tensely beside him, her hands clasped tightly in her lap, staring out the window. Every now and then he detected a tremor going through her.

God, could he truly be so frightening?

When he'd seen her in the terminal, he'd thought she was perfect, but now he regretted the impulse that had made him invite her. What appeal was there in befriending a trembling puppy? He had anticipated something more like coming to terms with a wild mustang.

At the village, he parked and stepped around to her door. "The way's a bit rugged from here on in. We'll be switching vehicles now."

He opened the door for her and waited as she stepped out.

"Hang on a minute." Sinna unlocked her bag and reached inside. Turning, she sat on the edge of the passenger seat and slipped off her heels, tugging on a pair of sturdy sneakers. She tossed the heels into her bag and zipped it shut. "Okay, I'm ready."

Goss grabbed her bag and led her to a snow-treaded, heavy-duty all terrain vehicle built exactly to his specifications. Sinna's eyes widened, but she said nothing as he handed her a helmet and climbed on board. She pulled the helmet over her head and hopped on behind him. "Let's go!"

He couldn't help showing off, gunning the motor and doing a three-sixty before they shot up the side of the mountain.

The wind's roar and the engine's rumble were all he could hear, music to his ears as they skated over the brittle snow toward his home. He almost forgot Sinna was there, until her arms tightened painfully around his middle and she yelled "Stop!" in his ear.

Goss killed the engine, sliding to a standstill. Sinna slid off the ATV, and stood in the knee-deep snow, panting heavily.

"Are you all right?" He thought she was scared, until she raised her eyes. The pupil was now a vertical slit, and her topaz irises rimmed in red. Astonished, he sat there unbelieving and watched as she tore at her clothes, kicking off her sneakers, peeling away her skin-tight jeans, tossing her thick sweater over her head.

There she stood, in all her jet-black glory. Goss swallowed, painfully aware of the bulge at his crotch.

"Fuck me," Sinna hissed. "Please."

Under any other circumstances, Goss would have turned and raced in the opposite direction. Yet those eyes, those inhuman, mesmerizing eyes were begging him to understand. There was pain there, and the promise of an explanation, but what she needed now was the one thing his body was all too eager to give her.

With a growl, Goss leaped to the ground and gathered her up in his arms.

Her lips, so hot against his, tasted of spikenard. Just like the Himalayan herb, Sinna was precious and rare, a prize to be cherished and guarded for all of his days. He grunted in surprise at his reaction. But God, she *was* sweet. Soft in all the right places, and yet firm and hefty in his embrace. With this woman, there was no fear of breaking her.

He shifted one hand to grip her shoulder, bending her back so that his tongue could savor the rapidly beating pulse at her neck. Moaning, she reached up, tangling her fingers in his hair, dragging his head to her breast.

Goss opened his mouth, covering the midnight-hued pearl of her nipple, drawing it deep into his throat. Sinna whimpered, arching, pressing into him.

Gods, but she was hot! Literally feverish. Her flesh where it touched his burned like wildfire, making him ache, but it was a delicious pain, a sensation that sent pleasure spiraling down to his groin. Supporting her with one arm, he reached down and ripped off his khakis, groaning with relief as this freed his painful erection.

"Now," Sinna cried. "Please, do it now!"

A part of him wasn't ready, wanted to savor the incredible heat of her forever. But she wriggled against him, her hip rubbing across the length of his cock. "Oh, shit!" He had one lucid moment in which to tug her on top of him as he fell back into the snow, hoping to protect her from the cold, and then she was on him, covering his chest with hot kisses as she buried his cock in the slick heat of her pussy.

"Oh, shit!" Goss roared, wanting to hold back but caught up in her desperation. The heat was unbearable, and yet at the same time he never wanted it to stop. "Sinna!" He grasped her waist and held her tight as he plunged into her. Once, twice, and with the third stroke he froze, ass tightening as pleasure flooded his groin, his cool seed pouring into the flames that surrounded him.

They both lay gasping when it was done, and then Sinna seemed to come to herself and struggled to stand in the snow.

Filled with a wonderful languor, Goss didn't want to move, but he made himself stand, then reached out a hand and pulled her upright.

Their gazes locked for just a moment, and then Sinna looked away, her lips tightening with shame. She knelt and gathered up her clothes, tugging her wet jeans on with difficulty, unable to fasten them, then pulling on her sweater. Still holding her shoes in her hand, she climbed back on the vehicle. "Let's go," she whispered hoarsely.

Goss's khakis weren't salvageable. He stuffed them into a strap on the back and hopped on barebottomed. As the engine roared back to life, he noticed Sinna very carefully wrapped her arms around his chest rather than his waist.

It was a blessing to finally reach the entrance to his home. He pressed his hand to an outcropping of what appeared to be ice, and a green light hummed for a moment, reading his prints. "Access granted," a precisely modulated computer voice announced. What appeared to be the wall of a glacier slid aside, and Goss drove into the cavern. As the wall closed behind them, he slipped off the ATV and turned to face Sinna.

She was looking around the cavern, examining the icy stalactites and stalagmites, the chairs carved of ice, the fluorescent lighting, everything but him. Not knowing why he did it, he reached out and picked her up, cradling her in his arms as he strode brusquely across the cavern to the smallish cave that served as his den. Depositing her on a couch carved of ice, he stepped over to the bar and poured them both a couple of fingers of vodka. Sinna accepted hers without comment, and tossed it back in one smooth motion. Goss drank his and poured another, but when he turned back, Sinna was on the floor, surrounded by a puddle. The middle of his couch was gone.

Tears filled her eyes, dropping to the floor, only to send spirals of steam undulating into the air. "I'm sorry. It's the heat. I can't..." She stood abruptly and turned as though to run, but Goss grasped her arm, carefully but firmly.

"It's okay. Come on." He let his fingers slide down her arm, and entwine with hers as he led her into yet another room.

Carved directly out of the rock, a large bed jutted out from the wall into the center of the room. Goss guided Sinna over to sit on the edge of the rock, then knelt before her.

Chapter Four
Curses

"Why don't you tell me about it?"

Goss knelt before Sinna, his voice gravelly, yet so gentle that Sinna felt tears rising again. For God's sake! She hadn't cried so much in her life. She took a deep breath, getting a firm grip on her emotions before she spoke.

"It's a curse," she blurted. She couldn't look him in the eyes. "Ages ago. An ancestor of mine offended a *bruja*, a witch. A very powerful witch. She placed a curse on the family line. We're not shifters originally, genetically. We were altered by the curse. In human form, physical heat builds up inside me until I shift into serpent form and allow it to dissipate, usually by taking a swim in the river."

He didn't say anything, but he hadn't drawn away. As a matter of fact, his thumbs caressed the inside of her wrists in a highly distracting manner. Sinna swallowed and forced herself to look up. "The physical heat represents professional jealousy. My ancestor, Asuri, wanted to be queen of our clan. She felt her mentor, Saya, was holding her back purposefully, and so she challenged her to a duel of magics, but she wasn't anywhere near as powerful as Saya, and challenging a *bruja* who was also your mentor and queen... it was unheard of. An unforgivable offense." It was so hard to look into those intelligent, concerned blue eyes and say the next words, but she made herself do it. "And... there was a man. Jealousy. Asuri was one of those people who seems blind to everything but themselves, and their wants and needs. She couldn't believe that Saya's lover didn't want her. So... Saya cursed our line with overwhelming..." She swallowed hard and pushed on. "Sexual desire. It's not like the other heat, where you can feel it building and prepare for it. It can strike any time, any place."

Goss's eyes widened in understanding. "I see."

"I tried to hold it off, but lately it's been happening more frequently, every time I—" She broke off with a gasp, her own eyes widening as she realized what she'd been about to say.

"Every time you what, Sinna?" Goss's thumbs caressed the pulse at each wrist gently, persuasively. His cool blue gaze bore into hers. "Tell me."

She so wanted to be with a man who knew. A man who knew everything. And yet, how could she tell him? How could she reveal the strange compulsion that came over her every time she looked into those sky blue eyes?

His grip tightened on her wrists. "Tell me, Sinna."

Before she could stop them, the words went tumbling out. "Every time I saw your face." She dropped her gaze. "Looked into your eyes."

He reached up, grasping her chin between thumb and forefinger and tilting her head up so that she had to look at him. "What did you do when that happened?"

Sinna closed her eyes, tried to shake her head.

"What did you do?" His voice, though quiet, held a note of authority that she couldn't seem to resist.

"I... I went into the city, and... and fucked the first man who was willing and disease-free. At least Saya gave us that. A sixth sense when it comes to a person's health. I think she didn't want us contracting anything that might kill us off before her punishment had run its course."

"How many times?" he asked softly.

Sinna swallowed, tried to shake her head again. The tips of the calloused fingers on his free hand caressed her cheek. "How many, Sinna? I want to know."

Her voice cracked when she spoke. "Every time we e-mailed." She opened her eyes, knowing she would drown in his, but no longer caring. "Every time I thought about you." The thumb caressing her cheek slid down, tracing the curve of her neck, her collarbone, the swell of her breast. Sinna moaned, spreading her legs as the heat rose in her groin. "Every time I turned on the computer and looked at your photo."

"How many times did you do that?" His icy thumb slipped beneath her sweater and teased the tip of her feverish nipple, sending delirious shivers through her body.

"I… I don't know." He freed her chin, his hands finding her jeans, tugging them down, then gliding along her sternum, across her belly. "A… a dozen times, at least. Oh, God!" The cool fingers of one hand glided between her feverish folds as the thumb and forefinger of the other twisted one ripe nipple.

"What about this, Sinna?" he whispered, his chill lips brushing her earlobe. "Did the curse do this, or is it me?"

The idea that she could feel desire for any reason other than the curse shocked her. "I… I don't know."

His lips laid a cool trail across the hollow of her neck, down between her breasts. Sinna whimpered and arched.

"You don't know?" His fingers stroked her hot folds.

Sinna drew into herself, analyzing her responses, trying desperately to block out his voice. With dawning joy, she realized that what she was feeling was nothing like the flame the curse lit inside her. This was… more patient. Oh, still eager, still desperate for his touch, but willing to wait. Wanting… no, *needing* to prolong the agony because then, oh then, the reward would be so sweet. "It's you," she breathed as his kisses dusted her bush with frost. "Oh, God, it's you!"

He covered her clit with the broadest part of his tongue, then drew the tip of it up, parting the clitoral hood and torturing sweetly the swollen bud beneath.

"Oh, Goss. Yes."

He twisted her nipple between his thumb and forefinger, pulling a short, sharp cry from her lips. He raised his head. "Shall I stop?"

"Nooo," Sinna moaned. "Whatever you want, Goss. Please." She opened her eyes and looked down at him, wanting him to know that she knew what she was saying. "I don't know how this two weeks is going to end, but until then... I'm yours. You're... in the lead."

His blue eyes seemed to flash. "That's good, Sinna. Very good." He stroked her G-spot, watching with pleasure as she arched, eyes locked on his.

He stood abruptly, tugging off his flannel shirt, baring that bronze chest of which she'd memorized every ripple over a fortnight ago. His white hair surrounded his head like a halo as he mounted her.

Her lips stretched taut as his thick, icy member pressed inside her. "Yes, yes," Sinna moaned, tossing her head. The chill of him burned, a cold fire that somehow set her pussy ablaze. "Oh, yes!" His fingers grasped her nipples, pinching them tight, and she gasped, arching as the unexpected pain sent shivers of pleasure racing through her blood.

He pressed into her, deeper and deeper. Good God, had he been this big earlier? She didn't remember him being so big. It hurt, and his coolness burned and soothed at the same time. "Oh, please, please," she moaned. "I have to come!"

With a sudden lunge, Goss buried the rest of his length inside her. Sinna sobbed and wrapped her legs around his waist. "Yes. Fuck me. Fuck me!"

With an animal roar, Goss drew back almost completely, then thrust in, fast and deep. Sinna tightened her legs, driving her heels into his buttocks. "Yes!"

His bright blue eyes clouded over, appearing gray and stormy as he plunged into her over and over, pinching her nipples, driving her over the edge with the pleasure/pain. "Oh, Goss, yes!" Sinna clutched his forearms, arching into him as she shuddered, almost climaxing. "Please, Goss. Come with me," she whispered hoarsely.

He gasped, his hands reaching out, pushing him up from the bed, driving his hips hard against hers as his cock swelled inside her. "Yes, yes!" A cool fountain filled her pussy, the sensation so strange and wonderful, so unlike anything she'd felt before, that she heard herself making animal sounds, primordial noises she never would have dreamed of making.

Goss shuddered, driving into her twice more as his cock emptied. Sinna locked her legs around him and held on, caught in the throes of an orgasm so intense she almost forgot to breathe.

And then it was over, and she was taking a huge, shuddering breath, and Goss was drawing back and then collapsing on the stone next to her.

Goss slipped his arm beneath her shoulders, pulling her against his side, planting a kiss on her damp, hot curls. Sinna sighed, letting herself relax. The last thing she remembered before falling asleep was drawing in a deep breath, allowing his strong musk to fill her nostrils as she drifted into dream.

Goss stretched and growled, rolling over. Opening his eyes, he stared at the ceiling for a moment, trying to figure out why he felt so content. The events of the previous day came rushing back, and he sat up.

Sinna was nowhere to be seen. "Crap." Goss scooted off the bed and stretched again, then padded out into the main cavern. No sign of her. With increased urgency, he began methodically checking all the rooms off the main cavern. No Sinna. She was either further back in the complex, or had managed to get outside.

Since the entrance would respond only to his voice and prints, Goss made his way down the tunnel leading into the depths of the mountain. As he approached the first doorway off this hall, he glimpsed a flash of red.

Anxious now, he half-ran to the opening. Staring inside, he felt his jaw drop. Coiled in the middle of this room that had been blasted out of solid ice was an enormous blood-red serpent.

As he stood gaping, the coils flexed. The serpent's head rose from amidst the heap, forked tongue flickering, tasting the air. It turned toward him.

Goss closed his mouth. "Sinna?"

The serpent regarded him warily, its head coming to rest on the topmost coil, like a dog resting its chin on its paws.

Goss stepped forward. Sinna's tongue flicked, its forked tip sampling his chest briefly. To his surprise, rather than offending him, the touch brought all the desire of the night before flooding back. He stepped closer, flexing his arms, initiating his own shift.

Sinna watched from inches away as his height increased by two and a half feet. Pale, nearly translucent fur that only looked white due to reflected light sprouted along his arms, his legs, and covered his torso. The palms of his hands and soles of his feet thickened and darkened, becoming tough black pads tipped with wicked claws. Goss arched and roared, his face flattening, lips thinning as his body filled out.

Sinna's upper portion slid forward, cascading down over the supporting coils and gliding across the floor. Her head circled his feet, her warm, dry scales gliding over his fur. Her powerful muscles flexed. She swirled around him, wrapping him like a candy cane, until her eyes were level with his.

It was like being inside her, except now his *entire body* was encased by the strange and wonderful heat of her.

He felt her strength, knew she could probably crush him if she tried, but he wasn't afraid. Instead, his cock ached. This powerful, exotic creature looked him in the eyes and waited. Waited for him to take control.

He ran his hand along her smooth coils. The muscles in her underbelly rippled against his thick fur. He reached beneath her, stroking the paler, softer skin there.

Sinna whipped her head up with a quiet hiss like a sigh. Goss stroked again, following the pale curves of her underbelly with gently questing fingers.

Ah, *there*. His fingers slipped inside a long, narrow slit in the lower portion of her body. Sinna writhed, her lower coils tightening around his calves even as her upper coils loosened, her head swaying.

Powerful muscles tightened around his hand, spasming roughly, drawing his fingers deeper. Goss groaned, pressing his erection into the gleaming coil wrapped around his groin. He felt a marble-sized prominence within her, and instinctively pressed two fingers against it, rubbing it in a clockwise motion as he would her clit. Sinna hissed again, sharply, body undulating as her coils loosened further. She worked her lower torso up, uncoiling herself until the slit was even with his huge cock.

Before he could react, a strong spasm thrust his hand from her. The next instant, his cock was buried inside her.

Sinna's serpent head blurred before him. More rapidly than he could focus, it shrank, the upper portion of the snake becoming an exotic hybrid of human and serpent. From the waist up, though bald and still covered in smooth scarlet scales, it was Sinna. Below that, she remained a serpent, and when her muscular pussy tightened around his cock, a wave of pure pleasure rocked his body.

Hairless and covered in the same thick black skin as his hands and feet, his penis wasn't as sensitive in Yeti form as it was in human form. Or so it had been in the past. None of that remained true with this wild and wonderful version of Sinna. Her torso was five feet in circumference and her body practically nothing but muscle, and all of that power seemed directed toward her pussy. Her lips didn't just surround him and press against him — *this* pussy suckled and nursed, massaged and caressed. The slightest ripples sent pleasure coursing through the marrow of his bones. And the heat of her — Gods! Groaning, he wrapped his arms around her ample waist, meeting her slit-eyed, red-rimmed gaze.

He covered her mouth, pressing his lips against hers, thrusting his hips shallowly as her forked tongue twined with his.

He broke away with a moan. The nipples on her red-scaled breasts darkened to the color of a burgundy wine at their peaks. He caught one in his mouth, nipping the tip sharply.

Sinna gasped, her pussy tightening even more. Growling, Goss crushed her to him, holding her immobile, suckling greedily at her breast as he worked his hips, driving himself deeper and deeper, until her hot flesh constricted around him so tightly that he couldn't take any more.

He snarled, his cock throbbing as wave after wave of his seed flowed into her in the midst of an orgasm like nothing he'd ever felt before. Sinna sobbed, whispering his name over and over, her fingers clinging tightly to the fur on his shoulders as her body rippled uncontrollably.

When the sensation ended, Goss felt weak as a newborn babe. Legs trembling, he guided Sinna gently to the icy floor, then sprawled out beside her, panting.

"I'm sorry you had to see me that way," Sinna apologized softly. "I needed to bleed off some heat, and it's easier to do in shifted form."

"Gods, no, Sinna. Don't apologize." He turned his head, surprised to find that in the few seconds that had passed, she had reverted completely to human form. He looked into her eyes. "You were magnificent!"

She made a face, as if she didn't believe him.

He rolled toward her, grasping her shoulders and gazing at her earnestly. "Really, Sinna. You're beautiful, in whatever form you take." He propped himself up on his elbows. "I have a confession to make." Sinna's eyes widened. "Even though I like to spend most of my time shifted, the Yeti form is not the most conducive to... well, pleasurable sex."

"What?"

He held out his hand. "Feel the skin."

Sinna reached out and caressed his palm gently.

"No. *Really* feel it."

She hesitated, then poked and prodded with her fingers. Raising her eyebrows, she rested the tips of her nails against it, pressing tentatively, then more forcefully as he failed to respond. "It's like rock!"

"Not quite, but pretty close. Thick and calloused and not very sensitive. Usually. But with you, in shifted form..." He traced the curve of her hip with one massive paw, shivering pleasurably at the memory. "Gods, you're so strong. I could feel the finest movement of your muscles. And the heat... when you wrapped yourself around me, it was like nothing I've ever felt before."

The beginnings of a smile tugged at the corners of her mouth. "Really?"

He grinned. "If we're going to continue this relationship," he teased, "I must insist we do that again. Soon. And frequently."

Sinna's smile faded. "Are we?"

"What?"

"Going to continue the relationship?"

Goss shrugged in confusion. "Don't you want to?"

Sinna sat up, fingers knotted in her lap. "I've just been... so different from the way I intended. I begged you for sex on the side of the mountain, broke down the minute we got here, turned into a monster first thing the next morning—"

"Stop."

Sinna froze.

"You're not a monster. Any more than I am. Do you think *I'm* a monster?"

"No!" Sinna's startled eyes met his. "But... you're a natural being, a product of your DNA. I'm... an abomination. A curse. There's nothing natural about me."

"You said this curse has been in place for centuries, right?"

Sinna nodded.

"And nothing's ever changed? The aspects of the curse never weakened? There's no stray male in the family line?"

Sinna shook her head.

"Then you're every bit as natural as I am, Sinna. Face it, whatever that witch did, it changed your great-great-whatever on a cellular level. That's the only way it could last this long."

She stared at him in shock. "Oh my God." She stood and began pacing the floor. "You're right. You have to be right. It's the only explanation that makes any sense." She stopped abruptly. "But that means... we'll never be free. We can never break the curse, never... redeem ourselves."

"Is that what you're searching for, Sinna? A way to break the curse?"

"Yes!" Her eyes glistened with unshed tears. "Don't you see? The endless procession of men. Meaningless sex. I feel like a whore! And none of it helps, I'm never sated!"

"Never?"

Sinna hesitated. "I... I don't know. I feel more... relaxed, now, than I ever have. But we've fucked three times in less than twenty-four hours. I—"

"Don't."

She stepped back, startled by the outburst.

"Don't say 'fucked' in that tone. Like it's disgusting. Like we did something unclean."

Sinna seemed at a loss for words. He stood. In his Yeti persona, he loomed three feet taller than she. He stalked toward her, following as she scrambled backward until she came up against the wall. Goss braced his hands on either side of her and kneeled, leaning close, looking her in the eye. "I like you, Sinna, and I want to get to know you better. But there have got to be some rules."

She swallowed audibly.

"Rule number one—be yourself. Don't worry about why or how you do what you do. Just go with it. Let life happen. See what develops."

He brought his lips close to hers. "Last night, the second time we *fucked*—" He said the word, but he made it into a gentle caress, a whisper, a promise. "You said it was the first time you'd ever felt that the desire arose from *you*. Were you lying?"

Sinna shook her head frantically. "No!"

"And this morning? Was that Sinna, or the curse?"

Her features softened. He sensed the tension draining away as she settled more comfortably against the wall. "That—that was me."

"Are you sure?"

Her soft, warm lips brushed against his, and for the first time, she smiled a complete, genuine smile. "Yes."

"But even if you *do* feel that heat, you're not going to be embarrassed by it, are you? You're going to act on it, knowing I'll understand. Knowing I realize it's a part of your nature I'm going to have to accept if we're going to be together. Right?"

"Yes," she breathed, her gaze locked on his.

"Good." He drew her into his arms, locking his hands at the small of her back. "There's just one more thing we need to clear up."

She raised her eyebrows questioningly.

"I just think we ought to hash things out now, before this goes too far. It's about who's in charge." She opened her mouth to speak, but subsided when he shook his head. "Just listen to me. I love that you're an independent woman—that you built your company from the ground up. If this relationship develops into something permanent, I will stay completely out of your business."

"But when it comes to the two of us, I'll be in charge." She started to speak again, and this time he pressed a finger to her lips. "No, just listen. I want you to know exactly what I mean."

He removed his finger and traced the curve of her shoulder, gratified when she shivered and shifted restlessly against him. "I will tell you what to wear. I will tell you what to eat. I will tell you what to do in your free time."

He'd expected her to protest by now, or pull away, but she hadn't. Encouraged, he plowed on. "Other than the times when your... nature... overwhelms you, in which case we've already established what you should do, I will be in complete control of our sexual relations. And by control, I mean that *I* will decide when you orgasm, how you orgasm, whether or not you orgasm at all."

Her breath quickened, and even with her dark skin, he saw the flush rise in her cheeks. She stared at his chest, seeming suddenly fascinated by the hair covering his pectorals. He let his hands travel down, cupping her buttocks. "I'll ask you to do things, Sinna," he whispered huskily. "Things you may not have tried before." His hands tightened on her cheeks, pressing her roughly against him. "You liked it last night when I pinched your nipples, right? And this morning, the way my teeth felt nipping your skin?"

Sinna shuddered. She nodded, but still refused to look at him. He reached up and grasped her chin, tilting her head so that her eyes met his. "You liked it."

She tried to nod, but he held her chin tight. "Say it."

She took a deep breath. "I—I liked it," she whispered hoarsely.

"What did you like?"

"What—what you said!" He frowned, and she tried again. "The... the pain. I liked it."

Goss smiled. "Why?"

Sinna shook her head. "I don't know!"

He looked at her sternly. "Sinna. You *do* know. And I want to hear it." He tilted his head. "No. I *insist* on hearing it."

It was a test, and they both knew it. For a moment there was the sense of teetering on a gigantic razor's edge, where the slightest misstep would send one or the other of them plunging to the ground.

Then Sinna spoke, and they stood firmly on solid ground. Squaring her shoulders, she looked him in the eye. "I liked it because... it's like there's a string made of pure electricity, tied to my clit. When you pinch my nipple, it's like you're a puppeteer. That string tugs on my clit, and it... God, I don't know how to describe it."

"Try." Goss's hands followed the curve of her back, coming to rest once more on her buttocks.

"It... pulses. It's electric. It hurts, but... oh, God. It feels so good." He kneaded her cheeks, letting the tips of his claws press into her skin—not enough to pierce it, but enough for her to feel it. "Oh, God. It's... it's pleasure... with an edge. A sharp edge that almost cuts, but not quite." Involuntarily, his fingers spasmed, and Sinna gasped. "It just... it takes me so close to something wonderful that I can't quite reach." He squeezed her ass rhythmically as her breath quickened, delighted at the way she responded to him, hardly believing that she desired him so much that the merest touch could make her come.

"Don't stop," he ordered, pulling her cheeks apart and reaching between them to catch her anus between his thumb and forefinger and squeeze.

"Oh, God!" She arched against him, bringing her legs together, pressing her thighs against her clit. He let her cheeks close, trailing his claws across her buttocks until their tips dipped into the indentations they'd made. He avoided their centers, circling each tiny wound again and again, with the barest tip of his claw, just at the edge of tenderness. "Oh! And then—" She gasped, panting. Her legs tightening, pressing her pelvis against his thigh. "When it finally happens—oh, God!"

She bucked, grasping his forearms, tossing her head back, but she kept talking, and he grinned. *Oh, yes, she was perfect.* Doing exactly as he said, revealing the most intimate sensations. His cock throbbed. Mmm. He was definitely going to enjoy discovering just how far she was willing to go.

"When it finally happens—" She was gasping now, talking in fits and starts. "I'm so raw, so sensitive, that—" He dug his nails in again suddenly, unexpectedly. Sinna arched, a half-sob, half-scream ripped from her throat. "Yes! Yes!"

"Don't stop!" Goss roared.

"It's—it's more intense than—" She gasped, swallowed. "Oh, God." Her hips ground against his thigh. "God! Than anything I've ever felt!"

Yes. Goss watched in satisfaction as she shuddered relentlessly for several seconds. When the climax had passed, he picked her up smoothly. "Mmm. You did very well, Sinna. When I ask you to tell me how something feels, you do it just like that, hmm?"

Sinna nodded, nestling against his shoulder.

"Need a nap, baby?"

"Yes, please," she whispered.

"Shall I put you in the bed, or would this room be better?"

Sinna shook her head. "The bed will be fine. I won't need to visit the ice for a couple of days now," she murmured sleepily.

"All right."

By the time he laid her gently on the stone, she was snoring lightly. He watched her for several minutes, admiring her broad black shoulders, her full rounded ass, and her nicely plump belly. Then he turned away, grinning from ear to ear.

And he'd thought she was insane in the beginning, suggesting that the two of them might be right for each other. He shook his head at the thought that he would have missed out on her. Maybe opposites did attract. Maybe they *were* perfect for each other.

Maybe, just maybe, he'd finally found his soul mate.

Chapter Five
Discovering Fun

Sinna woke to the smell of sizzling ham. Slowly, she stretched, not minding the dull ache in her muscles the slightest.

For the first time since she'd been old enough to truly understand what the curse meant for her, she felt happy.

She'd never been comfortable in her serpent form. The snake seemed to be the embodiment of all that was wrong in her life. The few humans who had seen her that way had run screaming in the other direction, of course. The idea that someone could find her beautiful, even desirable, in that form had never occurred to her.

But she liked it.

She hugged herself, remembering what it felt like to have his strong arms around her, to have a Yeti make love to her as a serpent. And afterward… Gods. Her cheeks were still tender where his talons had almost, but not quite, broken skin, and she didn't mind at all. It was a delicious reminder of their intimacy.

Sitting up, she looked around. At some point, Goss had brought her bag into the room. She stood and walked over to it. Rummaging inside, she pulled out a pair of jeans, a bra, and a low-cut sweater.

The delicious aromas coming from the kitchen made her stomach rumble, but she really needed a shower first. She carried her clothes over to a doorway in the opposite wall and peeked in. *Wow*. Not only was there a shower, but one that sported multiple shower heads aimed at various angles for an all-over body spray. That sounded delicious right about now.

She set her clothes on the counter and walked over to the alcove. She only required a moment to figure out how to control all the spouts. She left the water running so that it could warm, and studied herself in the mirror over the sink.

First and foremost, she was smiling, and hadn't even realized it. It had been a long time since she'd seen her own smile in the mirror. She liked the changes she was beginning to see in herself. For the first time in a long time, she felt genuinely happy. She turned slowly, admiring a body she hadn't really cared for all that much over the years. In the past, her thighs seemed too big, her ass too round, her tummy too thick, her shoulders too manly. Now, she loved them. At times, she had envied her sisters their petite, slim builds. Now, she was grateful. Goss was right, he needed a *substantial* woman, one that would fill those massive arms. One that wouldn't break in his strong grasp. And he seemed quite fond of her curvaceous hips and rounded tummy. She patted that tummy, remembering the weight of his head resting there the night before.

Humming quietly, she turned and stepped into the shower. "Holy shit!" The water was freezing! She studied the controls again. Despite what a person might expect, cold didn't usually bother her. There was enough heat built up inside her that she welcomed the release as her body transferred that heat to cold water, ice, whatever. But she hadn't been expecting it.

"What's wrong?"

Goss stood in the doorway, eyeing her anxiously. Sinna laughed. "I just didn't realize the water would be so cold." She glanced at the controls again. "I didn't notice there was no hot water."

He smiled ruefully. "Sorry about that. I *am* a Yeti."

"It's no problem." She stretched slowly, pleased at the way his eyes seemed to drink in the sight of her body. "I just wasn't expecting it."

Goss stepped forward. He had on a pair of tight black pants with silver rings sewn to the waistband. "I can have hot water installed. If you decide to stay."

Sinna's heart did a two-and-a-half twist with a somersault thrown in for good measure. "You mean, past the two weeks? You think — you think you might want that?"

Pausing just outside the step down into the shower, he peeled off his pants. "I think it's a possibility." He stepped into the shower. "Don't you?"

In this intimate space, she realized for the first time just how muscular he really was. She remembered thinking of him as some ancient ancestor to Conan the first time she saw his picture. With the water cascading over his bronze skin, forming rippling waterfalls along his washboard abs, she thought he was more like Adonis. But, no. Adonis seemed too pretty. Goss wasn't pretty. He was handsome, rugged. Pure male. More like Zeus, or… Hephaestus. She giggled at the incongruity of comparing this creature of ice and snow to the god of the forge.

"What's so funny?" he growled playfully, sweeping her into his arms.

"Nothing." She snugged her arms around him. "I'm just very happy."

He stroked her back gently. "I'm glad." Cupping her face with his palms, he kissed the tip of her nose. "Let's get you soaped up and out of here before you freeze."

She considered telling him again that the cold didn't really bother her, that she'd just been startled, but as he squeezed a mound of body wash into his hands and worked it into a lather, deltoids flexing, she decided it could wait.

He reached out and worked the suds into her short curls first, kissing her eyes shut when he was ready to rinse it out. Then he massaged her shoulders, her arms, her chest—nothing erotic, simply bathing her. Then again, *that* in itself was erotic—the idea that they were already comfortable enough with each other for a shower to be just a shower.

When he was finished, she smiled. "My turn."

She washed his hair, the fine strands slipping through her fingers like liquid silver. She soaped his chest, his arms, feeling delightful little twinges in her abdomen as her body responded to just how solid he was—his muscles like rock with a so-smooth bronze finish. It was nice, though, to feel that arousal, and not feel that she had to do anything about it right away. It was a pleasant ache in her groin, something that could be enjoyed, savored—not the burning compulsion of the curse.

When they were clean, Goss insisted on getting out first, grabbing a snow white, Yeti-sized towel to wrap around her as she stepped out. He hugged her for a moment, then pushed her away. "Get dressed quick. Breakfast is ready, and then we've got things to do." He turned to walk away, but stopped when he saw her clothes on the counter. He plucked out the scarlet sweater with its low, rounded neckline and held it up. He grinned. "Nice!" He shook out the black jeans, nodding approvingly. He set them back on the counter and picked up the bra, shaking his head. "No bra, baby."

"No bra? But my boobs are... well, I'm not exactly twenty. They'll hang, and bounce, and..." She let her voice trail away as she saw his grin.

"Exactly." He glanced at the counter, cocking an eyebrow. "No panties?"

Sinna shook her head.

"Oh, yes. Good girl."

He gave her a quick hug and kissed her forehead. "Those will do." He cocked his head toward the counter. "But from now on, I'll pick out your clothes." He grinned rakishly. "Some days, I may not let you wear any clothes at all. Meet you in the kitchen."

He walked out, and Sinna patted herself dry and tugged on her clothes as quickly as she could. The black jeans hugged her curves. The light sweater revealed ample cleavage, the red bringing out the gold flecks in her light brown eyes. She hurried out of the bedroom and followed her nose to the kitchen.

Goss pulled out a chair for her, and she sat. Piled on her plate were two thick slices of ham, a mound of scrambled eggs, and a heap of potatoes and onions.

She ate every bite.

He watched her, grinning as she placed the last morsel of ham in her mouth. "Been working up an appetite?" he inquired, wiggling his eyebrows.

She laughed, and the sound startled her. She couldn't remember the last time she'd laughed. Spontaneously, that is. She'd chuckled at clients' jokes before, laughed during business dinners, but it was forced. "There's this guy, see. He keeps me kind of busy."

"Speaking of which…" He pushed his chair back and picked up their dishes. "If you'll give me a hand with these, when we're finished I've got something fun planned."

She stood beside him at the sink, rinsing off the dishes as he handed them to her, then drying them with a towel and placing them on a shelf above the counter. It was such a comfortable, domestic moment. A deep feeling of contentment settled over her.

To her surprise, the kitchen had both hot and cold water. She commented on it, and Goss shrugged. "I have it for the dishwasher. No matter how hard you scrub, nothing sanitizes a plate like hot water. That's why it won't be any trouble, running a line to the bathroom."

She nodded, placing the last fork in the silverware rack. Goss pulled the plug on the sink and dried his hands on the towel. "Ready?"

Sinna shrugged. "Sure."

He led her to a doorway to the left of the main entrance. Two gleaming monsters sat side-by-side on a gray cement floor.

"What are they?"

"Snowjets. Like a jet-ski, only for snow."

"Cool!"

He pressed a hand to the security plate next to the main entrance and spoke into the receiver. The wall slid aside.

Goss wrestled the jets out into the snow, then made Sinna put on a helmet. "Hey, what about you?"

He rapped his head. "I'm built for the mountains. Skull like a rock."

Sinna shook her head, but didn't argue.

He spent several minutes going over the controls with her, and had her take a few spins around a flat shelf just below the cavern before he pronounced her ready for take-off. Together, they gunned their engines and shot over the snow.

"Woo-hoo!" Sinna whooped as she raced ahead, swishing back and forth down the slope. A cold wind scoured her cheeks. Goss caught up on her right side, and shouted, "Follow me!"

Sinna swung in behind him, and lost herself in the rhythm of the ride. The snowjet roared beneath her, sending a pleasant vibration through her bones. Plumes of snow splashed like waves in their wake.

They rode for an hour, describing a gradual arc toward the base of the mountain. As the trees began, Goss slowed, winding in and out between the thick trunks. Deep within the forest of boles, he halted, waiting for Sinna to catch up. He nodded his head, drawing her gaze between the two trees directly in front of them.

Framed between the trunks like a postcard, a tiny lake gleamed in the bright sun. Its surface frozen, it reflected the blue of the sky like a mirror, reminding her of Goss's eyes. "It's beautiful," she breathed.

"Yes," he agreed, but he was looking at *her*.

She felt her cheeks growing hot, and occupied herself by pulling off her helmet so that she didn't have to look into his perceptive gaze.

"Come on." He held out a hand and she grasped it, allowing him to lead her down to the lake's edge.

There were patterns in the ice, like gigantic snowflakes etched into infinity across the surface. Sinna shook her head in wonder. "I've never seen anything like it."

Goss moved behind her, wrapping his arms around her waist, resting his chin on the top of her head. "I know. It only happens here, with this lake."

"Wow."

They stood there silently for a long time, letting the beauty sink into their souls. Eventually, Goss stirred. "Hungry?"

Sinna nodded. Goss released her and walked back to his jet, opening a compartment behind the seat and pulling out an insulated bag and a blanket.

She helped him spread out the blanket, which turned out to have a waterproof backing. "I don't mind the cold," he explained, "but I do get tired of being wet all the time."

They sat down, and he handed her an apple and a ham sandwich. He stood and walked back toward the trees, bending down to rummage near the bottom of one, and came back with two frosty sodas. Popping the tops, he handed one to her and grinned. "Nature's cooler."

She smiled. They ate in companionable silence, then leaned back on their elbows and looked out across the lake.

"Goss," Sinna murmured. "I've never heard that name before. Is it Yeti?"

He laughed. "No. Actually, you won't believe how I came by it." He looked at her sternly. "You have to promise not to laugh."

Puzzled, Sinna nodded. "Okay, I promise."

"Cross your heart."

Sinna giggled, drawing a cross just over her heart.

"Okay. Well, when I was born, I already had a full head of hair, down past my shoulders and pure white, just like now. My mom said it was like spun gossamer, and that's what she decided to name me."

Sinna struggled to keep a straight face. "Gossamer."

"Yes."

"Goss is short for Gossamer."

"Uh-huh."

She couldn't help it. She burst out laughing.

He pounced on her, pushing her back against the blanket. "Hey! You promised you wouldn't laugh."

"Sorry." She choked on a giggle.

Goss straddled her, looking very stern. "I'm afraid I'm going to have to punish you." He reached out and tugged the neck of her sweater down, reaching in and cupping her breasts, tugging them out. Her nipples puckered immediately in the cold.

He brushed the tips of her ripe peaks with his calloused thumbs.

Sinna's chuckles faded as her breath quickened. Goss rolled off of her. "Kick off your shoes."

She pushed her feet free of her sneakers. He grasped her jeans, tugging. Sinna wriggled, pushing them down past her hips, and he pulled them off, tossing them aside.

He spread her legs, kneeling between them. Sinna waited breathlessly to see what he would do.

He looked her in the eye, trapping her gaze as his hands spread her labia wide. She swallowed thickly, heat rising in her groin. Her pussy spasmed, and Goss grinned. "Ready for your punishment, baby?"

Sinna nodded, unable to speak. His hands held her pussy wide while his thumbs slid inside her.

She moaned, cocking her hips.

"Don't," he ordered, in a tone brooking no refusal. "Don't move a muscle."

Sinna froze.

He buried his thumbs inside her, then pushed his forefingers together, trapping her clit between them. His thumbs danced, massaging her pussy as his fingers milked her clit.

Sinna clutched the blanket, trembling with the effort to remain still. Goss grinned, his thumbs moving more urgently, his fingers rubbing her clit rapidly, creating friction that made the nub burn pleasantly. "Oh, God."

"That's it, baby." He milked the sensitive nub relentlessly. "That's it. Come on."

Sinna held herself back for as long as she possibly could, but finally couldn't take any more. With a gasp, she brought her legs together, intending to trap him inside her while her hips rocked, freeing her from this exquisite torture.

Goss pulled himself free.

"Oh, no!"

He crawled up next to her, whispered in her ear. "You can't come yet, baby. Not 'til I tell you."

"Oh, God, Goss. Please."

He shook his head. "No." His grin softened the words. "You broke a promise, baby, and I'm very serious about punishment."

He scooted back between her legs, lowering his head. His cool breath swirled around her throbbing clit. She closed her eyes, clutching the blanket tightly.

His lips pressed tight around the throbbing nub. Sinna moaned and he drew them up, pinching her clit tightly until it popped free. Sinna gasped. He repeated the process, over and over, stoking the fire that danced between her legs.

"Please," she whispered. "Please." She tangled her hands in his hair, tried to push him toward her pussy.

He resisted, but a second later a thick finger worked its way inside her. "Oh, God. Yes." She pressed her hips upward, but he threw an arm across her pelvis, holding her down. His finger delved deeper and deeper, until Sinna whipped her head back and forth. "Oh, please, Goss. Please!"

He pressed into her G-spot, driving her up and up, until she was just about ready. "Oh, yes!"

Abruptly his mouth disappeared, his finger withdrew.

"No, no," Sinna sobbed. "Please don't stop."

"Don't worry," Goss rumbled deep in his throat. "I'm nowhere near finished."

He stood and walked toward the lake. When he came back, he held a rectangle of ice in his hands. "I'll bet there's something you don't know about the Yeti." He began running his hand over the ice. "We can shape ice with our bare hands."

His fingers worked rapidly, compacting and shaping, molding the ice into a perfect replica of a fat cock. He held it before her. "Oh, God," she whispered.

"Do you think you can take it?"

"I—I'm not sure." She had sex frequently, of course, because of her condition, and had heard that that could make a woman stretch and lose her tightness. She'd never had that problem, one of the few beneficial side effects of the curse, she supposed. There were still men whose cocks could hurt her. Goss's had stretched her lips to a point just this side of real pain, and it had felt delicious.

"Would you like to try?"

Wordlessly, she nodded.

He sat beside her right hip, facing her, holding the frozen dildo in his right hand. He placed it against her swollen lips.

Sinna hissed at the cold. He waited a moment, then pushed against her. She gasped, shaking her head. "I don't think I can."

He reached over with his left hand, pulling her labia apart. Sinna caught her bottom lip between her teeth as he worked the bulb of the icy wand just inside the rim. He looked at her. "How does it feel?"

"It hurts. But—" She bit her lip again.

"But what, Sinna?" His stern gaze promised more punishment if she didn't speak.

"But... I want more. I want it inside me." She drew in a sharp breath as he pushed harder, the dildo sliding in just a bit further. "Oh, God. It makes my lips ache." Noticing how his blue eyes clouded each time she spoke, filling with desire, she pushed on. "My clit's tingling." He thrust again, and a little more of the icy cock slipped inside her. "Oh, God. Yes. It's like fire!"

And it was. For her, flame was nothing, the equivalent to a tepid bath. Ice. Cold. That's what made *her* burn. And, God, was it HOT! Her pussy spasmed and she gasped as a mingled shock of pain and pleasure rocketed through her pelvis. "More," she gasped. "Please, more."

Goss was panting now, watching her as he pushed the cock in further. Sinna arched, moaning. "Oh, yes!"

She reached between her legs, covering his hand with hers. "Please," she whispered. "Please, Goss." She pressed against his hand. "All of it."

He hesitated, but his eyes became so dark she could almost swear they were black. "Are you sure?"

"Yes, yes," she chanted, clutching his hand. "Please!"

In one smooth movement, he covered her pelvis with one arm and shoved the cock in a bit further with the other. Sinna screamed.

He stopped, watching her worriedly. "Are you all right?"

"Yes, yes." She pressed hard against his hand, though it wouldn't budge unless he wanted it to. "Please. I want it inside me. All of it." She met his eyes boldly. "I like it," she said. "I like when it hurts."

"But you'll stop me if it's too much?"

"Yes!" She tried to jiggle her hips but he held her down.

"I'm serious, Sinna. This is a promise you can't ever break. Choose a word, a word you can say when something's too much for you. A word you wouldn't normally use."

"I—I can't think of anything."

"This is important, baby. Pick a word."

She shouted the first word that came to mind. "Jupiter!"

He grinned. "I guess we won't be having any planetary discussions, then." The grin faded. "I mean it, Sinna. If I ever go too far, you have to say that word. Sometimes, when we're... playing, I'll get... lost. It won't penetrate unless you say that word. I won't stop, until you do."

"I understand."

He stared into her eyes for a long moment, until he seemed satisfied by what he saw there. Still holding her gaze, he thrust the cock inside her and didn't stop until it was buried. "Oh, God, oh, God." Sinna's pussy burned like fire. Her muscles spasmed, sending waves of pleasure/pain skimming through her. "Yes." She looked into blue eyes seething with desire and begged. "Fuck me. Please. I want to feel it move."

He was breathing hard now, sweating. He drew the dildo out slowly, so slowly she wanted to scream. "Faster. Please, faster."

He thrust it deep again, drew it out, thrust it in, a little faster each time. Sinna gasped and grabbed the blanket. His grip on her waist tightened. He was thrusting deeper and deeper, able to go a little bit farther each time as her body heat melted the ice. "Oh please," she moaned. "Please." She tried to move her legs, but a flicker of his gaze stopped her. "Oh, God. I want you to bury it inside me. Please!" But he shook his head, fucking her faster and faster as the cock slimmed, but keeping her just short of gratification.

And then he drew it out. Holding it up to the light, he peered at it for a moment, then nodded.

Sinna lay trembling as he moved between her legs. He caught up her knees with his hands, pushing them back toward her chest, then drew her own hands up to hold them in place. "Close your eyes," he ordered.

She closed them immediately, then cried out as a brief stab of pain lanced through her anus, and then the smooth icicle was inching inside her ass. "Oh!" The melting ice worked as a lubricant, and Sinna moaned, tossing her head fitfully as Goss worked it deeper with quick, shallow thrusts, each one sending a new bubble of pleasure/pain bursting through her abdomen.

When he had buried it completely, pushing the rounded terminus in past her rim, he spread her legs and stood. "I think you've been punished enough." He peeled off his pants and knelt between her legs, entering her with one forceful thrust.

His cock felt so good inside her, like a flame licking her womb. She moaned and writhed. He chuckled and drew himself out, then thrust again, excruciatingly slowly.

Sinna whimpered. The icicle continued to melt inside her, but she could still feel it, shifting with his every movement, sending shivers of pleasure—no pain any longer, just pleasure— rippling through her. "Oh, please," she begged. "Please. I can't take any more."

He made her wait. Fucked her slow and easy, though she begged and writhed, sobbed and moaned. "Wait for it, baby. Wait."

Just when she'd convinced herself this was hell, and she was going to be trapped there forever on the brink of orgasm, his hands closed around her waist. His eyes blazed a brilliant blue as he forced his cock deep — powerfully, rapidly, over and over, grunting with each thrust.

Sinna threw her legs around him and arched. Goss straightened and wrapped his arms around her thighs, locking them together as she held her breath, pussy convulsing again and again as his cock pulsed inside her, sending a river of cool fire undulating through her.

When it was over, they lay side by side on the blanket, staring up into the clear blue sky. "I think I love you." Goss rose up and turned toward her, leaning on one hand as he traced lazy circles in her pubic hair.

Her breath caught in her throat. "Do you mean that?"

He nodded. "I never thought love could happen so fast, but... already, I can't stand the thought of you leaving." He watched her for a moment. "How do you feel?"

She *wanted* to shout to the whole world that she loved him, but something held her back. "I—" She plucked at the tail of her sweater with nervous fingers. "You don't think it's just the sex? I mean, we haven't really done much talking."

"That's true. I definitely think we need to get to know each other better before we settle down to a permanent commitment, like marriage."

Her body thrilled at his words. Just the fact that he was thinking about marriage warmed her, made her feel more secure with him.

"Still, are you in a position where you could work from here? I mean, do you have to be in an underground river cave in the Amazon, or could you stay here?" He met her eyes, seeming uncertain for the first time since she'd met him. "It'll keep, won't it, while we... explore each other?"

Sinna did think about it. She stared into the blue sky for a long time before she answered. When she did speak, she didn't answer, not at first. "You know, since that first time, there on the mountain, I haven't felt even a hint of the... *lust* that comes over me due to the curse."

She could see the confusion in his eyes, but was grateful when he remained quiet, letting her follow her thoughts. She picked up a handful of snow, letting it drift between her fingers. "And water is water. Frozen or in a river, it's just as good at dissipating the physical heat." She turned on her side, facing him, her gaze earnest. "I think what I'm trying to say is... maybe there's only a curse because of the way *Asuri* chose to live. I mean... through the centuries, we've just always done what she did, sucked in the first capable male as soon as the urge hit us, feeding into that instant gratification mindset that was the thing that got her into trouble in the first place. Maybe... what Saya was trying to do was... teach us how to tell the difference between love and lust."

He seemed to understand what she meant, nodding slowly. "Does that mean..." His voice cracked, and he looked away, as though afraid to let her see what was in his eyes.

Sinna reached out and caressed his cheek, and he caught her hand, pressing a kiss into her palm. "I think I love you, too," she whispered.

When he looked at her, she was shocked to see his eyes bright with tears. "Does that mean you'll stay?"

She nodded, and he stood abruptly and picked her up, swinging her around until she laughed breathlessly. When he stopped, holding her so that her hips were level with his chest and she looked down on him, she cupped his face in her hands. "Shall we celebrate?"

He let her slide down his length, stopping briefly to nibble a breast teasingly, then setting her feet on the ground. "Yeah. Let's go sledding."

"Sledding?"

He nodded. "Body sledding." He took off his flannel shirt, and his body rippled in the weak afternoon sun as he shifted. He shook himself after the change, his thick coat of fur settling into place. He nodded toward her clothes.

Sinna tugged her sweater up and pulled on her jeans. Since the cold didn't really bother her, it wasn't necessary for her to wear layers and layers of clothing, and for that she was grateful.

Goss picked her up, cradling her in his arms, and jogged up the mountain until they had passed the tree line, then jogged even further. When he finally stopped, it was at the apex of a steep slope that ran about three hundred yards and then flattened out into a pristine white plane. He set her down and squatted in the snow. "Climb on my back and hold on tight."

Sinna did as he said, and the next thing she knew, they were flying down the slope, the wind whipping tears from her eyes. "Ya-hooo!" she yelled, grasping Goss's thick fur tightly with one hand and holding the other high, riding him like a bronc until they slid out across the flat plane, losing speed and coming to a stop in a deep snowdrift.

Sinna jumped to her feet. "That was fantastic!"

Goss stared at her against the backdrop of sun and snow. A blazing black beauty, she *did* look like an Amazon, and she was *his* Amazon, now. He planned on loving her so well, she would never leave. "Want another go?"

She nodded enthusiastically and refused to let him carry her back up, laughing as she sank into the snow with each step, but loving every minute of the journey.

And that's how she felt three months later, when she and Goss sat down at their computer and removed their profiles from the Paranormal Mates Society website—something they'd been meaning to do for some time, but just hadn't gotten around to. When the pull-down menu asked why they were leaving, she happily clicked on "Found my lifemate! Please share your story with us in the box below—" Goss looked on, resting his chin on the top of her head as he usually did, as she typed.

I never thought I'd find love, but Paranormal Mates Society was the gateway to my dream." Goss snorted at the flowery prose, but she shushed him. "I met the Yeti of my dreams, and we started an incredible journey, one that we're still taking, and enjoying every minute. Do you love body sledding, ice fishing, ice cream, and bear hugs? I sure as hell do, and he's mine now, girls, so I suggest you visit the site and start your search, because the perfect mate may be just a click away and you never know what you might miss if you delay!

Rachel Bo

Rachel Bo is an award-winning author currently published in several genres. On the weekends, she works as a Clinical Laboratory Scientist. During the week, Rachel rides herd on her handsome husband, two wonderful daughters, a rabbit, a snake and several remarkably hardy goldfish.

Rachel loves to hear from her readers—you can visit her website at http://webpages.charter.net/rachelbo or email her at rachbo03@yahoo.com.

Paranormal Mates Society:
Chunkybuttfunky

Dakota Cassidy

For my good friend and fellow babe Pam. Thanks for sharing a good giggle with me every morning and for ending each day on such a high note! You're smart, funny, proud and fiercely supportive. For this and so much more—this one's for you, doll! And another thanks goes to the most wonderful man I know. R is a man who shares the other half of my warped sense of humor and my twisted brain, has the uncanny ability to read my mind and spew what's right on the tip of my tongue when I can't and most of all, loves me—every last wacky bit—because I'm "his guurl."

Love and kisses always,
Dakota :)

Chapter One

"Hey, all you Milwauuuukeeee night dwellers! This is CC, for the Nocturnal Journals, on B 105.5 FMMMMMMMM. Your lifeline to the nighttime. Call in and give me your views. Yep, I wanna hear them. The good and the oh-so-bad. Tonight's topic—online dating. It's the hottest thing in hooking up these days. Do ya think you can really find the match of your dreams in just one click? I wanna hear your story! Gimme a holler at *CC-in-the-eve*—that's 224-684-3383. Talk to me, Milwaukee. I'll be waaaaitiiiiing…"

Cadence Cranston clicked off her headset and swung her chair over to her computer while she waited for the commercial break to be over. Her topic tonight was inspired by her real life experiences, and she was curious to know how many people actually might be in the same sinking boat she was in.

The online dating Titanic-like sinking boat, that is.

Yes, Cadence Cranston, night time DJ and vampire, had joined an online date site to troll for guys. Not just any guys though. These men were of the paranormal persuasion and plentiful on Paranormal Mates Society.

Weeeeeeeee doggie—gazoodles of men to be had in every blessed paranormal category.

It was a new cyber haven, where hooking up with the mate of your dreams was finally a reality. Who knew a place like that even existed for her kind? It sure as hell made finding a date much easier on a vamp. There was no explanation involved if you wanted to hit the O negative for a little pick me up. It was refreshing and required far less hassle than dating a human.

However, this dating thing was becoming her favorite pastime as of late. The e-mail alone was enough to keep her amused for centuries on end. Cadence found herself glued to her computer every chance she got.

It couldn't be healthy.

Nay, it was downright pathetic…

Ooooh, but look! More e-mail.

Yee and haw.

Cheerist, she was sickly addicted to this bullshit e-mail, sadly compelled to check it every free moment she could dredge up.

As if the man of her dreams was going to pop up, and she might miss it because she was fixing her lipstick in the powder room or something.

Clicking on the date site, Cadence perused her inbox and sighed with defeat. It was too bad that most of the men who contacted her were stupidheads.

So many whacktards, so little time.

To: Chunkybuttfunky@paranormalmatessociety.com
From: Oncebitten2shy@paranormalmatessociety.com
Subject: Dayum!

Dear CBF,

Wow, could I ever sink my teeth into you! Looks like you got plenty to sink into <g>. How about we hook up and nail a herd of cows together?

Dave

Oh-my-God. A herd of cows? What kind of vampire sucked the blood out of cows anymore?

Cadence Cranston shuddered and then, for good measure, she shuddered again.

Fricken' vampire Neanderthal, knuckle dragging, Angus beef, blood sucking dork… God, what had she been thinking when she'd joined this damn online dating site?

She'd been thinking of sharing her Happy Meal instead of eating it alone…

"Oh, the Internet is the hottest thing in dating," her friend Pam had said. "You'll love it. Tons of men to be had," she'd boasted. "They even have a category for big and beautiful immortals and the like. You'll get loads of e-mail and have the social life of Paris Hilton. Trust me."

Cadence stared at the computer screen and flipped it the bird. She'd rather be dead than read one more flippin' loser's e-mail.

Oh, wait, she *was* dead.

Pam *had* been right. She did get lots of e-mail. It just so happened that for the most part, the e-mail was from psychotic nuts allowed Internet time for good behavior at the wacky farm. However, she was pleased to note that said psychos on the site rather liked her curves. She wasn't ashamed to call herself big and beautiful, and she was damn proud of the junk in her trunk.

Sighing, she grabbed her mouse and clicked on the reply button. *Someone* had to tell Dave he was a freak...

To: Oncebitten2shy@paranormalmatessociety.com
From: Chunkybuttfunky@paranormalmatessociety.com
Subject: Re: Dayum

Dear fucktard,

Cadence shook her head. That was mean. Probably true, but still, really not very good cyber dating etiquette. Backspacing and deleting the "fucktard," she began again.

Dear Dave,

Thanks for your response to my profile.
However, beef is *not* what's for dinner.

Good luck in your search,

CBF

There, Cadence thought, *buh-bye* now.

Oy.

How could it be that there wasn't a single vampire on this site that appealed to her? ParanormalMatesSociety.com was specifically designed for paranormals in today's society. It wasn't easy to be immortal, and finding someone to share that immortality with was harder still.

Yeah, everyone said her lifemate would pop up when she least expected him. However, Cadence was of the mind that until then, she needed to frost her Wheaties and for that, she had to find the Wheaties and some milk.

Paranormal Mates Society had everything from vampires to mermaids, alternative lifestyles and even demons. Surely there was someone out there that was a decent date? She remembered giggling over how funny the acronym for the site was.

PMS… that could well describe what finding a good date was like these days. She'd never forget how excited she'd been over the ad Pam had sent her for Paranormal Mates Society. Most of the sites she'd seen advertised on TV were not for chicks like her, but this site was specifically geared toward her kind.

www.ParanormalMatesSociety.com

Welcome to Paranormal Mates Society, where finding the love of your life is supernatural, super easy.

Tired of squeamish humans passing you over because blood is your beverage of choice? Do you long to indulge in intimate moonlit jaunts with a potential Pet Smart Companion? Are your fins fed up with the goldfish bowl of dating? Did the devil make you give up on ever finding your soul mate? Long to soar to the heavens with the match of your dreams?

Fill out our in-depth entry form. Browse thousands of profiles from paranormals just like you! Make new friends — find the immortal man or woman of your dreams with just one easy click.

Let us help you find the paranormal match of a lifetime at www.paranormalmatessociety.com — where meeting the perfect match can be out of this world!

Don't wait — join with our special offer for a free trial basis now. Choose the membership that best suits your search for the perfect paranormal mate!

The Heavenly Membership:
Allows you unlimited on-site e-mails to and from your own personal e-mail account. Send and receive as many e-mails as you'd like to find and communicate with the paranormal partner of your dreams! Upload as many as four pictures to the site — a premium mate-seeking tool! Our Heavenly membership also brings with it full access to all of the Paranormal Mates Society's member profiles and additional features such as "vibes" — the ultimate way to express your interest! — and Instant Messaging. Purchase a three or six month Heavenly membership package. The three month package is loaded with features and available for only $29.95 per month, or get crazy and take our value package for six months for just $22.95 per month!

The Purgatory Membership:
Our trial mate seeker package is totally free and includes sending and receiving up to five e-mails per day and allows you the option of sending up to two vibes a day!

Cadence had signed on for the Heavenly Membership almost immediately. It meant she might be able to get the hell out of the house or the radio station occasionally. Share a cup of blood with someone besides Granny Edna every other Tuesday. She loved her grandmother, but sometimes, when she saw couples strolling together or watched their hushed conversations at a secluded restaurant, her single status smacked her in the face with a resounding wallop.

So, how could it be that she'd been on the site for two damn months and not a single desirable vampire to be found?

The problem wasn't in getting a date. She'd been on a date or two since she'd joined, all right.

Cheerist, had she ever been on a date or two.

An inter-shifter date or two, a date or two she'd like to have amnesia as a result of, a date or two that involved coupons and a permanent chair at Starbucks.

The problem was finding a date that would hold her attention for more than the time it took to wipe her ass. It was becoming less like fun and more like trying too hard. No one sparked her interest for very long. No one even ignited an ember of a spark, let alone a flame. Hell, if she could get a good spark going, she'd be willing to get on the ground and blow on it to turn it into anything that was even remotely lukewarm.

But alas, no such luck as of yet.

Her focus returned to her newest obsession. It was time to get aggressive.

Ding dong, more e-mail calling.

Checking her watch, she decided to scan some more of the e-mails, before she had to go back on the air.

Cadence clicked on the profile of a particular e-mail caller whose user I.D. caught her attention. Niiice pic.

Fo shizzle, he was finger lickin' good.

Howling-ly hot, in fact.

A werewolf? Huh. That was one breed she'd not dated thus far.

Oh, God, please, please, please let him be normal… Okay, maybe "normal" wasn't the word she was looking for. At least let him be done with his prescription of Prozac. Was that too damned much to ask?

As she read the profile, Cadence smiled.

Rawmeatlover1969@paranormalmatessociety.com — Alpha Male seeks shifter's delight. Six-foot-four, dark and sometimes hairy, seeks mate for serious relationship. Must love hitting a field or two for a moonlight run — Steak Tar-Tar and a good back scratch. I love children and hope to someday have a whole litter. I'm open to an inter-shifter partnership — love a lady with junk in the trunk, but it isn't necessary. I foresee finding the woman of my dreams here and I won't leave disappointed. No players, control freaks, one-night stands or social climbers need apply. If the only game you like to play is Charades, I'm the guy for you — e-mail me and I promise you, you'll have a howling good time.

Cadence laughed at his use of the expression "junk in the trunk." It was her favorite way to describe her ass, which had far more trunk space than most mid-sized vampires, but still seemed to appeal to the opposite sex.

Glancing at his location, she realized he lived in England and his name was Carter. Carter, Carter, Carter, silly, but cute man. What were you thinking when you e-mailed someone who lives in God damned Wisconsin?

Fuck.

Well, England *was* nice.

Jolly good for him.

Not so jolly good for her.

Bloody men.

Cadence sent rawmeatlover1969 back a nice response, thanking him for his interest and mentioning that quite possibly, swimming the Atlantic to get to one another might be a drag for a first date. Besides, she didn't have a floatation device.

Damn it all, he was cute too. Cadence deleted him with regret.

The trouble with this online thing was people seemed to forget not only their inhibitions, but their locations.

It was like real estate. Location, location, location was everything and sometimes, one could get swept away looking at all of the pretty profile pictures and forget they lived fucking thousands of miles and a couple of oceans from their intended prey.

Cadence decided to add *Wisconsin residents only* to her profile. Admittedly, her photo was a smidge grainy but she was a vampire. They weren't exactly photogenic. Maybe she should rewrite her profile? Her eyes strayed to the small blurb that had taken her three days to get right before she'd uploaded it to the site. She was no writer, for sure, but she'd thought it was pretty self-explanatory and, most of all, direct.

> I'm thirty-two, work in radio and I'd like a date sometime before this millennium ends <g>. I'm friendly, funny and curvy. If anorexic chicks are your bag, I'm not the girl for you. I like animals, children and would love a family someday, but I'm in no rush. No serial killers, infidels, health nuts or guys who want to hit the Super Eight Motel on the first date, please. If you're interested, contact me at chunkybuttfunky@paranormalmatessociety.com.

Making the change, Cadence flipped her headset back on and positioned herself at the microphone, preparing to take calls from her listening audience.

"Helloooo, Gordon from Beaver Dam. You're on the air with CC! What's on your mind?"

"I just gotta say, that the online thing is crap. I signed up for one of those damn sites and went on a few dates. What a train wreck."

Gordon's thick, mid-western accent made Cadence chuckle. "What happened?"

"Well, I e-mailed a chick and her picture was hot, you know? I'm all juiced to meet her. We have some stuff in common — we got to know each other a little, shootin' e-mails back and forth — so I ask her out. I pull up to Bob's Big Boy for our date and I can't find her anywhere."

"Dude! She stood you up?" So far, that hadn't happened to Cadence, but she'd heard it often did.

Gordon snorted into his phone. "Hah! I wish. I get outta my truck and I'm lookin' all over and she comes up from behind me, ya know, callin' my name. I turn around and jumpin' Jehosaphat — she ain't the girl I e-mailed."

Cadence fought an on air giggle. "Ahhhh, what was wrong?"

"Wrong?" he squawked. "What was wrong was that her picture had to be at least twenty years old and her hips, twenty years older."

"So whadja do?"

"I feel kinda bad now, but I pretended like I didn't know her. Hit the bricks as fast as I could and took off in my Chevy pick-up like a pissed off daddy was chasin' me with his shotgun."

Cadence's chuckle was deep and resonant. "You just left her there? That sorta sucks, Gordon. She might have been nice if you'd given it half a chance."

"Ya know what sucks, don't ya, CC? What sucks is women think it's okay to put up a picture that's older than Methuselah. That's misrepresentation, if you ask me."

"Tell me something, Gordon?" Cadence prompted. "Did she have feathered hair and spandex in the picture on the site?"

"Well, yeah…" he responded, rather contritely.

"I don't wanna call a spade a spade, Gordon, but that might have been your sign. Did you read her profile? Look at her age?"

"I know, I know. I wasn't thinking, I guess. I got all caught up in the crap they feed you about finding your soul mate."

"Do you really want a soul mate, Gordon, or do ya just wanna get laid?" Cadence teased. Her listening audience was well aware of her lightly antagonistic, humorous pokes at them. It was what had made her a hit and had gotten her the show to begin with.

Gordon snickered. "I'm not gonna lie to ya. Sure, getting laid would be great. I'm a guy, but I really do want someone to hang out with and maybe someday, marry."

"Did you hear from her again?"

"Oh, yeah, I heard from her again, all right. She sent me a long winded e-mail about what a jerk I was and how looks aren't everything."

Cadence nodded her head in the silence of the studio. "I gotta agree with her, Gordon. Looks *aren't* everything."

"Yeah, but she lied. Maybe if she'd been honest, she might not have gotten much e-mail, but she sure as hell would have had someone who was interested in the real her, ya know?"

"So online dating leads to misrepresentation, then?"

"Hell, yeah, it does! You can be whoever you wanna be to rope some poor jackass in, and that just ain't right."

"Tell me, Gordon, have you had any good dates as a result of your online experience?"

"Nope. I quit after that."

"You gave up? Why would you do that?"

"I got tired of the same old crap. You get to e-mailin' with someone, they act like they're all interested, and then they give you some excuse for why they don't want to give out their phone number after you spent a week e-mailin' back and forth. Or you find out they just like all the attention, and they're talkin' to a bunch of other guys too. It's all crap." He paused and then he asked, "What about you, CC? You're single, right?"

"Yes, sir, I am indeed. What about me?"

"You ever think about joining an online site?"

Oh, Gordon... if cyber space had a tongue, it would have many tales to tell you about CC. "Do you think you'd answer my ad if I did, Gordon, or would you leave me high and dry once you saw me?" she joked in an effort to keep her personal life just that, personal.

"I'd never leave you high on anything but me, CC," he chuckled. "I love to listen to your show every single night. You have an awesome voice. I bet you're hot."

Cadence laughed into her microphone. The husky symphony of chuckles had become a trademark for her listening audience. "Yeah, Gordon, that's me. I'm one hot tamale. Hey, Gordon? Thanks for your input, and thanks for listening to The Nocturnal Journals. We'll be right back with a caller who says she married someone she met online and he married her too, but she's not the only one he calls *wife*... Stay tuned for more from CC. Your lifeline to the nighttime on B 105.5 FMMMMMMMMM." Cadence drew the last of the station's call letters out in her familiar sexy, low tones and went to another commercial break.

Cadence glanced again at her e-mail account at Paranormal Mates and opted to ignore it for now.

The next caller's dilemma left a bad taste in her mouth, and she hadn't even heard the full story yet.

You could be whoever you wanted to be online and sometimes, what you wanted to be wasn't anything like you really were. It was like playing dress up and pretending you were some movie star.

Cadence would be fucked if she'd end up swindled the way she was assuming her waiting caller had been. She had an eternity to spend. She sure as fuck wasn't going to waste time falling in love with a guy only to find out he was playing dress up.

No triflin' with her heart, thank you very much.

Chapter Two

Collin Grayson clicked open his account at Paranormal Mates Society and rubbed his hands together, hoping he'd have another batch of e-mails to choose from.

He was relieved to find that since he'd joined PMS, the chicks seemed to dig him, at the very least. Collin had received his fair share of e-mail. So far though, he hadn't had any luck in getting anyone to actually go out with him. He'd spent a lot of time pussyfooting around with the women on the site by e-mail and instant message, yet it seemed to peter out and lose its steam after awhile. But he *would* get one of these shifters to go out with him.

By God, he'd get a date with one if it killed him.

It just might too.

Fricken' paranormal women were as picayune as human women were. However, he was nothing if not a dog with a nice, new, rawhide bone, and he absolutely intended to get a woman.

A were-woman.

She-wolf.

Whatever…

All he needed was *one* and then, he was in, and he'd e-mail the shit out of every last one of them until someone, *anyone* agreed to meet him.

The user-ID Chunkybuttfunky in his inbox caught his eye and had him letting a small chuckle escape his throat. Funny handle she had there. Collin liked a woman who was secure in her curves. Her picture was a little cloudy, but her smile was nice.

Well, Ms. CBF, let's see what you have to say for yourself.

To: Ilikeminerare@paranormalmatessociety.com
From: Chunkybuttfunky@paranormalmatessociety.com
Subject: Nice profile

I was browsing the profiles and happened upon yours. You sound interesting. Would love to get to know more about you. If you're interested, e-mail me.
CBF

Collin pondered his profile. What was interesting about it? Not a whole lot. He'd kept it pretty generic…

Ilikeminerare@paranormalmatessociety.com
I'm thirty-seven, in excellent physical health, attractive and I'm a werewolf. I love women of all shapes and sizes, but I'm particularly attracted to a fuller figured lady. I'm here on a whim, searching for my lifemate because I can't seem to find her anywhere else. My future mate must love to take long runs beneath the light of the moon, have a strong sense of family honor, enjoy watching baseball from time to time and be willing to take it nice and slow if we dip our toes into the relationship pool. Read my in depth profile and let's see if we have something in common, then e-mail me. Only other werewolves need apply.

Collin glanced at Chunkybuttfunky's profile again and wondered what she looked like in person. She was under the BBW category on the site. He'd thrown the bit about liking fuller figured women in his profile because, well, it was true. He really did love a woman with curves, but it wouldn't matter much in the end.

Collin figured just getting a date was more than he could hope for at this point. His charm would have to work for him if he hoped to keep the connection and finally meet someone in person.

Swishing his coffee around in his mouth, Collin thought about how to respond to CBF.

From: Ilikeminerare@paranormalmatessociety.com
To: Chunkybuttfunky@paranormalmatessociety.com

Subject: Re: Nice profile

Hey, CBF!
Thanks, I like your profile too and we're in the same area.

Collin paused and decided that going for it was his best possible game plan. He needed to meet someone soon. Time was of the essence.

Would you like to get together for coffee? I know this is rather hasty, but I'm really interested in meeting you. Let me know and we'll make plans. Oh, and I'm Collin, by the way.

Collin

Fuck pride and fuck playing the dating game.
He had shit to do.

* * *

Cadence stretched her arms over her head and pushed away from her computer in her home office. If her face could flush, it probably would over this werewolf Collin.

Tired of the vampires on the site, Cadence had taken a more aggressive approach and e-mailed Ilikeminerare, or Collin as she now knew him. She must have been low on fuel when she'd done it because now she wasn't sure she'd done the right thing.

She never e-mailed a guy first.

Yet, his picture had sucked her in and she hadn't been able to take her eyes off it since she'd first seen it.

Hot wasn't exactly the word Cadence would use to define him, but rough and lean would. Collin had this sex and sin label stamped on his thoroughly luscious lips, and it virtually made Cadence squirm in her office chair.

She'd spent a long night surfing the profiles listed under many different categories on the site, including Wild Thang (hairy critters and more), and decided that maybe a werewolf had something up his sleeve some of the other creatures didn't. A werewolf wasn't too far out of the realm of vampires. Well, not a whole lot, anyway. It was closer than flippin' Yetis, that's for sure.

A Yeti... Even Bigfoot needed a date, she guessed.

Then, she'd seen Collin's picture, read his profile and her mouth had watered, her thighs trembled and the gut she didn't have because she was a vampire twittered.

Twittered, mind you. Not just a little flutter, but a full-on twitter.

His request to have coffee made it even worse. Now her no-holds-barred attitude about man hunting was making her rethink her aggressive approach.

Sitting back down, she clicked on Collin's picture again.

Jesus effin', he was the shit.

The picture on the site was full body, full on fantastic. He was just five inches taller than she was and, at six-two, he had a lean honed look to him. He wasn't bulked out, and he didn't look like he spent all of his time in a gym. His hair was as inky black as the felt tip pen she used to make sticky notes about the men who e-mailed her, keeping track of what she liked and didn't like about each of them. It was thick and shiny under the glare of the sunlight in the photo, brushed back and cut just above his ears.

He was leaning against a brick building of some kind. One foot braced against the wall with his hands in the pockets of his blue jeans. Collin's grin spoke volumes to her, cocky and sardonic all at once, with a slight arrogance to the tilt of his jaw.

Again, Cadence found herself tingling all over just looking at him.

Hookay, no more friggin' around. Cadence sent Collin back a quick "coffee would be great" e-mail before she lost her last nerve.

Maybe they should spend more time getting to know one another via e-mail?

Shaking her head, Cadence snorted. She was tired of playing the e-mail tag, you're it game. You could get to know one another over a cup of coffee just as easily.

It wasn't like she had anything to worry about physically. She could take care of herself. She was a vampire with superhuman strength. If Ilikeminerare Collin tried any funny shit, she'd open up a can of whoop ass on his doggie tookus and drink him dry.

Bet he had some sweet blood too…

Closing her eyes, Cadence clicked on the Send/Receive button on her e-mail. It showed Collin as "online" and, loser that she was, she realized she was waiting to hear back from him. Popping open one eye and squinting at the computer screen, Cadence smiled in relief, then frowned.

Yeah, he'd e-mailed back all right.

Collin wanted to know if she was a werewolf… Oh, yeah, his profile *had* said werewolves need only apply. Some shifters just didn't dig a good inter-species relationship. They stuck to their own kind, and that wasn't boding well for Cadence's fangs and bat wings.

Shitpissfuck.

But—but—he was so damn delish.

Frustration rose and stuck in Cadence's throat like gooey peanut butter. How was it that the cutest guy she'd seen since she'd joined this damn site was off limits?

Or was he?

Drumming her fingers on her desk, Cadence thought hard.

Then, harder still.

And in mere moments, a plan was hatched.

Devious with intent.

Demented with desire.

Defiant in nature.

Freakin' desperate…

How hard could it be to *pretend* you were a werewolf? She was black. Her skin tone wasn't as pale as most vamps. It had a light caramel hue to it…

It could be done…

She could howl just as well as anyone else. Hell, all you had to do was watch Animal Planet and woof along if getting the pitch correct was the problem, right?

Ahhh, but the fluffy stuff might be an issue. She wasn't very hairy. Were werewolves hairy in their human forms? Shit, she didn't know any werewolves personally. Damn, she needed to get out much, much more. Broaden her otherworldly horizons. Not spend so much time cruising the blood banks and spend more time like moon bathing or something, getting to know her fellow paranormal-ers. Was that even a word?

For fuck's sake, you are one sheltered sista, Cadence Cranston.

Her mind raced and when Cadence was nervous, she became impulsive. Sometimes her lips flapped without censor and she did stuff that required more time in her "thinking spot."

Cadence e-mailed Collin back before she allowed herself to over-think this werewolf thing.

Was there a *How to be a Werewolf for Dummies* at the bookstore?

* * *

"You're black."

Cadence glanced down at her arm and gave him a mock look of astonishment. She gasped, "Ya think? Oh, my God! I'm a sista?" Cadence slapped her hand to her forehead in mock surprise. "Thank *God* someone told me. Imagine if I'd kept going on believing I was white? I had no idea! I can't believe my mother never told me. After all this time too. I mean, I'm thirty-two years old and I've spent all of these years thinking I was some damn Anglo Saxon. Shit, no wonder the White Supremacists turned my picture application down. I'm adopted. My folks are white, so I guess they reeeallly went overboard with the unification thing, huh?" Turning her body, Cadence took a defensive stance, jamming her hands into the pockets of her jeans and swinging her cute pink Macy's half-off purse over her shoulder.

Instead of being riled, Collin surprised her and chuckled at her joke. "I'm sorry. I didn't mean to offend you, but you didn't look black in your photo on the site."

"Well, if you want to romanticize it, I guess I'm more of a light caramel, huh?"

"You're beautiful, no matter your skin tone."

"This would be the part where I preen and thank you for your 'I want to get in your plus size panties, first date' bullshit, right?"

Rocking back on his heels, his body seemingly relaxed and Collin flashed her a cocky grin. "No, this would be the part where you graciously have that cup of coffee you agreed to have with me and stop harping on me for making a simple mistake. Your color is unimportant, but my lips work faster than the censor in my brain, i.e., I have a big mouth."

Oh.

Okay.

Cadence took a deep breath and expelled the air into the chilled night.

She was getting all up in his face for no good reason because she was a nervous wreck now that she'd met him, seen his hunky self in real life, decided she wanted him and planned to lie every step of the way to get him. Her lips took the roller coaster ride of defensive with the big dip into flapping your gums. In essence, Cadence Cranston was a big, plus sized liar and lying wasn't her strong suit. In an effort to cover her boo-tay, she became surly and developed diarrhea of the mouth.

In her defense, every so often she'd catch herself being overly sensitive about her color. Being raised in a clan of white vampires often made Cadence very aware of her adoption. She loved her family with a ferocious possession, but she also longed to know where she came from and why she'd been left in the first place.

"I'm sorry. I think I go overboard sometimes. It's not easy being a shifter, let alone a black one raised in a white family. I have a big mouth too. So, how about we start again? I'm Cadence, of the big mouth, nice to meet you." Cadence shoved her hand at him, giving her goose bumps when his larger, broader hand took hers.

If he was surprised that she'd been adopted, he was good at hiding it. "I'm Collin, of the loose lips, nice to meet you. I say we have coffee and forget the first few minutes of this date. You?"

Cadence cocked her head to look up at him in the parking lot's light. Fuck, he was as fine in person as he was in his pic.

Only with animation. Like hunky muscles rippling under his snug sweater animation. Like thighs that were taut and visibly bulky beneath his jeans animation.

Real life animation was taking on a whole new meaning.

So was the suggestion she planned to send to Paranormal Mates Society the moment she could breathe again after whiffing paradise Collin.

Smell-a-mail.

Surely with all the technology today, one could find a way to send a man's scent via e-mail? It could be a deal maker with vampires.

Coffee was the last thing on her mind at this point, unless coffee was a new flavor in condoms.

Cadence shivered and straightened her shoulders, remembering that the Holiday Inn was for vacations, not first date boffing. "Okay. I think we have a deal. Unless you drink sissy coffee, then I'd have to reconsider," she joked as she began walking toward the same coffee shop she'd parked her ass in for as many first dates as she had fingers and toes.

God, she hoped just this once, it would be a different ending to the same old song.

Play that funky music, white boy.

* * *

She had prayed for different, hadn't she?

Sleeping with the stone fox you'd met like an hour ago could certainly be classified as a different ending, couldn't it?

Oh, yes. This was different.

Unique.

Diverse.

Crazy, right?

Not so if you found you'd begun to wholeheartedly believe crawling across the coffee shop table and pouncing on your intended prey was a perfectly logical course of action to take three minutes into your first date.

Chemistry was a funny, instantaneous, lightning rod of reaction versus a solid, well formulated plan. All Cadence could claim at this juncture was Collin had set her Bunsen burner on fire.

One minute they were sipping non-sissy-like coffee while Cadence busily dodged talking about werewolf packs and the full moon, the next, they were in Collin's car, out of it five minutes later, and tearing the bejesus out of each other's clothing in their rush to get naked.

Now, as Cadence looked at the virile, lean, tan, many-yummy-adjectives Collin, she couldn't even pinpoint exactly what had happened after she'd come to the conclusion she'd thought was so logical.

Three minutes into their coffee drinking, mind you.

Three minutes.

That might appear hasty to some, wouldn't it?

Hasty is as hasty does.

There was no turning back now. They'd very firmly taken the first date rules and crumpled them up, throwing them out the window with abandon and crashing through the door of wanton, forbidden lust.

Oh, and it *had* been lust. Thick and redolent, quick silvered and flaming.

At least she'd been smart when she'd decided to go all werewolf in her date search. The lunar loving folk were damned gifted in the sack.

Collin stirred beside her on his bed (yes, *his* bed) and reached out to caress her spine, making her forget any and all misgivings.

His large hand swept over her back, soothing and hot. Cadence moaned and her eyes rolled back as she tried to focus and maybe, just maybe, have a conversation with a man she'd spent all of a New York minute with.

"Collin?"

"Cadence?"

"We just had *sex*."

"Yep, and now, we're going to have more."

"Don't you think this was rather sudden?"

"Ahh, I know what's worrying you."

"Do you?"

"I do. You're worried this will be a one-night stand."

"Well, yeah. Isn't it?"

"Oh, hell no it isn't. Not after that blow of the old meat whistle you just gave me."

Cadence began to laugh, her shoulders shaking and tears forming at the corners of her eyes. She should be insulted by his crack about a blow job, but what little conversation they'd had at the coffee shop had been enough to know Collin was the wisest of asses. "That should really piss me off."

"But it doesn't because you already know I'm a smart ass." He grinned at her again. "I mean it. We just had some of the best nookie I've ever had and, begrudgingly, mind you, I am willing to admit that openly. I definitely want to get to know a woman who can make your kind of mattress magic."

Cadence lay back against the hard muscle of his arm and he curled it around her, dragging her across his chest. Collin's hand cupped her breast, thumbing her nipple and moving with the rise and fall of her breathing. "I don't get it. I'm a firm believer in exclusivity before sex. But—but—we—I…"

"We clicked. There's no denying that. We're adults, Cadence. It really is okay to be this attracted to someone and then act on it. It also doesn't mean you'll never see me again. I dare you to try to keep me away from you after *that*."

Collin's reassuring, slightly arrogant words were followed by his lips, skimming the outline of her own, slipping a silken tongue into her mouth, drawing her into a kiss that left her mind blank and her mouth greedily pressing into his for more.

The kiss said it all.

It was one of Cadence's determining factors in a date, and Collin was game on when it came to a lip lock. He didn't just ram his tongue down her throat like most of the men she'd granted a kiss. Collin consumed her, devoured her, used that tongue of his like a weapon of mass destruction out to eliminate all other kisses.

Cadence moaned into his mouth with husky approval.

Collin tugged the sheet away from the grasp she didn't realize she had on it. "Don't cover yourself up with me *ever*, Cadence. You're beautiful in the moonlight. I want to see you when my cock slips inside your pussy."

Man, these werewolves really had an unrealistic hard-on for the moon. Cadence shifted under his penetrating, blue gaze. His eyes roved her body with apparent, hungry appreciation. Gazing at her lush breasts, he commented on the color of her nipples. "They're like dark chocolate," he mumbled as he pushed her to her back. Her nipples rose in response, turning taut and hard. Collin dipped his head to capture one between his lips and suckle it as Cadence undulated beneath him.

Her hips rose, encouraged, begged for his thick cock to press between them, but Collin took a different path, the path that led to her aching cunt. Wet and glistening with desperate need. The first touch of his tongue to her swollen outer lips had her lower body fighting for control as he swiped that silken tool of pleasure over her, licking and nibbling.

He took several passes, avoiding dipping into the bundle of nerves that was screaming for satisfaction while his hands smoothed over her thighs, lifting them, parting them so he could position himself between them.

Collin's head rose and he hooked her legs over his forearms, hiking her up to his mouth. When his tongue finally touched her clit, it seared Cadence, burned with a painfully pleasurable sting of the release that was sure to come. His tongue slithered around the nub, stroking with precision, swirling around in rhythmic circles until a force of heat slammed into her like a head on collision.

Cadence bucked against his mouth, lifting herself up on her elbows and letting her head fall back as she ground into his lips.

The sweet sound of flesh being licked, suckled drove Cadence to lose the last thread of control, and she bit the inside of her cheek to keep the yelp from escaping her throat.

Her panting was a sharp noise in the still of Collin's bedroom, rasping and ripped from her lungs.

Collin let her legs fall to the bed and levered himself over her body. His erection bobbed against her abdomen, teasing and straining against her hot skin. He bracketed Cadence's head with his strong arms and she ran her hands over the taut, tension filled surface with pleasure, sighing when he sat between the cradle of her hips.

Cadence reached between them and circled his shaft with a firm hand, caressing the head of his cock and the tiny slit that seeped pre-come. Collin's groan was muffled against her forehead as he nestled between her thighs and zeroed in on the heated, slick entrance of her passage.

Chapter Three

Collin wanted to drive into her much the way he'd done the first time they'd fucked, but he also wanted to savor the exquisite heat that encompassed him when he slid into her welcoming, tightly fisted cunt. So he tortured himself, letting his cock taste but not fully indulge in the sweetness of her pussy. He sat back on his haunches, admiring the fullness of Cadence's lush curves in the moonlight, her plump rounded breasts, reaching upward. She was as sweet as the caramel candy she claimed her skin was like, as hot and thick as when it was melted over vanilla ice cream.

His senses roared, licking at the tight sacs that had drawn up snugly against his body. Collin's will to take this newly erotic ride of lust barely kept him in check, but when Cadence's pink tongue slipped over her lips, wetting them, he almost lost the rein he had on his primal urge to drown himself in her cunt.

"I think *now* would be a good time to make this happen, Collin," Cadence demanded from beneath him. Her command was breathy and anxious.

Collin kneaded her full thighs and laughed a wicked reply, "I suppose it would, but then I like to do things in my own time and you'll thank me for making you wait." He palmed a breast as he dragged his cock between the plump folds of her pussy, lingering at her clit.

Watching as her eyes slid closed and her hands gripped the sheets on either side of her, Collin took enormous pleasure in her reactions to his teasing. Each moan was a victory.

As she fought her obvious impatience to have Collin in her, he gained the time he required to master his need.

And need her he did. Like nothing before.

Collin had had plenty of sex, but it wasn't like this. And if he allowed himself to dwell on it, he'd hit the ground running like the hounds of hell were chasing him and never see Cadence again

because it was freaking him out. Not to mention it was wrong…
but he wasn't letting something this fucking fantastic go.

Not likely. Not after tonight.

So he chose to focus instead on her flesh, spread before him
like a feast fit for a starving man. He inched his cock into the firm
grip of her cunt, until Cadence groaned, low, and sexy as hell.

Collin clamped his jaw shut as he watched her pussy
swallow his length, tighten around it, milking it with a slick,
greedy grip. His hips began a slow circle while he lowered his
frame to the soft, smooth fullness of hers. An "ahhhh" drove from
his lips as he settled in her and her arms went around his back,
clutching at him and grinding her hips into his.

Spikes of electricity arced through Collin's veins, heating
them, clawing at his cock, driving him to find relief. Yet he
remained almost motionless, shoving his arms under Cadence's
back and drawing her close. He gritted his teeth as her breasts
scraped his chest and she rolled her upper body to press them
closer. Sweat clung to them, making them wet and slippery.
Collin's hand strayed to her ass, positioning them to lie almost
sideways, and he clamped a hand to one full globe, grinding her
into him. He threw a thigh over hers, locking her body to his.

His cock throbbed as he began to stroke, using the strength
of his legs and feet to drive deep. Cadence clung to his neck, her
eyes opening, then widening in surprise when Collin hit the spot
he'd found she liked best.

Lunging into her, he then drew back so that the cool air
sifted between them, only to plunge into her again, linger, grind
against Cadence's pelvis and draw back again.

Digging her hands into his hair, Cadence's body went
immediately rigid and she mumbled into his ear, something
incoherent and hushed, but defined and urgent in need.

The roar of his orgasm clutched his balls, tearing through
his resolve to hold back. Cadence's body pressed so tight to his,
her skin flushed and smooth against his own, her cunt wet and
welcoming, was more than Collin could refuse.

So he came, with fury and thick come spewing from his engorged cock, jolting out of him and releasing him in a downward spiral of relief.

They gasped together, collapsing against one another but still clinging to each other.

Cadence raised her head and her eyes, glazed and shining, sought his. "Dayum," she said on a laugh as she gasped for air. "You werewolves sure know how to throw down, huh?"

Collin stared back at her and something flitted across his gaze before he kissed the tip of her nose and said, "Yeah, we can really howl. You oughta know, being one yourself." He grinned.

Oops. Yeah, she oughta know, werewolf wannabe that she was. Cadence dismissed the fleeting, odd look on Collin's face as leftover confusion—something she too was experiencing. If she was a little freaked out about this whole encounter, Collin had a right to be.

Whatever the hell had just happened, it had been life altering.

No one had ever known her body as instinctively, as carnally, as Collin had. She hadn't had many lovers, and none compared to the sync their bodies shared.

She knew it and she knew Collin knew it too. Her vampire senses were keen, aware, and something, whatever it was, something monumental, something she knew instinctively in her gut, had just happened and it was huge.

Maybe all the romantic bullshit really was true?

Maybe when you found "the one," it happened like this?

Yeah, all happily married couples will tell you they found their soul mates on a one-night stand.

Jesus Christ in a miniskirt.

She buried her head in the strong column of Collin's neck to hide her embarrassment.

"Cadence?"

"Collin?"

"Don't question it."

"Oh, okay. If you say I shouldn't, then I guess I shouldn't." Her sarcasm was scathing, but she bit her tongue to keep from flapping her big ole lips in the breeze. Nervousness would only make her tell more lies she'd never be able to explain if the time ever came for explanation.

Leaning back from her, Collin lifted her chin and rubbed a thumb over it. "I say something just happened between us that was pretty fucking intense. I dunno about you, but I want it to happen again."

"So we'll be fuck buddies?" She flung the words at him like hard stones skipping on a pond and fought the undeniable urge to tell him his newly found fuck buddy was sportin' fangs.

"Fuck buddies don't fuck like that, Cadence. They find relief for their sexual itch and see each other every other Tuesday to do it. That's *not* what's going to happen here. That wasn't just some itch. It was more than that."

"I think the males of the werewolf species have a high bullshit factor when they don't want to be caught red-handed spewing crap."

"And female werewolves are too stupid to figure that out?"

Well, she'd have to actually be a werewolf to know for sure... Fuck. What had she gotten herself into? "No, we're not too stupid. We're cautious and my doggie instincts are always in fifth gear."

"Good, then they should tell you I *never* say anything I don't mean. Now let's go make a sandwich and get to know each other like we were supposed to in the coffee shop."

Talk.

He wanted to talk?

That meant getting to know one another and sharing intimate details. Like the ones that would involve more lying about her paranormal origins.

This was a predicament.

A very heinous one indeed.

She hadn't planned past meeting him. She'd just wanted to see the yummy hunk in person. Now she'd had yummy sex with the yummy hunk, and he thought she was a fricken' werewolf.

Fuck, fuck and fuck again.

Collin tugged at her arm and offered her a robe. "I never wear it. My mother sent it to me for Christmas last year. It'll keep you warm."

Cadence's mind raced as she tried to remember what she knew about werewolves. He was bound to ask questions about her people… oh, wait, pack. Werewolves lived in packs. Her limited knowledge was going to fuck her over if she wasn't careful.

The less said the better, especially with her big mouth. She could go all mysterious on him and evade, avoid, fly low under the getting-to-know-you radar. Answer a question with a question.

Cadence slipped into the warmth of the terrycloth robe, even if she couldn't really feel the cold per se, and followed Collin into his tiny kitchen, plunking down in the chair he offered her.

"Hungry?" he asked.

No, um, *yes*. Yes, if she were a real werewolf, she'd be starving right now, right? Surely after two rounds of a sex-a-thon, werewolves would need nourishment. Thank God her breed of vamp actually enjoyed food. It wasn't necessary for their survival like blood was, but to fit into society, they could and would eat just like the rest of the humans. Hell, Cadence loved pepperoni pizza. "Yeah, I am a little."

"I'm not much of a cook, but I can make a kick ass sandwich. Turkey and Swiss?"

Turkey? Didn't werewolves eat rare stuff? "You eat turkey?"

He shrugged and turned his back to her as he perused the contents of the fridge. "Yeah, don't you?"

Answer a question with a question. "Um, yeah?" she squeaked.

Turning to put the cold cuts on the counter, he narrowed his gaze in her direction. "You okay?"

Cadence's discomfort grew. *Breathe in, breathe out. Do not hyperventilate from the lies you're about to spew.* "I'm fine. I've just never done this before and I'm a little at a loss for words."

"Believe it or not, I've never done this before either."

So he wasn't as much of a dog as his ancestry would claim. "Really?"

Collin crossed the small square of linoleum and captured her chin in his broad hand. "Really. Relax, Cadence. I'm not the big bad wolf."

Yeah, well if you wanted to get technical, neither was she.

Chapter Four

Fabricator.
Falsehood teller.
Fraud.
Fucking liar.

Those words and more winged through Cadence's head as she sat at her computer and researched werewolves. After playing Secret Agent Man with Collin for the last seven nights, Cadence knew that *fucked* had become a literal scenario in more ways than one.

She'd dodged, avoided, and ducked all of his "pack" questions on their first night while they'd eaten sandwiches in his dimly lit kitchen. He sure was inquisitive. Collin wanted to know all about her family. Who was the Alpha in her pack, where did they eat small wildlife, was it hard to keep yourself well groomed, et cetera, et cetera.

She had to tell him. How long could she go on keeping him believing she was going to turn into a fluffy puppy when, in reality, she had incisors and a lust for O negative?

Nervous tension and guilt were ugly bedfellows. She'd slept with them for a week now, all while she and Collin did each other in as many free hours as they could find and e-mailed all day long when they couldn't.

For Cadence, Collin was the kind of man that once you learned something about him, you wanted to learn more. Each tidbit he revealed was a tender, juicy morsel of information she kept and she got back in the buffet line for another helping.

Their conversations weren't just about the sex they had and their seemingly insatiable need for one another, but ranged from favorite television shows to politics. The gamut was enormous and it depended solely on the ease with which they were able to communicate. Their brains functioned on the same wavelength or something. The more time they spent together, the more Cadence knew she'd eventually have to tell him the truth.

She had to tell someone. Someone who would understand why she'd done something so utterly impulsive and completely out of character for her. Someone who would help her to understand what the fuck she was thinking when she'd hatched this plan. Her guilt wouldn't allow her not to confess.

To someone...

Pam. Pam would help.

Cadence grabbed her phone and hit the speed dial.

"Hey, Elvira! We still doin' lunch on Friday?"

Did Pam have lunch with liars? Oh, God... "Hey, Pam. Yeah, we're still on for lunch. I need to talk to you. I mean, I *really* need to talk to you."

"Did you have another shitty date?"

If only Collin had been an asshole extraordinaire, this would be so much easier. "Not exactly."

"Okay, so talk. What's wrong?"

"I had sex. The best sex I think I've ever had."

Pam whistled into the phone. "Did you get new batteries for B.O.B.? This calls for a celebration!"

Cadence would have laughed at Pam's crack about her prudish nature if this involved anything prude like. "No, I had it with a real live guy."

"Guuuurrrlll! Go on with your bad self! How the hell did this happen? Last I knew you hadn't met anyone you even liked enough to have *two* cups of coffee with."

Damned coffee... "It just happened. I don't know why it happened or how we got from a coffee shop to his bed. It just did."

Her cackle was maniacal. "Beats B.O.B., don't it?"

With a stick... "Yes, yes, it beats B.O.B. That's not the problem, Pam. I have a serious problem and it isn't just that I had sex three minutes into my first date ever with this guy. It's that he's a werewolf!"

Silence.

Cadence waited for Pam to digest.

"I don't see the problem, Cady. Your clan isn't against inter-species relationships. I would think that's obvious, seeing as they adopted your black ass and they're white."

"No, I don't mean my family will object either." Crap, how was she just going to say this and not cringe when the words left her mouth?

"Was the sex bad?"

Oh, no, no, no. "No. It was pretty hot. Actually, it was more than hot. It was amazing. I know I'm not the most experienced girl of the millennium. I know I have trouble leaving my morals back in the eighteenth century, but this was a whole different kind of sex than I've ever had."

"Does he feel the same way?"

"I think so."

"I'm not seeing the problem. So why don't you just tell me what it is so we can stop beating the shit out of this dead horse?"

Say it, Cadence. Get it over with. "He thinks *I'm* a werewolf too." There. Done. No looking back.

"Say again?"

Cadence grimaced. "He thinks I'm a werewolf too, damn it, and now I'm in a bind I can't get out of!"

Pam's screech of horror hurt Cadence's ear. "Are you fucking nuts, Cady?"

Macadamia for sure. "Yes, yes, I'm nuts! I don't know why I did it. I just did. He was so damned hot on that stooopid site you sent me to. I couldn't help myself. Look, go to your computer and I'll send you his picture. I'm telling you, you'll see just what I mean. He's irresistible." Cadence clicked on the picture she'd saved of Collin and forwarded it to Pam.

"You get it?"

"Yep, I got it and yep, he's real cute, but he's a werewolf, Cady. A dog. Canine. You are a *vamp-ire*," she emphasized. "Why can't you just tell him that?"

"Because he specified in his profile that he only wanted to date other dogs! I can't believe I've done this, Pam. What the hell was I thinking?"

"Shoot, Cady, I don't know but I'm no priest. You're confessing to the wrong person here. Why not just tell him the truth?"

Oh, sure. After she'd lied like a pro. "Then he'll dump me."

"Not if he really likes you."

"Don't werewolves have some sort of pack rules or something? I mean, can't they only mate for life with another werewolf?"

"I don't know. I can't say as I watch much of the Discovery Channel these days to find out. He's half human if he's a shifter. Maybe the same rules don't apply. I do know that you ain't no werewolf, and when the time comes to shift, your pearly whites and gossamer bat wings are going to give you away, Mistress of the Dark."

"Gee, thanks, Pam, for being so damn supportive." Cadence knew Pam was right, but it hurt just the same.

"Hey! I got yer back, but your back has no fur this time. I'm just stating the obvious, Cady. You have to tell him the truth. There's no getting around it."

* * *

"I said I'd have it done by the end of the month, God damn it! Have I ever fucking screwed you when I give you a date?" Collin barked into the phone. He ran an impatient hand over his stubbled chin and listened to the drone of the voice at the other end.

"Don't bark at me, Collin," came the unfalteringly calm reply. "You know the deal. Now get it the fuck done and get busy giving me the updates I was promised when you went off on this half-assed, bullshit wild goose chase! We need her and we need her soon."

The click on the other end left a resonant buzz in his ear and fury in his veins.

Collin threw the phone at the wall with a violent flick of his wrist and watched as the shiny, black pieces cracked and splintered, scattering on his bedroom floor.

Dick.

Collin reached for the bottle of antacids he'd bought yesterday and poured some into his hand, popping the palm full in his mouth and crunching them into oblivion. The chalky aftertaste made him wander to the kitchen and pull out a beer from the fridge. Opening it and clamping his lips around the neck, he drank until it was bone dry.

The sound of his inbox tinkling drew him to the living room where his laptop sat on the beat up old coffee table he'd found at a thrift store.

Cadence calling…

Collin opened the e-mail and his lips cracked a reluctant smile. She knew how to fuck with a guy's innards, and the last bit of pissed off he had left from his phone call vanished when he read she'd agreed to meet him for dinner.

Visions of her gorgeous body, naked, willing, erotic, flooded his vision. The sweet taste of her nipples lingered on his tongue. Her thighs parted, her pussy glistening, the juices of her desire drove his senses to overload. His cock hardened if he let her linger in his mind. Her chocolate brown eyes, alive with laughter, darker in passion, gnawed at his gut, eating away at his defenses.

When she shuddered after they made love, Collin wanted to hold her until she slept, soothe and consume her all at once. When she lay beneath him in the dark of his bedroom, rounded, full, lush, he wanted to lock her up and keep her there until he could exorcise her from his every thought. When he kissed her ripe cherry red lips, he wanted to devour them. Each taste of Cadence that Collin took made him hungrier, greedier for more.

And he didn't know why.

Was there really an explanation for this kind of chemistry? The kind that simmered and burned just beneath the surface, spattering and spilling over into a rolling boil he seemed to have absolutely no control over?

He'd had girlfriends in the past. Shit, he'd even had a wife way back when, but he'd never had this kind of voracious, insatiable need to spend every spare moment with anyone like he did with Cadence.

What had begun innocently enough was turning into something decadent, forbidden, headed for disaster. Collin didn't do fucking one-night stands.

Well, he reasoned, it hadn't been a one-night stand. It had been explosive as he'd watched Cadence's lips wrap around the rim of a coffee cup. Something had taken hold of him in that coffee shop and gripped his balls with an iron vice. One minute they were talking and the next they were heading to his apartment.

Now, they were decidedly involved. Collin didn't get involved unless it suited his purposes. Yet, here he was, going against all of his ingrained rituals. Bucking every friggin' rule he'd given himself about getting involved.

Half of his sexually, intellectually overworked brain almost didn't give a flying fuck. He hadn't been lying when he'd told Cadence adults did this all the time, and he wasn't lying when he'd told her he wanted more.

But that was a week ago. He sure as shit didn't plan on *still* wanting more much. Maybe this would burn itself out in a couple of weeks and he could skip the fuck back off to where he'd come from with little or no guilt.

He clicked on her picture. The picture from the site he'd saved to a file on his laptop. She was so damned fine his groin twitched in response to just a grainy picture.

Smart too. Cadence was sharp.

Having a conversation with her was as easy as breathing. It was mental gymnastics keeping up with her, and that was a new experience for him. He didn't spend much time talking to women who knew so much. It could be his job kept him from doing that often, or the women he'd dated didn't find much interest in what he did.

Cadence did. She was like a walking encyclopedia of knowledge and it intrigued him.

Once again he thought, *fuuuuuuuuck*.

Collin couldn't get enough of Cadence and that wasn't supposed to be a part of the plan right now. But he couldn't go through with it, and that meant Collin was seriously fucked.

* * *

Pam's words came back to haunt her later that evening while she and Collin strolled through the mall after dinner and saw a stand with some calendars. They'd seen each other every day for the last week, in one fashion or another, and the more time they spent together, the more Cadence shoved her guilt aside in favor of Collin's ongoing company. He'd kept true to his word about their liaison being more than just a one-night stand. It had turned into a week-long stand and then some.

He was standing at one of the many racks that held all kinds of calendars, flipping through it. "Hey, look. The full moon is in two weeks."

Oh, good. Maybe they could howl together under it. Woof-woof.

Cadence gave him an absent smile and chose to focus instead on his cute ass in tight, faded blue jeans. A full moon was when packs ran together. Maybe she could lie some more and say that her pack had plans that night?

"Did you hear me, Cadence?"

"I did."

Pulling her nearer, Collin whispered in her ear, "The moon will be full in two weeks. Will you show me?"

"Show you what?" Dumb. She would just play dumb.

His chuckle rumbled in her ear. "When you shift."

Cadence turned into the solid warmth of his body and winked. "I'll show you mine if you show me yours."

His expression changed for a fleeting moment, then returned to its usual playful grin. "I think I've shown you mine plenty."

A giggle bubbled in her throat. "Oh, and I was fully clothed?"

Collin pressed a kiss to her lips. "Speaking of clothes. We have too many on."

"You want me to disrobe right here in the mall? People will talk."

"Then let's go back to my apartment where we can't hear them."

Cadence gave him a sly grin, thankful his talk of all things lunar had passed, even if it was only momentary and sure to come back to haunt her later. "I'll race you to that truck of yours."

"You're on," he called over his shoulder as he took long strides toward the double doors of the exit.

Cadence blew a breath out of the side of her mouth and raced after him. *Keep distracting him with sex, Cady. That'll do ya.*

Damn, Cadence thought briefly when, ten minutes later, Collin elicited a groan from her with hands that were still new and exciting. Werewolves were insatiable. They hadn't even made it into the elevator of Collin's apartment building, and they already had their tongues firmly planted in one another's tonsils.

His lips seared hers, burning them with the kiss of his lust. His tongue found her own, warring with it, sliding its silken surface along hers until she arched against him, shifting her legs between the muscled steel of his. Collin's hands splayed over the soft swell of her belly, tracing small circles around her navel through her thin skirt, dipping into the waistband of it, then pulling back.

Cadence tore her lips from his with a whimper of discontent. "Collin," she rasped as he pressed her against the wall of the elevator.

"Cadence?" he replied, his voice throbbing and smoky in the small space.

"Maybe waiting until we get into your apartment would be prudent, considering our rather revealing location?"

His warm hand wrapped around hers, placing it on the bulge of cock, now prominently displayed in a large outline beneath his jeans. Collin groaned as he rubbed it over his flesh, pushing into her hand, guiding her. "*This* is all that's prudent."

She chuckled into his mouth when the elevator dinged and the doors opened. "I think you'll have to wait, Mr. AKC. It would seem we've arrived, and we have company." Collin ignored her, keeping her hand in his and tugging her behind him as they wormed their way past the small crowd of giggling teenagers and down his hallway.

Slipping the key in the lock, Collin popped the door open and pulled her into his apartment right behind him. He swung her around and pressing her up against the door, shutting it behind them with a bang. His body covered hers, hard, chiseled and hot to her cooler skin. A rushing heat slithered up her spine, resting in her nipples and setting them ablaze with the need for Collin's mouth.

His eyes were unreadable, dark and piercing, as he let his hands roam over her abundant curves, watching her intently.

Collin wasted no time in relieving her of her clothes as his confident hands tugged her sweater up and over her head and nimble fingers unclasped the front of her bra with a simple tug. Her breasts hit the cool air and Collin cupped them, bending his head to snake his tongue out over the rigid flesh.

Cadence hissed as he laved each nipple, pushing her breasts together and kneading them with impatient hands. Heat, sweet and sharp, hit her cunt and she let her fingers slide into his mouth, running them over the silk of his tongue, circling his lips. Collin rolled a nipple in his mouth, tugging it between his lips.

Her hips bucked as she strained to press him closer, burying her hands in his thick hair and arching into him. She gasped when Collin slid his hand along her thigh and under her skirt, pushing her panties out of the way and sliding a finger between the plump lips of her pussy. Deft fingers spread her swollen flesh with ease and fondled her clit.

Cadence cried out when Collin inserted a finger into her slick passage and drew back with a long pull, pushing into her in agonizingly slow strokes. She came instantly, writhing against him, forcing his finger to move with rapid fire strokes. Hands that had been immobile now clasped the bulk of Collin's thick shoulders, shrugging his jacket off, tearing at the shirt he wore, yanking his jeans open and reaching in to stroke the cock that made Cadence wet with the mere thought of it.

Stroking him, she let the hard shaft, thick and pulsing, glide in the tunnel of her hand. Grasping it, she ran her fingers over the smooth head of his cock.

Collin ground against her, kicking off his pants and pulling his underwear off, leaning into her, capturing her lips with a kiss that seared her mouth.

Cadence tore free of him and planted her hands on his lean hips, sweeping kisses along his chest, brushing his nipples as her tongue roamed over the rigid lines in his stomach until the throbbing shaft rested against her lips. She let her mouth engulf his cock, fighting a small cry of victory when his hands knotted in her hair and he hissed her name.

A slow descent of tongue and moisture was the path Cadence chose, taking his cock deeply between her lips and driving down on the hard flesh with a painstaking glide. Her fingers dug into his tight ass, forcing him deeper into her mouth, licking at him, sliding over the head of his rigid flesh, cupping his balls now tightly drawn up against his body.

Collin's hand moved to the top of her head, gripping her hair, pushing her mouth toward him, driving into it until she heard him say through clenched teeth, "Stop! Stop, Cadence. I need to fuck you now." Collin hauled her up against him, his voice gritty and hard. "Bend over the back of the couch, Cadence."

Ripples of electricity wove a new kind of lust in Cadence, and she responded by following his command and crossing the room to splay herself across the back of his couch. Her heart slammed against her ribs in anticipation of his hot cock driving into her. Cadence braced her hands in front of her, quivering with a desire that ruled her senses.

Collin was immediately behind her, trailing kisses that were wet and hot along her spine, hooking his thumbs into the waistband of her skirt and dragging it over her hips. The rasp of his tongue slid over her ass, between her legs, darting out to caress her clit before he rose behind her and let his cock slide between her trembling thighs.

His presence was heated, electric and blistering as his muscled frame wedged against hers sprawled on the back of the couch. His strokes were slow, letting the juice of her cunt wet the thick rod. Cadence lifted her ass high, feeling his hard abdomen against it, finding herself on the brink of begging Collin to fuck her.

She didn't have to beg.

Collin entered her with a growl, his strong arms trembling as he gripped her hips and drove upward into the fire slick passage. Her pussy clamped around his cock instantly, taking her breath away. Her fingers clutched wildly at the cushions of his old couch. The fit was snug and deliciously wicked as he plunged into Cadence. She was at his mercy and her senses reeled from it.

He demanded her response to his strokes, lifting her hips hard against him, draining her of her last will to hold back for more.

Cadence came with a silent scream on her lips. It clung to her throat and picked up speed when she felt Collin tense behind her. His thighs grew harder against the backs of her own, his grip tighter on her hips, his roar of release harsh as he spilled his seed in her with one last forceful stroke.

Collin drew her to him, wrapping his arms around her waist, still inside her, cupping her breasts and pressing his jaw to her neck.

Cadence's arm immediately wrapped around his head as they both took gulps of air into their lungs.

"Cadence?" he rasped in her ear.

"Collin?"

"That wasn't half bad."

Her grin spread across her face. "Yeah, I guess it was okay."

"Just okay?"

"Well, not *half bad*."

The rumble in his chest vibrated against her back. "All right, it was pretty good."

"Yeah," she responded absently. "It was pretty good. I was wondering if you were ever going to have your way with me like that."

Collin's body stiffened behind hers. "Whaddaya mean, like *that*?"

"You know, from behind. Don't all werewolves like to do it from behind? Ya know, doggie style?"

"Haven't you been with your own kind before? Did they all do it doggie style?"

Oh. Her own kind. Like the kind that wasn't really hers. Woof, woof. Shit. When would she learn to drink a cup of shut-the-fuck-up? "Contrary to popular belief, I haven't been with many before you."

Collin withdrew from her and turned her to face him. "Good. I don't know why I'm glad to hear that, but I am."

It pleased her to no end that he was happy she was such a novice. If he only knew how many centuries she'd been hanging around all novice like.

"Tell me about your family. You said you were adopted. Your pack is white?"

Um, oy. More lies… "Yes, they're white." She couldn't bring herself to call her clan a pack. It was like denying who they were.

Brushing her hair from her face, he asked, "Where did they adopt you from?"

Oh, this was just insane. *Tell him, Cady, m'love, before you get in even deeper.* "A church, believe it or not. It's really pretty clichéd, huh?"

In the eighteenth century, but a church nonetheless. Her grandmother had found her. Thank God for Grandma's acute vampire senses back then. They weren't as good now, but they had saved Cadence from a death that was sure to have been painful. Drained and nearly dead, Cadence's adoptive grandmother had taken her home and handed her to her daughter Leticia and her husband Martin.

Her parents, like many vampires, were unable to conceive. Despite Cadence's obvious differences, they'd raised her like they'd given her their own DNA and, most of all, they adored her.

"That is pretty clichéd, but nice. I didn't mean to dredge up anything painful," he said, kissing the tip of her nose.

Cadence shook her head at him. "I don't remember it, so it isn't something that troubles me now. My parents are my parents and they love me. I love them. It's that simple." The not so simple part was they weren't fucking baying at the moon anytime soon.

"I'd like to meet them sometime." His request was perfectly natural, normal even, considering how involved they were becoming, she supposed.

But for fuck's sake, it just couldn't happen. Maybe she could fake it?

Oh, good. That worked. Hey, Ma, could ya pretend you like your steaks rare and howling at the moon has meaning? How about you don't shave your legs for the next millennium so we can make like we're furry?

Cadence's stomach clenched. "I'm sure they'd like that," she said noncommittally as she slipped under his arms and went to his bathroom to clean up.

"What about your fam—er, pack? What are they like?"

Collin had followed her into the bathroom and he took the cloth from her, washing it under the warm water flowing from the faucet and running it between her legs. His ministrations were gentle and so tender Cadence felt shittier than ever. "My family is a lot like yours, I'd suspect. Nothing out of the ordinary."

"Is it that they don't like other shifters?"

His gaze was questioning as he washed himself too. "What do you mean, *other shifters?*"

"Well, your profile said 'werewolves only need apply.' I thought maybe they didn't like inter-species stuff. You know, vampires and werewolves hooking up and making baby werebats or whatever."

Collin turned away and his hard jaw clenched. Cadence watched the tic in his jaw and thought about why he was so tense when they talked about his family. She could almost taste his tension.

Ahhhh, maybe that was the trouble. Werewolves didn't want were-bats messing up their family tree.

"Yeah, they kind of want me to stick to my own, I guess. It doesn't matter because you're a werewolf."

Yeah, that was her. She-wolf at large. Oh God, the guilt would chew at the lining of her stomach if she had one.

Encircling her waist, Collin pulled her to him. "I had a thought just now."

Reaching between them, she latched onto his cock, growing in size again. "Does it have to do with some more of what we just barely made it out of the elevator for?"

His groan was low, feral, filled with renewed desire. "Sort of. We've been pretty hot and heavy with each other for over a week unprotected, Cadence. Shouldn't we be more careful in the future?"

Birth control... did werewolves worry about that like humans? Vampires didn't have to worry overly much because they couldn't get a disease, and they sure as hell didn't procreate very well. So she hadn't been thinking in terms of preventing something very unlikely from happening.

Fuck.

Then a thought hit her. A factoid she'd garnered from the Discovery Channel. "There are specific seasons to mate for wolves and possibly make babies, Collin. You know that. I have to be in heat to do it." Thank God for the Discovery Channel online.

"Are you?"

"Am I what?"

"In heat?"

Oh, she was in something. And it was hot, and deep. Some deep, hot shit. "No, silly," she replied as if she knew what the hell she was talking about. "I won't be in heat until later this year. Didn't those shifter discriminating parents of yours teach you the birds and bees of werewolves?"

His chuckle was deep and like honey as he molded her to him and kissed her again. "I think I've got a pretty good handle on the whole sex-ed thing."

Cadence sighed when he took her breast in his hand and ran his fingers over her nipple. Yep, he had a handle on it.

She had to tell him soon, she thought fleetingly. But when he captured her lips for a kiss that stole her breath, Cadence forgot all about the coming full moon and working on her howling.

Chapter Five

"This is CC for the Nocturnal Journals, your lifeline to the nighttime, on B 105.5 FMMMMMMMMMM on your listening dial. Hey, all you night dwellers—tonight's topic, one-night stands. Anybody out there had one? Of course you have! Anybody out there had a successful relationship as a result of one? Talk to me, Milwaukee. I wanna hear it all. The good and the oh so baaaaad."

Cadence clicked off her microphone while the station went to commercial and hung her head in her hands. Why she tempted fate like this she'd never understand. She was virtually asking her listening audience at large to tell her their horror stories so she could hear firsthand how doomed she and Collin were. It would bring nothing but trouble and plant more seeds of doubt in her head. She already had a flower garden in full bloom residing in her brain.

She and Collin had been spending every available moment together, and when they weren't nailing each other, they were e-mailing each other. It was bound to fizzle, yes? How long could an attraction this smokin' hot survive?

How long can you continue to pretend you're a werewolf, you lying sack of shit?

Cadence groaned. Not much longer. She didn't have much time until the full moon, and he'd want her to shift with him. The specifics of this ritual jaunt were a bit blurry for Cadence, but she knew that, come the full moon, werewolves shifted together and Collin would fully expect that she run with him.

She hated to run.

Maybe she could tell him her sports bra was in the wash?

She could kick herself for not asking about the details of it, but she'd been afraid to stir up too much suspicion. If she were a werewolf, she'd know all there was to know about this full moon nonsense.

She had to tell him and she'd only told herself that a million times since they met. But after he'd said his parents wouldn't be so thrilled about an inter-shifter mating for their son, well, it solidified that not only was she a friggin' liar, but she was making some trouble for Collin he didn't want or need. Worst of all, trouble he didn't deserve.

According to Animal Planet, this pack shit was serious. Packs formed for life and they didn't bond with bats. Alpha males found their Alpha females and that was, in essence, that.

Of course, Animal Planet wasn't taking into account the fact that Collin's breed of werewolf was half human. Maybe those rules didn't apply to the shifter crew.

Who did she know that was a werewolf? Or even hairy enough to qualify as one?

Nobody.

What difference did it make? She just wasn't a werewolf and that was that.

Maybe she could let the hair on her legs grow…

Cadence rolled her head on her shoulders and blew out a frustrated breath. No amount of Rogaine would help. No amount of watching werewolf flicks was going to magically make her one either.

No matter how great it'd been getting her ya-yas off, she was eventually going to have to tell Collin the truth. And though they had no official commitment to one another, Cadence knew it would be over. Collin wasn't the kind of guy who'd stand for a lie, let alone the whoppers she was making up as she went along.

If her vampire instincts were good for anything, they were good at reading someone's moral fiber and Collin had plenty of that. He didn't much like liars.

Cadence groaned again and swung her chair over to the lit up switchboard to answer phone calls.

She *had* to tell him.

* * *

It was bound to happen.

And it did.

In the most out of the way place.

Quite by accident and like most circumstances do when you're a fucking bold-faced liar, covering your tracks left and right and keeping secrets the size of Montana.

Collin and Cadence were happily in their corner of an out of the way, small Italian café, huddled together and sharing some fettuccini when her name, sharp and crystal clear, was called.

"Cadence? Cadence Cranston?" a voice, none too quiet, yelled.

Cadence's head bobbed up, smacking into Collin's because they were sitting that close to one another. Her eyes focused on a vaguely familiar, round shape making its way to their table.

"Oh, Cadence! It's so wonderful to see you. Your grandmother was just telling us all she hadn't seen you in a couple of weeks and now I know why!"

Eudora. Eudora Livingston. One of her grandmother's poker/knitting circle buddies and a fellow bat-girl.

Well, fuck.

Cadence inwardly cringed, but outwardly rose to give Eudora a kiss and introduce her to Collin. "Collin, this is Eudora Livingston. Eudora, Collin Grayson."

"Your...?"

"Um, my — my — *friend*."

Eudora's laugh was deep and rumbly as she patted Collin on the back and took the hand he offered. "Look at you! Aren't you a nice looking boy?"

Collin smiled and thanked her. "It's nice to meet you. Are you a friend of Cadence's?" His inquiry was innocent enough, yet somehow it left Cadence feeling something she couldn't quite pinpoint.

Eudora's smile was wide. "I've known Cady since she was a little one. Such a blessing to her parents. I play poker with her grandmother, every Friday night like clockwork."

Collin chuckled. "Poker, huh? I like poker. Maybe I could drop in sometime and get in on a hand?"

Oh Christ and a sidecar. Cadence grimaced and stumbled around in her muddled brain for something to say. "We'd love to have you, Collin. I know Cady's grandmother would anyway. Oh, Cadence, I can't believe your grandmother couldn't sense this."

Cadence's glance flashed between Collin and Eudora. Collin's eyebrows rose as he disentangled his hand from Eudora's. Cadence giggled with a nervous twitter and jumped in between them. "Well, you know Grandma. She's pretty good, but sometimes she misses things."

Eudora's eyes sparkled, blue and crinkling at the edges. "How could she have missed *this*? You have a beau. That's not something she's not likely to be able to tap into, miss."

Eudora's question had an astonished tone to it and she was right. Grandma knew everything. If Grandma sensed a shift in Cadence's aura, she would know. It could explain why she'd called Cadence ten times in the past two weeks, wanting to know what she was up to.

Cadence shrugged her shoulders and tried to keep the panic out of her voice, even if her chest felt like it was going to explode. "I dunno, Eudora. I've been pretty busy lately so I've missed our Tuesday night get-togethers." Avoid, avoid, avoid is what she'd been doing.

Eudora clucked her tongue and patted Collin on the back again. "I don't get it. I don't think she's ever not been right on the money in all the centuries I've known her."

"Centuries?" Collin tilted his head and looked at Cadence for an answer.

Cadence grabbed Eudora by the arm and swung her around to face her husband, Arnold, who was waiting patiently by the door of the café to leave. "Look, Eudora, Arnold looks like he wants to go and you know what he's like when he misses Oprah."

Eudora snorted. "That man. We've been married for two hundred years now. I don't know what he did before Oprah showed up."

Cadence gave Eudora a quick kiss on her cheek and waved at Arnold. "Well, you'd better hurry up or he's going to pitch a fit."

Eudora hugged Cadence and whispered in her ear, "Is this our little secret, Cady? If you haven't told your grandmother, I suspect you're not ready to."

Relief flooded Cadence's stomach. "Do you mind, for now anyway? At least until I know where it's going? You know what they're like. They'd just badger me to bring him over and I don't know if I'm ready to."

Eudora gave her an affectionate pat on the back. "No, Cady, I don't mind. Is it because he's, well, you know, er, white? You must know I don't think your family would care."

A tear stung Cadence's eye. No, her family wouldn't mind. They were the least narrow minded people she knew. It was Collin's family that would, and it wouldn't be because she was black. "I know, Eudora. That's not it at all. I just don't know where we're going with this yet."

"Good on you, Cady. I'm glad you've found someone you like. Mum's the word, sweetie."

Cadence sighed as she watched Eudora zip around the tables and latch onto Arnold. Turning back to Collin, she let the worry of running into Eudora seep from her face and slapped on a smile. She slide back into her seat, her hand trembled slightly as she picked her fork back up and began to twirl her pasta.

"Soooo, Cad-yyy. She's your grandmother's friend?"

Cadence smiled and stuck her tongue out at him for mocking her about her nickname. "Yeah, they knit and, of all things, play poker together every week."

"How old is your grandmother? She must've been a young one because that woman didn't look a day over forty at most," he observed.

Oh, yes. The old vampire thing. They didn't age much. Crap. Here we go, yet another lie to add to your coffer, Cady. Go on, you're soooo good at it now. "Good genes?"

He tilted her chin up and held her eyes with his. "What did she mean by centuries?"

Dumb, dumb and dumber. "Centuries?" Had that come out squeaky? *Of course it did, you're a liar, dipshit.*

"Yeah, she said she'd known your grandmother for centuries."

Lowering her eyes to her pasta, she said, "It's just an expression. You know, like we've known each other forever?"

"Yes. I know exactly what you mean."

What did that mean? Exactly? He knew exactly what she meant? He knew she was a lying piece of shit, or he knew the expression? "Do you?" Her voice wobbled a bit and her words were spoken with soft tones.

"Yeah, I do. It kinda reminds me of us. Feels like I've always known you."

Her smile was coy. "Really? Huh, that's a pretty big admission for a guy who doesn't say much." Cadence's stomach settled back into place, glad that the conversation had taken a different turn.

Twining his fingers with hers, Collin grunted, the soft lighting of the café highlighting his squared jaw. "I'm not much for the girlie, share your feminine side bullshit. You're right about that. But I can admit when I feel a connection."

Cadence squeezed his hand. "You waaay like me," she teased.

"Yeah, you're okay for a girl."

"Yeah? Well, you're okay for a stinky boy."

"You wanna consummate our newfound like?"

"Sex, sex, sex. Is that all you can think about?"

"Sure seems like it lately."

His honest admission made her burst out laughing. "Maybe it's just the sex and we'll fizzle out?"

"Maybe, but I don't think so."

She'd damn herself later for asking, but she had to know. "What is it exactly that you're looking for, Collin?" When she thought about it, she didn't know many details about him. He freelanced as a writer, lived in an apartment that would make Martha Stewart cringe and he was a werewolf with a family that wanted him to meet his werewolf mate.

"Do you mean in life?"

"Sure, life, the future… from me…"

"Life? I just want to find my own piece of the pie, I guess. You know, the American Dream. From you? Another shot at trashing some more of your panties," he said with a grin that defined lascivious. "The future? I want a big screen TV. You know, the flat screen, high definition kind," he said with a cocky grin.

"So you just want to bang until we tire of each other?"

His face grew serious and his jaw clenched again, much like it did when they talked about anything too personal. "I don't know what will happen with us, Cadence. The only thing I do know for sure is this, I think about you all the fricken' time. I can't get enough of you and I haven't ever felt like that *before* you. It isn't that I just want to screw your brains out. That's a perk I won't deny is great to have, but it isn't everything. I like talking to you. I like being with you. I like hearing your views on anything and everything. Do I want to hear that you aren't seeing anyone else, yeah, I do. I can't explain why, but it would make me fucking nuts if you were playing the dating game on that site. Right now, that's what I have to offer."

Well, okay, then. That was honest enough and she was in no position to say otherwise because she was a liar. Oy. "I'm not seeing anyone else, Collin, and I haven't been back to the site since I met you."

"I won't say that doesn't make me happy, Cadence."

Ahh, but will you say it's the same way for you? she wondered.

"I haven't been back there either."

Whew. Nice save. "What made you join the site anyway? I mean, you're attractive and you have a job. Why did you resort to online dating?"

"Why did you?"

"I work primarily alone, Collin. I'm a DJ at night. I don't meet too many people, but the occasional night staff. They're mostly college students that don't interest me. I don't have a hunky co-host. There's no happy hour we all get together at and bond, know what I mean? My options are limited to bars and the produce section at the grocery store. I don't shop much," she joked.

"I was tired of meeting the same people over and over. I wanted to meet someone who wants what I want out of life."

Yeah, a werewolf was what he wanted out of life. You are a vampire. Can you spell that, Cady? V-a-m-p-i-r-e. Vampire. Say it with me, now. Vampire. As opposed to werewolf. Double-you-e-r-e-double-you-o-l-f. Werewolf. Like the one in London. Big difference, night dweller. Cadence shoved the ever present warning of her conscience firmly away. "Have you ever dated a human?"

He bent his dark head when he replied. "Yep."

"And? It didn't work out because your parents want you to date werewolves?"

"No, it didn't work out because it didn't work out. I can and do date whomever I want, Cadence. My parents won't have a say in the end. I put werewolves in my profile because…" He paused for a mere moment, making Cadence's acute senses flutter. "Because it seemed like the easiest route. You know, to meet one of your kind, er, one of *our* kind."

Right. *Our kind* being the kind who didn't lie like a Persian rug. Oh, God, she had to tell him.

"Hey, let's go back to my place and watch a movie," he said, pulling his wallet out to pay for the check the waiter had discreetly left on the corner of the table.

Okay, so now didn't have to mean now. Like right now. Now could mean a little bit later. "Yeah, let's do that, but I'm not watching *Gladiator* again, Collin. It's my turn to pick and I pick anything but *Gladiator*."

Grabbing her hand, he pulled her to him. "Like it really matters anyway. We haven't finished a single movie since we began seeing each other."

She tweaked his side with a playful pinch. "Sex, sex, sex, it's all about the sex, Mr. AKC."

Collin wiggled his eyebrows and grinned, that boyish grin he let slip sometimes when he wasn't keeping it to himself. "Yeah, so let's go do that, you know, sex, sex, sex thing," he whispered, convincing her that she could wait just a little longer to tell him the truth.

As they made their way out to his truck, Cadence caught a glimpse of the moon in the dark of the sky.

Another week or so and it would be full.

And she would be, essentially, fucked.

Fan-tab-u-lous-ly, royally ruined.

She had to tell him.

Just not right now.

Chapter Six

"I think I'm in love."

"That's nice, Cady. I can tell by the dreamy look on your face it's love. Love is a many splendored thing, chica. However, it might not be so splendiferous when you go into it lying like Pinocchio," Pam reminded her.

Oh, yeah, there was that.

"So when do you plan to tell the nice, furry guy you ain't no werewolf?"

The twelfth of never seemed a suitable time frame. "Um, soon?"

"Yeah, soon seems to be the right answer. Cady, you can't go on like this. You just can't. If what you say is true and werewolves shift when the moon is full as like some sort of ritualistic, bonding thing, you'd better either get hairy quick, or tell him, because you've got two days to do it."

Two days and it would be over. Two days and Collin would be using the word liar like it was her first name. Two days and she would lose the man she was falling in love with because she was a bat, not a werewolf. "Don't you think I know that, Pam? I think about it every waking moment and then, I have horrible dreams about me out under the full moon with him, squeezing hard to try and shift into something I'm not! I know I have to tell him. I just don't know how."

Pam flicked her napkin across the table at Cadence with annoyance. They were sharing a pint of blood at Cadence's kitchen table, while trying to figure out what the hell to do next. "Oh, I know how, Cady, and so do you. You say, 'Hey, Collin. I'm a big fucking liar. I don't like steak and I don't prey on small woodland creatures. I'm not a werewolf like I've led you to believe all of this time. I'm a vampire. A bat, essentially, and when

I shift, I have wings and fangs and I drink blood.' That's what you tell him, Cady, and you'd better do it soon."

Cadence laid her head on her kitchen table and scrunched her eyes shut. She supposed if vampires got headaches, she'd have a migraine by now. "I know, I know," she whimpered into the cool Formica.

Pam got up, the chair legs scraping on the linoleum as she did. She lifted Cadence's head and looked her directly in the eye. "Guurrl, you keep saying you know, but you haven't done jack shit to make it right. I'm your friend and I just want you to be happy, but I don't want you to base that happiness on a lie. Even if you were able to escape the full moon thing, you'd have to tell him eventually. How long do you think you can keep hiding the fact that you drink blood for nourishment?"

"I like Pepsi…"

"Yeah, so do I, but it won't keep me undead for very long and it won't keep you that way either, Cady."

Point.

"Maybe he won't care, Cady. Maybe he's as nuts about you as you are about him and a little thing like being a vampire isn't going to faze him. He might be pissed at first, but he can't ignore the connection you've made."

Maybe. Doubtful, but maybe.

"Cadence Cranston, get a fucking grip, would you? This guy likes you just as you are. Well, *almost* just as you are. He likes the person you are. He likes talking to you. He obviously likes twisting your panties in a knot. He likes spending time with you. So why wouldn't he like you despite the fact that you're a vampire? You have all of these elements working in your favor and if you added the truth to them, this could be it."

Oh, it would be *it*, all right. The *over* kind of it.

Pam let her head flop back on the table. "I'm done trying to talk some sense into you. I have to go meet Larry for our bowling tournament. Call me when you need my shoulder to sob on, and you will, Cady. If you don't get this over with, you will. Bye, Elvira." Pam left, her words ringing in Cadence's ears.

She would need a shoulder to cry on.

That was okay. Pam had big shoulders.

* * *

Collin slugged back his second beer and looked at his watch. He'd better get his ass in gear if he was going to pick up Cadence on time.

His phone chirped. Flipping it open, he frowned into it. "Grayson," he answered in clipped tones.

"Collin? What the fuck is the hold-up here?"

"I can't make the moon full on command, bud. It didn't come with my special super powers welcome kit." *You asshole.*

The crackled laughter over the line made Collin narrow his eyes. "You always were a wiseass, Grayson. Did you make a date to meet her yet?"

He toyed with the peanuts in the bowl on the bar and sighed with exasperation into the phone. "I told you I'd take care of it and I will. Now if you don't stop fucking calling me, there's gonna be a time she catches me on the phone with you and then we're fucked. So get the hell off my back and wait all nice and patient like a good boy." *Dumbass.*

"Yer hangin' by a thread, Collin. This better be the right one and it better be done right," he warned.

Thread this, shit stain. "I told you I'd be in touch in a couple of days when it's done and I will. I gotta go. I'll get back with you in a couple," Collin spat and flipped his phone shut before he could listen to more of his objections. He wasn't going to do it and that was simply that. Fuck him.

A hard thump on his back made Collin swing around on his stool, forgetting his phone call for the moment. "What the—"

"Hey, buddy. Long time no see. How's it goin'?" the half-snockered drunk asked.

It took a minute before he registered with Collin and then, he gave him a good natured thump back. "It's goin' okay. How 'bout you?" Obviously, not much had changed since he'd last run into him. He smelled as drunk as he had the last time they'd spoken.

"Issss good. Hey, you get a date on dat sssite?"

Collin stiffened. "Yeah, yeah, I did and I gotta hurry up and meet her."

He smiled at Collin, watery and lopsided, revealing his chipped corner tooth. "Thasss good. I didn't get one. Bunch of picky vampires out dere, I tell ya. Maybe I'd be better off trying the demon category?" He wobbled forward and his breath fanned Collin's face.

Collin tried to gasp for some clean air without being obvious. "I'm damn sorry to hear that. Who wouldn't want a nice guy like you?"

He shrugged his shoulders and leaned on Collin. His rumpled suit jacket reeked of smoke and a smell Collin didn't want identification for. "I dunno. I jus' know dat dem women should be grateful I sent 'em an e-mail. I'm glad it worked out okay fer you. You got a nice lady werewolf now? You said you was lookin' for a wolf."

Yeah, he had a nice lady werewolf that he'd managed to fall in some serious like with.

Screw like.

He knew it was beyond that and Collin also knew he was in knee-deep crap. Or he would be. How the fuck this had all turned into something much more than he'd bargained for was beyond him. The goals he'd begun with were not the ones he was now left with. "Yeah, man. I got a nice lady," he said, wincing at the words as he spoke them for the first time to anyone out loud. Cadence was nice and he was going to lose her because he was an asshole, but he wasn't going to keep lying to her either.

"Thaaaassss so niiiice. Yer niiiice. You need a nicccee lady. Maybe I'll go back to the site and see if anybody new is there. If you got lucky, then I can toooo," he slurred as he weaved his way back toward the tables near the bathrooms.

Collin threw some money on the bar and ran a hand over his stubbled chin. He'd gotten lucky, all right.

The problem was, he was pretty sure Cadence wouldn't feel the same way.

Chapter Seven

The moon hung low in the sky, full like the ripe belly of an expectant mother, pale and the color of softly whipped butter. It played hide and seek behind the clouds, airy and grey against the black sky. Tomorrow it would be full and Cadence had no plans as to what to do next.

She couldn't keep floating along in this limbo, kidding herself into believing Collin would accept her lies and move on as though she could be considered trustworthy. He'd probably never speak to her again and it made her stomach turn.

How did you do that? Tell someone that nearly every word out of your mouth since you'd met was a lie?

I am not a werewolf, Collin.

I do not like my steak rare.

I like O negative and I have incisors the size of shark's teeth. Fangs, if you will.

But on the plus side—I do really dig the moon. It's pretty. Nighttime is my thang.

Oh, punkin', don't stress. I could always fly beside you while you run beneath the moon…

It wasn't as if she was telling him she was once a man…

This was not helping. What she was doing—had been doing for almost a month now—was lying.

She had to tell Collin and she had to tell him tonight.

Strangely, Collin hadn't said a word about the moon when he opened the door to Cadence and she had taken the opportunity to distract him, even if it was just for a little while by doing what they did almost as well as they conversed.

Boink.

This would more than likely be their last night together.

Unless, of course, a miracle occurred and Collin was sidetracked by something like the parting of the Red Sea.

Unlikely, but there was that thing called hope and something eternal springing up that she could latch onto.

Nevertheless, she intended to make the most of what would likely be the end of the best thing that had happened to her in centuries.

A tear stung her eye, but she was determined to tell him tonight and let the chips fall where they may, but not before she treasured every last moment with him.

She'd cut off any more thought and dove into the task at hand. Now, as their kiss lingered, growing more heated, and their tongues tangled, dipping into one another's mouths, she fought her fear. Cadence caressed his throbbing cock, stroking the satin of it with firm passes of her hand.

Collin stirred against her, thrusting his hard body to hers and cupping her breasts with hands that were forceful and gentle all at once.

He was right, they never finished a movie. They never even made it off the couch. In fact, they weren't even on the couch. They were on Collin's reclining chair. Curled around one another with Cadence draped across his lap. She wormed out of her skirt and slung a thigh over his lap to straddle him.

Clothes flew in their impatience to feel naked flesh. Cadence sighed as her breasts rubbed against his chest, sprinkled with just a bit of crisp, dark hair. His arms wound around her back and he pulled the tip of a cherry red nipple to his mouth, circling it with his tongue and capturing it between his lips.

Her groan overrode the noise from the television as Collin slid between her thighs, leaving her clinging to the back of the recliner while he slinked his way between her legs and parted the wet flesh of her cunt.

His tongue slipped into her, stroking the swollen nub of her clit, evoking small moans of pleasure from her lips. Cadence rocked her hips against the smooth, silken glide of his mouth, letting his tongue fuck her, devour her. Tendrils of heat swept her pussy when he cupped her breasts, thumbing her nipples.

His hair, dark against her belly, was reason enough for Cadence to cradle him to her and she did so with writhing hips, crying out when she came.

Collin wasted no time sitting back up, pulling her down to him and simply unzipping his pants to free his hard cock. He settled her on it with a groan against her neck and soon, they were driving against one another. His hips crashed upward in short, rapid strokes. Cadence gripped him inside her, clamping around him and squeezing his hard, silken length.

Collin's cock pulsed within her, driving deeply, his abdomen scraping her clit when she leaned into him, absorbing the sensuous rhythm they rode.

Gripping his shoulders, Cadence leaned back, letting the sheer invasion of him take over.

"I can't wait anymore, baby. Come with me, Cadence," he demanded, hotly against her ear.

His words skittered along her spine and into her ear, decadent, forbidden and carnal. Cadence howled in response, clinging to Collin. Her orgasm clawing at her until she could no longer stave it off. It was powerful in its force, deeply rooted and roaring in a tidal wave of pleasure.

They came together and Collin held her with arms that were tense, rigid, quivering. Sweat had gathered between them and Cadence stroked her hand over his brow, rocking with him to a beat only the two of them could feel. Tears threatened again when she considered what she had to do. Holding him tight to her, she took a shaky breath and prayed for the words she'd need to convince him that despite their differences, they belonged together.

It wasn't impossible.

Nothing was impossible.

Cadence had to wonder who'd said that. Someone who'd obviously not tried to pretend she was a werewolf.

"Wow," Collin said, pressed to her chest.

She smiled against the top of his head. "Indeed."

Gripping her ass, he kissed her and chuckled. "I think you like me."

"Maybe."

"Oh, there's no maybe about it. It's a definite."

"You like me more."

"Maybe."

"Oh, you do too."

His eyes lifted and held hers. The blue of them grew serious and Cadence couldn't quite pinpoint what was next. "Yeah, I do too and I'd like to talk about that if you don't mind."

Hoo boy, here it came. Full moon talk. Cadence gulped and decided naked probably wouldn't be the best way to tell him she was a vampire… "I don't mind at all, but can we clean up first?"

Kissing the tip of her nose he agreed with a "You got it. I'm going to go dig for a sweatshirt. It's cold tonight. Are you cold?"

No, I'm a liar. OY. "No, I'm fine. Go change and I'm going to wash up."

He slid out from beneath her and headed toward his bedroom. "You know, baby, your skin is always so cool. I would think you were always cold, but you never complain."

Cadence might laugh if the circumstances were different. No, she wasn't ever cold, even in the dead of a Wisconsin winter. Because she was a *vampire*. Not a living, breathing, warm-blooded werewolf. She gripped the edge of the sink for stability.

Oh, this sucked big, fat weenies, but there was nothing left to do. She had to come clean.

Tonight.

Now.

Cadence remained immobile.

Now means put some lead in it, vampire.

She made her way back out to the living room on legs that trembled, with a lump lodged thickly in her throat. She found Collin in the kitchen, rooting around in the fridge.

"I'm going to get a beer. You want one?"

Cadence didn't answer. What was on the television had riveted her and she dug in the recliner to find the remote, turning up the volume.

It was Collin.

On TV.

A bit younger, his hair shorter and more conservative, but that was her Collin.

A voice was narrating a sort of "Where are they now" documentary bit and the announcer posed a question—where is ace reporter Collin Grayson now?

Cadence cocked her head. He was right here in Milwaukee was where he was. Right here in a shitty apartment with his sort of, but not official, girlfriend and, well, it would seem, Collin had some splainin' to do.

Cadence turned the volume up even louder and when she did, she listened in utter astonishment to the speculation about what Collin had been up to since some big story he'd botched had ruined his credibility.

Apparently, at one time, he'd been a pretty noteworthy guy.

Well, huh.

Her confusion grew and so did her anxieties. Were werewolves big-shot reporters on television? It was her experience that most shifters had low-key jobs that kept them out of the limelight. Her job was fairly public, but no one saw her on television everyday. They heard her voice and nothing more. When her show was over, she drove home from her job in the dead of night. No one but the station's owners knew what her real name was. She was CC of the Nocturnal Journals and that was essentially that.

Collin had come to stand by her, a beer in each hand. Looking up at him, she noted his face had taken on a grey cast and his eyes glittered.

Cadence turned to face him. She'd begun to put some of what she hoped were crazy thoughts together in her head and she needed to rein them in until she had answers. "So, got some thoughts on what you've been doing all this time, Collin Grayson, ace reporter? Cuz your public would like to know."

"We need to talk, Cadence" was his answer. Solemn and with a hint of what she was certain was remorse.

"We need to talk about what, Collin? That show says you've been out of circulation for five years in the big bad world of reporting the news. So where ya been and if you're such a big shot, what happened to all of your money? This apartment sure as hell doesn't reflect greenback, Collin." Her voice was rising with each question she asked and her instincts told her this was going to be something she wasn't ready to hear.

Collin's voice was stiff when he spoke. "I have been out of circulation for five years. I've been writing articles under pen names and working for a shitty supermarket rag. That's what I've been doing for five years, Cadence." His words reflected a whole lotta bitter and it seemed to be aimed at her right now.

"I'm thinking I'm supposed to be sorry to hear that and I guess I would be if my radar wasn't telling me the supermarket rag has something to do with our meeting."

"I'm not going to excuse what I do to make ends meet. It's shit," he spat, running his hands over his hair. "Look, Cadence, I lost my job five years ago because a source fucked me over on a big drug ring I'd been investigating. My source was my friend and he led me around by the nose, thinking I was going to have the scoop of the decade because the guy who was heading this drug ring was a United States Congressman. He'd given me plenty of falsified documents, tons of pictures. All sorts of stuff that said this guy was into some crap that shouldn't leave him sitting in his nice brownstone in Georgetown. My *friend* failed to mention the Congressman he had me chasing around was the *wrong* Congressman. Naturally, he had the right one all along. In essence, he scooped me, the bastard, and then, because of the aftereffects of my report, I found out just how influential a nice Congressman with lots of connections can be. I lost my job, my house, my money, my *wife*."

Er, wife? Like the kind with a ring on her finger and his last name? "Whoa, there. A wife? You had a wife and you didn't tell me?" Holy shit. Collin had mentioned girlfriends, but never a wife.

A wife. That was pretty fucking important information in their getting to know each other process.

Sighing with exasperation, Collin paced the small space between them. "Yes, I had a wife. A wife who liked the prestige my job offered and the money it gave her to have fat injected into her lips. When there was no more money and she had to cancel her collagen injections, she split."

Cadence's head spun. A wife. "Do you still love her?" It was agony to ask, but she needed to know what else he might have kept from her.

"Love her? Um, no, Cadence. I don't know that I ever loved her, but I sure the fuck knew I didn't love her when I found her naked in my kitchen with my golf buddy."

Ooooh, that was sooo bad.

Tramp. Whore. Infidel. Jesus!

She felt a moment's pity for Collin before she sat down, trying to catch her breath. "Okay, so tell me, was this wife a werewolf too? You said your family wasn't into inter-shifter romances, so she must have been."

He was silent, looking down at her with that stoic, unreadable expression he seemed to be so damned good at. "My family is dead, Cadence. I don't have a family."

Well, color her confused.

Disoriented.

Knocked for a loop.

And then, it hit her almost at once and connecting the dots to this picture in her head was drawing a clear portrait of exactly what was going on here.

Let's see... reporter plus bad reputation equals needing a really big scoop to seek retribution for said soiled reputation, equals hitting the fucking story jackpot on a dating site for paranormal beings.

After all, the Boogey Man, not to mention Count Dracula and An American Werewolf in London, really *did* exist.

Collin Grayson was no werewolf.

And because she'd spent so much time wallowing in her own guilt over lying, she hadn't been paying attention to the signs he'd given her all along or now, where the blame should really lie.

With Collin.

The non-paranormal Collin.

She'd lied too, no doubt, but she didn't lie in order to eventually hurt anyone else. No one but quite possibly herself.

If Cadence had organs, she'd suppose by now they'd have all stopped working.

Collin was going to get the proof he needed to write a story that was sure to sell to every newspaper and television station across the land and he was going to use her to do it, making her a freak. A spectacle. Hurting her family, forcing them to hide because they were very different.

Cocksucker.

Cadence rose again, her legs shaking in tempo with her voice. "You lying son of a bitch! You're no werewolf, are you? You're a human who spun the wheel and hit shifter-lucky, aren't you?"

Collin's face was tight and his jaw twitched, but he remained in front of her, standing his ground. "Listen to me, Cadence—"

"The fuck I will, you shit!" she interrupted with a shout. "You've been lying to me the entire time we've dated. You were fucking me to get a story, Collin. A big, fat, juicy story to gain back the recognition you'd once enjoyed!"

"No, Cadence! I mean, yes. Yes, I lied, but no, I am not, and was not fucking you for a story." He put a hand on her arm, but Cadence pulled away with a sharp yank.

Oh, bullshit that's not what he'd been doing. "You're a liar, Collin Grayson. You joined that site so you could get a scoop. I don't know how you found out about it, but you did and you were going to expose me and anyone else you could to get back your prestige. Do the real reporters—reporters who are notable and respected—sleep with their exposés, Dan Rather? You fucking story whore! Is that what you're about, Collin? Ruining people's lives so you can reap the kudos for a job well done? For a little fame, maybe?" Her rage had boiled and every last bit of her shook with it as she stood in front of him with her fists clenched to keep from clocking his ass.

His face was pale and his calm approach was tweaking her. "Look, we need to talk about this rationally. I just want you to hear me out, Cadence. All I'm asking is that you listen to me. I don't care about any of it now. Not my job, or the money, or regaining my reputation, but I do care about you."

Her face twisted into a mask of infuriation. "Do you, Collin? I don't think so. I think you care about getting a story. I think *I'm* your story. Ain't you feelin' like you won the story lottery? All your talk about full moons and your pack. How did you intend to pull that off, Collin? You had to tell me sometime. Tomorrow is the full moon. So then what? What would you have done?" Vaguely, she remembered she'd intended to do the same thing, but she shrugged that off in favor of her fury. She was a shifter. She might not be the hairy, meat loving kind, but she was one. Collin was a *human*. An interloper out to expose her family and Cadence just wouldn't allow that.

Shoving his hands in his pockets, he said through clenched teeth, "That was why I wanted to talk to you tonight, Cadence. I don't know what I was going to do, but I wasn't going to let it go on."

"Well, that's mighty fine of you, Collin. You were going to tell me all about the lies you've been feeding me since day one. How very altruistic of you, *reporter*." Cadence stood on her toes and hissed in his face. "I won't let you hurt my family, Collin! They've worked long and hard as vampires…"

Oops. My bad.

Collin's eyes narrowed. "As what?"

Oh, fuck. Double fuck even.

Collin's gaze grew hard and cold. "As what, Cadence?"

Suddenly, the idea that they were both liars was both ironic and infuriating. Fuck Collin Grayson. She was a shifter. She might not be a dog, but he was still a threat to her family and for that, she couldn't forgive him.

"You heard me, Mr. AKC. I'm a fucking *vampire*! Yeah, I lied too, just not with the obvious intent you had. Got that, Peter Jennings? A *vampire*. A bat. A night dweller. I'm surprised with your reporter nose you didn't put that together. I mean, I do a radio show, Collin, called CC and the Nocturnal Journals. It's sort of hiding in plain sight."

"A vampire." His reiteration was cold, distant, but Cadence no longer cared.

"Yep," Cadence said as she strode to his one, lone window streaked with dirt, and turned to take a last look at what a fool she'd been. "A vampire. Pay attention now, you piece of shit, because I'm going to set your little reporter's pen to twitching and I swear to you, Collin, by all that's dear to me. I'll jack you up if you hurt my family!"

Cadence spun around, unable to look at Collin anymore, warring with her anger and the tendrils of sadness that clawed at her.

She concentrated with fierce determination, letting her fury take over and allowing her shift to take control.

In the blink of an eye, Cadence transformed before Collin.

The rapid-fire flutter of her wings echoed throughout his apartment. She flew over and around his head in a wide arc before zeroing in on his window and flitting out into the night.

Cadence left without looking back.

She couldn't bear to look back because it was tangible proof that she was, indeed, a fool for love.

Chapter Eight

"I can't let you go, Collin, and you know that, don't you?" Pam's words were firm, eerily calm and undoubtedly said with the deadliest of intentions while she let her slender hand rest on his forearm.

Collin's bleary eyes assessed Cadence's friend. If he was three sheets to the wind a moment ago, he was now, officially, done with his laundry. He'd been drowning his sorrows in booze when she'd presented herself to him with "Collin? Pam. I'm Cady's best friend and your friendly guide to all things vampire. You are officially toast." She'd then gone on to explain her purpose in this dive.

Sitting up straight on his barstool, he wanted to posture, but found he had little energy left to do much but question the obvious. "So what you're telling me is that in order for me not to die, I have to become one of *you*. Which essentially means—I'm going to die."

"Yep, because I'll see you dead—like the real kind of dead, before I'll let you expose Cadence or her family and you won't be exposing anything if you're one of us, now will ya? You'd be icing your own ass." Her menacing statement was crystal clear. She'd kill him before she'd let him expose her friend.

It was nothing less than he deserved. He was a scumbag for ever thinking he could go through with it to begin with. His writing had never been about wanting to hurt someone else. It was about justice and fair reporting until he'd been fucked over by an unreliable source and blackballed at every major newspaper, television station and magazine worth its weight in font.

All Collin Grayson wanted to do was reenter the world of reporting with a story strong enough to erase the past and give him back his credibility. To have stumbled on what he did in a seedy bar had seemed like just the manna Heaven had denied him so far.

He'd been juiced on the story of the century. Hell, it was the story of the fucking millennium and when that drunk had approached him in the bar that night a few months ago with talk of an online dating site for vampires and werewolves, Collin had thought the guy was about as soused as you could get, but he'd taken that card from him and gone online to research it anyway because the business card looked damned legitimate and the idea of a site like this was too funny not to at least poke around in.

He'd honestly believed that some bunch of nuts had started an online dating site geared toward a paranormal *theme*. Like the idiots who dressed up like vampires and pretended they were night dwellers. He sure as fuck hadn't thought they were anything but groupies, kind of like alien watchers. People convinced aliens were coming to take them away on a particular day and while life moved on around them, they spent all of their days preparing for "unification."

But he'd been wrong, very, very wrong and even now he couldn't believe it.

What he'd found had rendered him speechless. Once he'd gathered his wits, his reporter's instincts had set in and there was no stopping him. It hadn't been easy to fill out the forms to subscribe to Paranormal Mates, but he'd figured it all out.

He wasn't thinking about anything but making some cash, clearing his name in the industry and getting the fuck away from the job at the rag mag he'd hated so much. He never would have sold a story like that to Ronald Atkins at *Tell All*, a cheesy supermarket piece of crap. Collin had artfully strung his smarmy ass along so he could keep collecting a paycheck, with the idea he was going to get the story of the century for Ronald, and good ole Ron had fallen for it.

But he couldn't deny he'd planned to sell it to a reputable source. That was until he'd met Cadence… Everything had changed after that and selling a story hadn't become as important anymore.

But the paranormal really did exist.

Cadence just wasn't a werewolf, she was a vampire. Either way, shifters *did* exist.

And he was about to become one of them. If he had known how to find someone that would have turned him sooner, he'd have done it. But he'd already involved enough of the innocent. To go back to the site and seek someone out to change him was playing with a hand grenade and taking the chance he'd end up dead, rather than a bat. He'd spent the past few days trying to figure out just how he was going to achieve vampire status to prove to Cadence he'd never hurt her or her family.

In his mind, becoming one of them was the only way.

"How did you find me?"

Pam's laugh was sharp, punctuated by a short intake of breath. "I smelled you, you asshole. Cadence mentioned you hung out here and I've seen your picture. So I knew what you looked like. That was all I needed. She's pretty screwed up over you. She felt so much guilt over lying to you and it looks like you were both lying to each other. The games people play, huh?"

"She's upset over me?"

"Of course she is, even if you are a jerk. Sometimes, you can't help who you love."

"Why did she lie about being a werewolf anyway? I don't get her motivation."

"Like you deserve an explanation?"

"I *need* to know."

Pam seemed to think about that for a moment and then said, "You said you would only entertain the idea of hooking up with other werewolves, according to her. She kinda fell in super lust with your picture and she wanted to meet you in person. Sometimes, Cady can be a smidge impulsive and then she worries about the consequences after it's too late. You are case in point. Cady didn't have any idea you and she would end up liking each other the way you did. None of the dates she'd been on meant anything to her. Yours obviously did."

So she did want him. What a freakin' mess. "Do ya suppose this will work in my favor?"

"I can't make any predictions about a future with her, Collin. Your lie supersedes hers, if you ask me. Yours would have hurt a lot of people and made her and her family social pariahs. It could have seen her dead. You know, humans kinda freak and break out the garlic recipes if they think a vampire is their neighbor. Cady's lie just meant she might be hurting herself."

What Pam said was without a doubt all true. One problem at a time, he thought. First up, the Count Dracula thing.

"So, how shall we do this? You want a quick rundown before I turn you? Vampire one-oh-one?"

"Nope. I've had a couple of days to research it on the Internet. I think I know what happens next and I wouldn't let you do it if it weren't for Cadence."

Pam cocked her head at him. "What are you talking about? You were going to write a tell-all story on Cadence. What were you doing for her but looking to ruin her damned life and the rest of ours with it? Besides, you couldn't stop me, Collin. I'm far stronger than I look. If you researched us, then you know I have some serious superhuman strength. You'd be wasting your time fighting me. Just be glad I offered you the chance to live. I could have just killed you. I should just kill you…"

She was remarkably calm, which led Collin to believe that she'd done this before. "Do you do this often?"

"What?"

"Kill people? Ya know, drain them or whatever?"

Pam shoved at his shoulder. "No, you idiot. I've never drained anyone dry. None of us have. Well, wait, maybe Cady's great-uncle Jackson, but that was centuries ago. Contrary to popular belief, we don't kill people. At least the breed of vamp we are doesn't or won't. We get our blood elsewhere. We just want to live peacefully with humans. Another reason I can't let you expose us. But don't think that doesn't mean I can't *start* killing people now, especially if it means saving Cady."

Collin stood, towering over Pam, and got his coat. "Okay, let's do it."

She looked up at him, her eyes narrowed and her lips pursed. "You're not going to put up a fight?"

Collin stared back down at her. "Nope."

"Are you serious? What kind of nut are you?"

"The nut that loves Cady."

"Ohhhh, be still my non-beating heart," Pam mocked.

Collin remained silent and waited to go wherever it was that vampires went when they sucked the life out of people.

She looked confused. "You're fricken' serious, aren't you?"

"Deadly so" was his answer.

"Oh, my God! You love her... You really do."

"Yep."

"Why'd ya have to go and make this so easy on me?"

"Because I deserve nothing less and I love Cady," he said again with more conviction.

"I can sense that."

"Sense it?"

"Yeah. We have acute senses and my vampire instincts tell me you really do love her." Pam shook her head again, obviously with disbelief.

"I do. So let's get going and get this over with."

"I really don't have a choice, Collin. It should be Cady that does this, but right now, you couldn't get her near you to save your life."

How ironic she should mention saving his life. Pam was looking regretful at this point and Collin wasn't sure how to take that. He deserved anything but her remorse. "So let's stop talking about it and do it."

"What the hell? Shouldn't you be fighting me tooth and nail? I should have to drag you out of here, not skip out together hand in hand like we're best friends."

"I told you, Pam. I deserve nothing less and I love Cady. If this is the only way to prove it to her, then so be it."

"You are one fucked up white boy, Collin Grayson, but you must love Cady to do this willingly. C'mon, we have some turning to do and then, I have an idea. It's crazy and I shouldn't even consider it, but I'm going to give you a hand here, big guy. Now let's go."

"Can I ask you one question?"

"Shoot, pardner."

"Do I have to sleep in a coffin?"

Pam's laughter rumbled from her chest as they crossed the bar's dirty floor to the exit.

* * *

"This is CC for the Nocturnal Journals on B 105.5 on your FM dial and tonight's topic is…" Cadence paused to take a breath and fight the sting of tears. Fuck that. She would not cry over the *human*. The human *reporter*… "Star-crossed lovers. People who should be together, but can't for whatever reasons. Ya know, political, religious, ethnic. I wanna hear your views. The good and the oh so bad. Gimme a call, Milwaukee!"

Cadence took another deep breath. It shuddered on its way out, ragged and depleted. She couldn't believe the station had chosen this topic. Of all the topics they might have picked, this was not the one she felt much like addressing tonight.

But she and Collin weren't star-crossed, they weren't anything. What they'd begun had begun as a lie. His just happened to be much bigger and with a far different ulterior motive than hers.

Yeah, that's right. Put the blame where blame belongs, Cadence. On the big, fat, lying white boy, human reporter. It's not like you lied too, Ms. Wannabe Car Chaser… Ms. Bay at the Moon. Ms. Isn't My Lustrous Coat Pantene Perfect?

Fine.

She'd lied. But she'd continued to lie because she'd fallen in love. Not because she wanted to expose shapeshifting werewolves in some seedy damned rag of a newspaper to the human population. Not because she wanted to make shifters look like freaks of nature and certainly not because she wanted to get the inside story.

She'd been attracted to someone and she'd been foolish enough to believe she could pull off this werewolf thing. So she'd been wrong to go into something like this believing she could keep lying, but she hadn't gone in looking to ruin anyone's life.

Collin had.

Okay, maybe ruining someone's life wasn't what he'd set out to do, but surely he knew nothing good could come for the person he attacked in his expose. They'd never be left alone by the paparazzi. They'd be made to live like freaks, outcasts in society — pointed at — poked and prodded.

It was fucking hard enough to keep her vampire origins to herself without raising suspicion, but a story like that could ruin her life. Her family's lives. The paranormal really did exist and they'd do whatever they had to to keep people from knowing.

Cadence would do her part to help.

She'd fought long and hard to blend in with the rest of society for too many centuries to become a Jerry Springer sideshow freak.

You have no one to blame but yourself, Cadence Cranston. No one. If trouble comes from this, it's your fault. You were impetuous, impulsive, in-fucking-fatuated. Honestly, did you really think you could fool anyone into believing you were a werewolf, Cady?

Question was, how the hell had Collin planned on doing something like that? At the very least she really was a shifter.

The answer was he'd never planned to do that. He'd planned to get pictures of whomever the poor soul ended up being his scoop long before he had to reveal any such animal.

Fucktard.

Never once had it occurred to her that anyone on the site could be a fake. How he'd gotten past that long list of Nazi-like questions from Paranormal Mates was beyond her.

You could be whoever you wanted to be on the Internet.

Collin was living proof.

You could also get your heart broken.

Cadence was living proof.

No more Internet rendezvous. No more dating for awhile, period. Men were no longer on Cadence's diet plan. They were high in heart calories and low in friggen' poundage loss.

Her switchboard was lit up like a proverbial Christmas tree and one of the night staff was frantically waving his hands and a big sign on posterboard that said, "Take the caller on line thirteen. It'll kill you."

Ugh, if he only knew. Cadence pressed the button for line thirteen and put on her happy face. "This is CC, your lifeline to the nighttime. Talk to me, night dweller! Have you had a lover you've lost due to circumstance? The one and only person in the world that's perfect for you?"

There was a long pause on the other end. Normally, Cadence would prompt the caller with another question, but she was distracted and losing her will to focus. She rubbed her thumb and forefinger over the bridge of her nose.

"Um... yeah, I did, er, I mean, I have lost a lover to circumstance."

Her head whipped up from its hanging position and her throat clogged. No way. It couldn't be. He wouldn't.

Oh, but he would.

"Did you hear me, CC? I said I lost a lover to circumstance and I regret that that circumstance was lying to her from the beginning of the relationship. I pretended to be something I'm not."

Cadence remained silent. She had no words and somewhere in her haze of disbelief, she knew she needed to speak up, but she couldn't. All of her thoughts were stuck in her throat and her hands couldn't connect quickly enough with her brain to press the button that would end the call.

"CC? I screwed up. I mean I really screwed up. I was involved with this woman for the wrong reasons to begin with and all of a sudden they became the right reasons. I didn't know when I first met her I'd fall in love," the caller continued.

Love?

Yes, love.

He'd said love.

Yep.

The lying son of a bitch.

No, I think he means it.

Still, words escaped her, sitting in her darkened studio.

But he plodded on. "So I kept on lying and it was wrong, but I didn't want to lose her. We had a lot in common. There isn't anyone I like talking to more than her. She's smart and funny and sexy. Everything a guy could ask for. Yet, I managed to do that, er, lose her and she has every reason to hate my guts, but I want her to know, here on live radio, that I never would have lied if things in my life hadn't been the way they were. I'm a man, I do stupid stuff, and this time, I did something that was so stupid, it cost me my life, but I don't care. I'd do it all again. Are you there, CC?"

Whoa, whoa, whoa. His *life?* Cadence's antennae went up and finally, she was able to speak. "Your life?"

"There you are." Collin's voice was warm. "Yeah, or my life as I knew it, if you know what I mean."

No, she didn't know what he meant, but she had a funny feeling.

"So, what should I do, CC? What would you do if you were me? How do you make something like that up to someone?"

Cadence keyed the microphone. "We'll be right back to ponder this crisis — after this Public Service Announcement, brought to you by the United States Marine Corps."

Her cell phone rang just as she was struggling to concoct some kind of answer. "Hello?"

"Cady?"

It was Pam. "Yeah?"

"You okay?"

"Well, no. No, I'm not okay. Why do you ask?"

"Listen to me. Come outside to the parking lot."

"Pam, what the hell is going on?"

"Just come down to the parking lot." Pam hung up with a click.

Cadence sat astonished for only a moment before she quickly spoke to her audience. "I'll be right back with more Nocturnal Journals. I'm gonna have to give our caller's dilemma some thought. It's break time for me. While I'm gone, give a listen to Iron Butterfly with 'In-A-Gadda-Da-Vida.'"

Seventeen minutes. She raced out of the studio door and down the back stairs of the station toward the parking lot. She threw the heavy door open and it crashed against the wall as she burst out of it.

Pam and Collin were there, leaning against his crappy car, waiting for her, side by side, each smirking.

Approaching them, Cadence squawked, "What are you doing with him, Pam? What the hell kind of friend are you anyway?"

"The kind that knows what's good for you."

"How can *he* possibly be good for me? He's a liar, Pam!"

"And you're Mother Teresa?"

Jesus effin'. How could she possibly defend him? "You're joking, right?"

"Look, Cady, I'm not going to defend either of you. One lie was just as bad as the next, but it can be fixed. It's already sorta fixed. Show her, Collin."

Collin, long and lean, muscled and sexy as hell, opened his mouth and smiled.

No fucking way.

Her jaw dropped open. "Wha-what have you done?" she screeched.

Pam crossed her arms over her chest. "I did the only thing I could do, Cady. He went willingly enough because he really does love you."

"What kind of drugs are you mainlining today, Pam? He was going to ruin our lives! Do you hear me? He would have exposed us for the vamps we are and fucked us *forever*!" Cadence slapped her hands on her thighs in exasperation.

"Well, he can't do that anymore, now can he? He'd be fucking himself too in the process."

Collin's newly acquired incisors gleamed in the dark of the evening, but he remained silent.

"Look, Cady. He was willing to do whatever it took to prove to you that he loved you. I would have turned him whether he was willing or not, but he went like an innocent lamb to slaughter. In the turning process, we spent some time together and I don't care what you say, I believe him when he says he loves you. So make nice and figure this out."

Cadence rolled her eyes in disbelief. Rooted to the parking lot, she could do nothing more than stare at them in disbelief.

"It's true, Cadence," Collin spoke up for the first time. "I do love you. I was going to tell you that night, but I realize now you wouldn't have believed me. What I set out to do was wrong. The point is, I didn't do it. I realized after our first night together I just didn't have it in me to hurt someone, especially you. I'll admit, I wanted payback for losing my career and I got all caught up in the werewolf thing, but not as caught up as I got in you." Collin smiled then, letting his fangs sparkle under the streetlamps.

"Okay, you two," Pam said. "I have a date with my Larry. I can't hang around all night and play host to the *Dating Game*. Work out all of your stuff and call me when you do. We'll do blood shots or something. Double date or whatever."

Pam turned to go to her car, but stopped midway. "Oh, and, Cady? Don't worry about any of this ever getting to that rag Collin worked for. We fixed that, didn't we, Collin?" she said with a husky giggle. "I did that Vulcan mind-meld thing on his boss for the first time, Cady. Guuurl, I tell you, it was a hoot. Ronald never knew what hit him. Doesn't remember a thing. Bye, guys." Pam sauntered off to her car, starting it with a rumble, and became a small pinpoint of nothing as the night swallowed her up.

"Vulcan mind-meld?" Cady finally asked, refusing to look at Collin.

He moved forward and tipped her chin up to make her look at him. "Yeah, you know, the whole suck his memory out of him. It was pretty screwed up when he couldn't remember who I was before we left."

Cadence pulled her chin from his grip. "So he doesn't remember the scoop of the century?"

"No, Cadence. He doesn't remember anything."

"I guess I'm supposed to feel better about that?"

"Well, yeah. I'd like to think it would ease your mind."

"Collin?"

"Cadence?"

"Are you fricken' crazy? Why did you let Pam do this?"

"My choices were kinda limited, babe. I had to prove to you that I wouldn't hurt you or your family. This was the best way."

"But you have no idea what it is to be a vampire."

"Well, I was hoping you'd teach me the finer points."

"Wow, that *is* hopeful, huh?"

Collin chuckled. "You know you like me."

"Yeah, I *love* liars."

"I don't want to throw stones here, honey, but you lied too..."

"Yes, yes I did, but I didn't do it for the reasons you did."

"Nope, you're right. You did it because you way like me."

"I don't know how much I like you anymore..."

"Yes, you do, Cady, but I understand your hesitance."

"Shouldn't I be hesitant?"

"Yeah, you should, but I'm willing to try and make this right. I'm just waiting on you."

"We started off all wrong, Collin. How will we ever know if either of us is telling the truth?"

"Because I can read your mind and now you can read mine too. I think we'd catch each other."

Well, there was that. "I don't know what to say."

"How about we don't say anything? We'll just start over." He paused and then stuck out his hand to her with that cocky grin. "Cadence Cranston, I'm Collin Grayson. A once well respected reporter who's pretty crazy about you. Wanna have coff — er, a pint of blood together and get to know each other?"

Cadence could no longer contain her amusement. She threw her head back and laughed before taking his hand. "It's nice to meet you, Collin. I'm a vampire. Not a werewolf like I once led you to believe."

Collin pulled her to him and planted a kiss on her lips. "So, ya wanna hang out, you non-lupine?"

"Okay, fine," she mocked disinterest. "But there will be no funny stuff, mister."

"Oh, fine. I'll have to woo you some other way, then."

Cadence laughed again and put her arms around his neck. "You know, there is one thing you might be able to do that might help you in the wooing process."

"Really? I'm all ears," he teased, gathering her close to his side while she pulled him in the direction of the studio.

When Cadence finally addressed her audience again, she smiled in Collin's direction with a sly grin. "Well, my nighttime dwellers, I think I've come up with a solution to our caller's dilemma and you know what? I'm not gonna tell ya what happens till next week." She gave a smug chuckle. "This is CC, for the Nocturnal Journals, signing off for now. Gooood niiiight Milwaukee..."

She had one more request. "Yeah, I loooove Charlie Gibson. You know, the guy from *Good Morning America*? You know him? I mean, like personally? Cuz he is beyond hot. I mean, when I see him on TV, I melt. Literally, I do. If I had a heart, it'd flutter for Charlie. Do ya think you could hook us up? Have you ever seen him in that black suit with the red tie? Oh, my God, he's so smokin'. I get all atwitter…"

Collin kissed her moving lips, pulling open the studio door, his hearty laughter echoing in the stairwell.

Epilogue

Cadence kissed Collin square on the mouth and giggled. They were sitting on his beat up old couch, preparing to leave Paranormal Mates Society's online dating service.

They'd spent a lot of time together since that night in the parking lot, working things out, figuring out where Collin could go with his career in such bad shape.

Where they would go as a couple.

Little by little, things had begun to fall into place for them and Collin now had a good job at a local newspaper. He wouldn't get rich, but it was honest work and he was happy to have a reason to get up each day.

Happier still that he didn't have to sleep in a coffin.

Two nights ago and six months since they'd met, with a full moon shining overhead, Collin had popped the question and Cadence had accepted with complete confidence.

"Look, honey, they want to know why we're leaving the site," Cadence said, looking at the exit form on Collin's laptop screen.

Choose one of the following reasons for leaving Paranormal Mates Society:

____ Too expensive.
____ I'm taking a break from dating right now.
_X_ Found my lifemate! Please share your story with us in the box below.

"Well, you're the writer. Tell them why we're leaving — and hurry up about it, stud. It's time to make some noise." Cadence flashed him with her cute new nightie and a wicked grin.

Collin smirked at her and began to type.

Thanks to Paranormal Mates Society, I found the woman of my dreams. It was rather by mistake. Well, actually, it was on purpose, but by mistake. Sort of. Either way, I'm really glad it happened. Our story began...

Dakota Cassidy

Dakota Cassidy found writing quite by accident and "it's been madness ever since." Who knew writing the grocery list would turn into this? Dakota loves anything funny and nothing pleases her more than to hear she's made someone laugh. She loves to write in many genres with a contemporary flair. Dakota lives with her two handsome sons, a dog and a cat. (None of them shape shift—that we know of.) She'd love to hear from you—she always answers her e-mail! Visit her at www.dakotacassidy.com or email her at dakota@dakotacassidy.com.

Changeling Press E-Books
Quality Erotic Adventures Designed For Today's Media

More Sci-Fi, Fantasy, Paranormal, and BDSM adventures available in E-Book format for immediate download at www.ChangelingPress.com—Werewolves, Vampires, Dragons, Shapeshifters and more—Erotic Tales from the edge of your imagination.

What are E-Books?

E-Books, or Electronic Books, are books designed to be read in digital format—on your computer or PDA device.

What do I need to read an E-Book?

If you've got a computer and Internet access, you've got it already!

Your web browser, such as Internet Explorer or Netscape, will read any HTML E-Book. You can also read E-Books in Adobe Acrobat format and Microsoft Reader, either on your computer or on most PDAs. Visit our Web site to learn about other options.

What reviewers are saying about Changeling Press E-Books

Heart's Blood: Make Love, Not Money — Kate Hill

"Make Love, Not Money touched me on so many levels. Felicia and Drake are a fiery, passionate couple and each one knows how to push the other's buttons."

— Amy Wynn, Ecataromance Sensual

Members Only: Rx for a Dom — Ann Jacobs

"[Trace and Ellie] are wonderful characters who are willing to sacrifice in order to be together and thankfully all they really need to do is be honest with one another. This reviewer highly recommends Rx for a Dom!"

— Mandie, Love Romances

Rookery Cove: Make Mine a Double — Michele Bardsley

"Bravo! This book made my morning."

— Hayley, Fallen Angel Reviews

Making Memories — Elizabeth Jewell

"I found this to be a very different and touching tale that explores what it is to be human and vampire."

— Roxy Blue, Just Erotic Romance Reviews

Children of the Dust 2: The Factory — Eve Vaughn

"The plot moved at an electrifyingly, swift pace and before I knew it I was upon the end.... And, let's not forget about the strong attraction between Sydney and Jack — talk about an instant electric shock."

— Contessa, Fallen Angel Reviews

Dr. Jacobs and Mr. Hyde — Vashti Valant

"A sizzling tale full of unbridled domination and pleasure [Dr. Jacobs and Mr. Hyde] will conquer the senses while bringing one woman's deepest secret to life."

— Sheryl, Ecataromance Sensual

Office of Kink and Karma: Serve Me — Celia Kyle

"When the pair come together, no matter whose turn it is to be in charge, the sex is hot and laced with a teasing humor that will have you blushing and smiling simultaneously."

— Megan, Erotic-Escapades

Rookery Cove: Faun of a Time — Jade Buchanan

"Both amusing and hot... Watching these two very different men come together was a lot of fun. If you're in the mood for a lighthearted paranormal story with unusual heroes, pick up Faun of a Time."

— Cassie, Joyfully Reviewed

The Battles of the Sidhe 2: Fountain of Pleasure — Beth Kery

"This story is erotic with a capital E. The plot is good, and Ms. Kery now brings her readers into the world of the Sidhe where Cheveyo and Dristan are kings and mighty warriors."

— Valerie, Love Romances

Bound in Lust — Dawn Montgomery

"Bound in Lust is a devilishly sexy tale that you will not be able to put down."

— Mandy Briggs, Rogues and Romance

www.ChangelingPress.com

LaVergne, TN USA
12 May 2010
182442LV00002B/57/P

9 781595 968111